Free spirit—or kindred spirit?

"Is that what you believe?" she probed. "That life is futile?"

"What I believe is that life is futile, so you might as well have a ball while you're passing through. Important distinction, Brooke."

"And why are you trying to convert me?"

Because...because of what he saw in her face, Sky almost said. Because he saw in it the resentment and hurt he'd once suffered himself. He saw sadness in her eyes, and withdrawal. Because her eyes were so lovely, so delicate in color, and her lips seemed to beg to be softened by a kiss....

"Call me an unfulfilled evangelist. I can't resist a soul in need of saving."

"I'm a Methodist," she informed him dryly. "I'm sure my soul has already been saved many times over."

"I also can't resist a soul in need of sinning," he teased.

"Brooke Waters—whoever's shirt you're wearing, you need it unstuffed."

ABOUT THE AUTHOR

Judith Arnold says she can't remember ever
not being a writer. She wrote her first story at
age six and pursued a successful playwrighting
career after getting her master's degree from
Brown University. Judith devotes herself to
writing full-time. Now she is also penning
novels under the pseudonym Ariel Berk. She
and her family live in rural Connecticut.

Books by Judith Arnold

HARLEQUIN AMERICAN ROMANCE

104—COME HOME TO LOVE
120—A MODERN MAN
130—FLOWING TO THE SKY

These books may be available at your local bookseller.

Don't miss any of our special offers. Write to us at the
following address for information on our newest releases.

Harlequin Reader Service
P.O. Box 52040, Phoenix, AZ 85072-2040
Canadian address: P.O. Box 2800, Postal Station A,
5170 Yonge St., Willowdale, Ont. M2N 6J3

Flowing
to the Sky
JUDITH ARNOLD

Harlequin Books

TORONTO • NEW YORK • LONDON
AMSTERDAM • PARIS • SYDNEY • HAMBURG
STOCKHOLM • ATHENS • TOKYO • MILAN

Published December 1985

First printing October 1985

ISBN 0-373-16130-1

Chapter One

Brooke couldn't take her eyes off the bearded man on the bench.

The gentleman talking to her, one Orlando Florida, according to the gummed label affixed to the collar of his blazer, was shorter than she by two inches, not counting the wedge-heeled sandals that augmented her height, and older than she by at least fifteen years. As he chattered in a thick Spanish accent that Brooke might at another time have considered remotely interesting, he gesticulated with his hands. She knew she should watch the plastic cup of wine he held—large drops of Chablis continually splashed onto the grass at her feet. She didn't want Nancy's blouse to get splattered. She ought to pay attention.

But her eyes kept drifting to the bearded man.

She couldn't read his name tag. It was glued to his plaid flannel shirt just above the chest pocket. She recognized the bright red shapes of the printed letters: "Hello! My Name Is," but she couldn't decipher the two words inked in below it. His shirt appeared fairly new, its recently pressed creases concealing the shape of his chest. His jeans, however, concealed nothing. It wasn't that they were so tight, but that they had obviously been worn enough times to have adopted the shape of the man's long legs as their own. What fascinated Brooke most about them—because, as a rule, she found blue jeans not to her liking, and she assiduously avoided wearing them herself—was that the denim had faded so evenly. No white blotches at the knees or along the fly.

Why was she looking at his fly? Her cheeks reddening, she turned back to Orlando Florida.

"You are *muy bella*," he said, laying his accent on heavily. His gaze was fastened to the deep slit shaping the neckline of Nancy's blouse. The fact that Brooke's breasts were almost exactly on the same level as Señor Florida's eyes didn't allow her to forgive him.

Impatient, she began to wonder whether he was faking the Spanish routine. She was vaguely aware of his embarking on a verbose discourse on Latin lovers.

She lifted her own cup of wine to sip. The more she drank, the more this entire escapade would make sense to her, she hoped. She didn't even want to be here. If only she'd gotten home before Nancy the day the invitation arrived, she would have thrown it out and forgotten about it.

But Nancy had picked up the mail that day, and the invitation wasn't enclosed in an envelope. It was a folded, unstapled mimeographed sheet that read:

Dear Brooke:

As someone saddled with the rather bizarre moniker of Corny Cobb, I have spent much of my life indulging in the hobby of collecting equally appealing and appalling appellations. You should not be surprised to learn that your name is on my list.

To celebrate our unusual names, I will be hosting a party at the western end of the Central Park Sheep Meadow on Saturday, April 20, at 3:00 P.M. (Rain date, April 27.) Please join me in the mirthful festivities.

Sincerely, Cornelius S. "Corny" Cobb

Brooke didn't want to celebrate her unusual name. She considered having been christened Brooke Waters one of the great burdens of her life. The unfortunate name hadn't even been a result of wit on her parents' part. Brooke had been named after her maternal grandmother, whose name at birth had been Brooke Humphries and after marriage Brooke Jennings. A wealthy and powerful woman—to say nothing of an incredible egotist—Brooke's grandmother had announced to her offspring that whoever named a daughter after her would receive a grand sum of money. Brooke's parents had immediately embarked on a family, but were disappointed by the arrival of two sons preceding their daughter. To this day, Brooke still hadn't forgiven her first cousin Jane for having been born three weeks after Brooke. And Jane's parents had never forgiven their niece Brooke for having been born three weeks before their own daughter.

Blessed with the beautifully meaningless name of Nancy Carlin, Brooke's roommate didn't understand. "Brooke, you've *got* to go to this party. Come on, you're one of the chosen."

"If I were chosen to inaugurate Sing Sing's new electric chair, I wouldn't care to celebrate," Brooke had retorted. "Going through life being called Drip and H_2O is not something I choose to celebrate, either."

"Oh, come on," Nancy had admonished her. "Lighten up. It'll be a gas."

"Nancy, I refuse to attend any affair hosted by someone named Corny Cobb."

"Why?" Nancy had pressed her. "Maybe if you meet enough people with weird names, your own won't seem so awful in comparison."

Brooke had conceded the point. Still, she prayed for rain, and when the first scheduled date dawned drizzly, she'd been relieved all out of proportion.

But Saturday the twenty-seventh arrived with an obscenely bright sun. "You've got to go." Nancy had insisted.

"Why don't you go in my place?" Brooke had offered.

Nancy had appeared indignant. "That wouldn't be honest. You've got to go yourself."

So Brooke had gone herself—but not quite herself. Nancy had refused to permit Brooke to leave the apartment dressed in her idea of casual clothes: tailored trousers of lightweight gray wool and a starched white shirt. Too sedate, Nancy had maintained. If Brooke was going to do something as whimsical and utterly unlike herself as attend Corny Cobb's bash, she ought to do it the right way. That meant wearing a shocking turquoise tunic of Nancy's, which dropped halfway down the thighs and was cinched at the waist with a black satin sash, and slim-fitting black satin slacks to match. And no, Brooke's brushed-gold stud earrings wouldn't be right. She would have to borrow Nancy's silver hoop earrings and, while she was at it, a silver bangle bracelet that resembled a snake eating its tail.

One of the reasons Nancy had asked Brooke to be her roommate was so they could swap clothing. Both were five feet six, one hundred twenty pounds; both could fit into anything from size five to size nine depending on the cut. "I want a roommate who's neat, who doesn't smoke, and who can double my wardrobe," Nancy had declared when Brooke had responded to one of the advertisements Nancy had placed about the city. Brooke had just joined the staff of Benson & Broderick, and she was desperate for a place to live. And she was neat and didn't smoke.

The fact that she and Nancy didn't share the same taste in clothing didn't emerge until after Brooke had moved in. Actually, Brooke liked Nancy's flamboyant wardrobe. But Nancy was the sort of woman who could get away with wearing anything from haute couture to Goodwill castoffs. She was slim and dark, with wildly frizzy hair that she rarely bothered to trim. Her job in the city's Department of Cultural Affairs allowed her to mingle with artists and weirdos, and the unusual apparel she preferred served her well in that capacity. Brooke, however, was an accountant. From Boston. She favored tweeds and wools, the most impeccable, inconspicuous conservative clothing she could find. When one was cursed with a name like Brooke Waters, one did everything possible not to call attention to oneself.

Still, she'd gone along with Nancy's advice and donned the uncharacteristic ensemble. If she was going to attend this ridiculous shindig, she might as well do it incognito.

She had already met her host, Corny Cobb, a plump, elderly gentleman who had inherited an enormous sum of money and took pleasure in frittering it away on nonsense such as this party. He had been posted by a portable table alongside the paved walk circumventing the Sheep Meadow, a large, rolling stretch of grass near the southern end of Central Park. The tabletop was covered with jugs of cheap wine and plastic cups, a sheet of gummed name labels and pens, and a large stereo from which oozed treacly string arrangements of early Beatles tunes. Brooke had conversed politely with Corny and with a skinny black man named Van Driver, a chubby black man named Chuck Wagon, two withered sisters named Olive and Cherry Pitt and a loudmouthed cabbie with the appropriate name of Glad Hand. She'd already consumed two cups of wine.

Now she was guzzling her third cup and listening to Orlando Florida describe to her the sublime thrill of being made love to by someone of the Hispanic persuasion. Her eyes drifted back to the bearded man on the bench.

A blond woman in a blindingly bright magenta dress that loudly proclaimed the spectacular dimensions of her bustline had plopped herself onto the bench beside him. The woman was talking, giggling, leaning intimately toward the man.

His hair was much too long, Brooke noted. It was dark, nearly black, falling in thick, untamable waves that partially hid his ears and curled over the collar of his shirt. The beard, while neatly trimmed, covered his jaw all the way to his temples and extended in a mustache across his upper lip. When he grinned at the blond woman, the beard split to reveal incredibly white teeth. If only he shaved, Brooke mused, if only she could see his chin...

He turned from the blond woman and stared at Brooke. His eyes were as dark as his hair, large and round and startling. Brooke colored and turned away.

"To my lovely *casa* on Staten Island," Orlando Florida was saying. "I have both a bed of the water variety and one of the dry variety. To make for variety, you see...."

"I need a refill," she muttered, hastily swallowing the last of her wine so she wouldn't be lying. She excused herself with a chilly smile and roamed through the throng back to the table, wincing as a cloying violin rendition of "Norwegian Wood" poured through the speakers of the stereo.

She filled her cup with Chablis from one of the jugs. The wine was particularly rancid in flavor, and she knew she'd wind up with a headache from drinking it, but even the risk of a headache was worth removing herself from Orlando Florida's clutches.

She turned from the table and her eyes immediately zeroed in on the bearded man. The blond woman beside him was seductively peeling the gummed label from his shirt. He cast the woman a bemused glance, then turned and stared at Brooke again. For some reason, she hoped he wasn't searching for her nonexistent cleavage in the depths of the slit of her tunic.

If he had any sense at all, she considered, he'd recognize that the blouse wasn't hers. Her face was much too prim and ordinary. Her skin was smooth and clear enough for her to have modeled for soap commercials if she wanted; she considered her complexion her best feature. Her nose and chin were a bit too pointy, her eyes seemed to vanish into her cheeks thanks to their pale hazel color and the equally pale lashes that fringed them, and her sandy-colored hair was cut in a demure page boy that didn't quite reach her shoulders. It was a proper hairdo for an accountant, a proper hairdo for a well-bred Boston lady trying to live down the horrible name of Brooke Waters.

The bearded man continued to study Brooke's face, even as the well-endowed blond woman babbled into the dark curls covering his ear. Unlike Señor Florida, the bearded man seemed to have no interest at all in Brooke's slender figure. His eyes toured her face an inch at a time. They shimmered with intriguing shadows.

"This is absolutely ridiculous," Brooke mumbled into her wine. "No," she corrected herself. "Stupid. Dumb. Idiotic." She glanced at her wristwatch, a slender gold Bucherer hidden beneath the cuff of the tunic.

She'd been at the gathering nearly an hour. That was long enough to satisfy Nancy, she decided, certainly forty-five minutes longer than Brooke had intended to stay. And the wine tasted dreadful. Her mouth felt numbed by the quantity she'd consumed.

She set down her cup and meandered through the crowd, forcing a plastic smile at Cherry Pitt, who had touched her arm as if about to confide something to her. Gotta run, Brooke's smile conveyed. So terribly sorry we can't talk further. She hoped to high heaven that Nancy wouldn't be home. All she wanted to do was curl up in bed with the *Internal Revenue Code of 1954*.

She made it to the asphalt path, having successfully eluded both Señor Florida and Corny Cobb. Escape! she thought, her spirits lifting slightly.

And then she felt another hand on her arm, turning her around. She shaped a new artificial smile as her body followed her shoulder.

He was much taller than she'd estimated. She ought to have been surprised that he'd approached her, but all she could think about was his towering height, his broad shoulders, the implicit strength of his fingers. With all that hair, both above his eyes and below them, he looked as if he'd just climbed off a mountain.

"Brooke Waters," he murmured, reading the label she'd stuck onto the tunic. "I like that. Brooke Waters."

She fixed her gaze on the spot above his chest pocket where his tag had been before the buxom blonde had removed it. She should excuse herself from him as she'd excused herself from Orlando Florida and Cherry Pitt. She really didn't want to stay at this ludicrous party any longer.

But the words that rose to her lips instead were: "You have me at a disadvantage. Where's your dog tag?"

"I haven't even got a dog," he told her. His eyes were uncanny, she mused, almost too dark to be brown. Like his hair. Dark, dark brown, striking in their intensity. "Sky," he said.

"I beg your pardon?"

"My name is Sky."

"Guy?"

"*Sky.*"

"Oh." Why should she be surprised? At a party like this, the only surprising name he might have spoken was John Doe. "Sky. How interesting," she managed. "Why Sky?"

"Why not?" His beard parted around a stunningly warm smile. "My last name's Blue."

"Sky Blue." Her brain was mildly fuzzy from all the wine she'd drunk, or she never would have added, "How awful!"

Curiosity flashed in his eyes. "You think it's awful, Brooke Waters?"

"At least Brooke is a real name," she pointed out, recalling Nancy's comment about having her animosity toward her own name assuaged by attending the party and meeting people with even worse names. "I've never met anyone named Sky before."

"And you'll probably never meet anyone named Sky again."

"What do people call you?" she asked.

"Sky."

"Oh." She realized that his hand was still on her arm. She was amazed to find herself responding to the inherent strength in his clasp. A mountaineer, she pondered. Maybe a logger. His shirt was plaid. Didn't loggers wear plaid shirts?

"It's not that I'm ashamed of my name," he explained the absence of his tag. "It's just that Joy Foy pulled the label off before I could stop her."

"Joy Foy?"

He angled his head toward the magenta-clad blonde. Brooke was pleased to discover that Orlando Florida was now gawking at Joy Foy's chest and evidently finding much to inspect in the décolletage of her dress. "If you're planning to leave, you'd be wise to steer clear of her. She latches on and doesn't let go."

"She's met her match." Brooke laughed, watching Señor Florida's eyes bulge as the flouncy woman jabbered at him. Perhaps there was justice in the world after all.

"Are you planning to leave?" Sky asked.

"As a matter of fact..." Yes, she was. *The Internal Revenue Code of 1954,* remember? Yet Sky hadn't let go of her, and until he did, she simply couldn't leave—not for any reason she could come up with. She knew if she shifted her body a millimeter he'd release her. But she didn't. She didn't move at all.

"We could leave together," he suggested.

Was this a proposition, she wondered. Men generally didn't come on to her that way. Brooke generally didn't put herself in positions where they could. And whenever she found herself in a group with someone who looked even remotely like Joy Foy, men generally didn't notice Brooke at all.

She touched the tip of her tongue to her lips. Sensation had returned slightly to her mouth, though the metallic taste of the wine still lingered. "What did you have in mind?" she asked.

"I've got to drop in on someone in the neighborhood. Business," Sky informed her. "And then dinner. Care to join me?"

"For business or dinner?" Lord, what was wrong with her? Why should she even be considering a dinner invitation from Paul Bunyan? Correction: Sky Blue. Who was he, anyway? What if he was a sicko, a pervert, someone far less safe than he appeared?

"Both. The business won't take long."

"I don't know," she demurred. "I mean, I didn't come here to pick up a man." She cursed inwardly. She never spoke with men like this. The entire encounter struck her as vulgar. It must be Nancy's blouse, she decided. Nancy was always meeting men in strange places.

"Why did you come here?" Sky asked.

She risked peering up at him. His eyes, for all their infinite darkness, seemed rather gentle to her. His lashes were short but dense. Another glass of wine might have given her the courage to tell him that he ought to shave. She suspected he'd be remarkably handsome if he ever emerged from beneath all that fur. "My roommate made me," she replied. "I was afraid that if I didn't come she'd change the locks on me. How about you?"

He had come to look at faces. He was always looking at faces, always looking for them. Faces had become his professional trademark, but his interest in them predated his career by some time. He imagined that if he'd ever discussed it with his analyst she would have told him that he was obsessed with faces because he'd grown up knowing that his own wasn't unique. Another boy had been born with a face identical to Sky's, and so he'd spent his entire life looking for unique ones.

He was unnervingly drawn to Brooke Waters's face right now. He was intrigued by the smooth white stretch of her brow beneath a faint fluff of bangs, and the arrowhead shape of her chin, and the slender line of her nose. Hers was a face of lines and angles. Her pale brows were nearly straight, her lips narrow, her cheeks high, her eyes tilted upward at the outer corners. She had lovely skin, he mused. All in all, it was a face he'd like to look at for a long time.

He didn't tell her that, of course. She'd probably be put off by such a statement. Most people didn't like to

be stared at. Even those he flattered by hiring and re-
warded by paying at scale felt oddly uncomfortable
when they realized that Sky Blue was fixated on their
faces. Instead, he said, "Why is the sky blue? I came
because it seemed like the right thing for somone like
me to do."

"Then why are you leaving so soon?"

"Because you are," he declared bluntly.

Well, Brooke thought, now what? What would
Nancy do? She'd probably go traipsing off with this
hirsute stranger, drag him to some outdoor craft fair
or folk festival or something, and come home Sunday
morning wearing a Cheshire cat grin. Brooke admired Nancy's flair, but she couldn't very well imitate
it. It simply wasn't her style.

"Uh...look, Sky." She had a bit of difficulty saying his name with a straight face. "That's quite a line,
but I'm not really susceptible to lines."

"I didn't intend it as a line," he earnestly told her.

"Then what?" she challenged him. "What if I
hadn't shown up? Would you have left alone?"

"Alone and disappointed," he replied.

Positively ridiculous, Brooke muttered silently.
"You're laying it on rather thick, Mr. Blue," she said
aloud.

He smiled, and something about his smile made his
beard appear enchantingly soft to her. She wondered
what it felt like. Velvet, she imagined. A soft strip of
black velvet. "Other than you," he commented, "this
get-together is pretty disappointing. The wine is
wretched and the music sucks the big wazoo."

"I beg your pardon?" she blurted out.

"It's music to drill teeth by. Montavani sticks it to Lennon and McCartney." He perused her thoughtfully. "You don't like it, do you?"

"No," she admitted, matching his smile. *Sucks the big wazoo,* she repeated silently. This guy certainly had a bizarre way of expressing himself. "And I agree, the wine is wretched."

"Then let's go." He said it with such sensibility that Brooke found herself accompanying him down the paved walk.

Central Park teemed with people enjoying the warm spring afternoon. Most of the Sheep Meadow was overtaken by several rambunctious softball games and an assortment of kite flyers. The walkways bustled with food and drink vendors, dog walkers, lovers holding hands. It really was a delightful afternoon, Brooke acknowledged, feeling a waning of her resentment about her name and the invitation it brought. She wasn't an impulsive person, but the sun was high and the park was crowded enough that she didn't think she was in any great danger strolling beneath the leafy trees with Sky Blue.

"What sort of business do you have to attend to?" she asked.

He nodded her toward Central Park West, his hands plunged into the pockets of his jeans. He was wearing hand-stitched loafers, she noticed as he picked his way across the bridle path, pointing out the places she should avoid. Expensive shoes, she mused. "I have to see a client," he answered.

"What sort of client?" It was admittedly a nosy question, but he had to expect as much. Certainly he didn't think she'd go marching off with someone she knew nothing about.

"A famous one," he responded cryptically.

Across the bridle path she halted. "I'm asking a legitimate question, Mr. Blue. No need to be so secretive about it. If you honestly want me to have dinner with you—"

"I honestly do," he interrupted pleasantly. "And I'm answering your legitimate questions. If I'm not answering them to your satisfaction, my dear Ms Waters, perhaps you ought to phrase them more precisely."

His tone seemed strangely stilted, and Brooke realized that he was mimicking her own stodgy manner of speech. She pursed her lips and said nothing.

He laughed, a soft, husky sound. "Where are you from?" he inquired.

"Boston," she said.

"*Bwah-ston*," he teased. "That would have been my first guess." He hesitated, then continued, "You didn't come all the way down from Boston just for Corny Cobb's jamboree, did you?"

"No, of course not," she replied. "I live here in New York now."

"How do you suppose he found your name?" Sky asked. "Are you listed in the phone book?"

She shook her head. "I wondered about that myself. I think he got my name from the newspapers."

"Oh? How'd you end up in the papers?"

"I sat on a panel at Hunter College last winter, and it was written up," she told Sky. "A discussion on women and their alleged fear of numbers. He must have gotten my address from the college."

Sky's gaze traveled down her body and then back up to her face. "Are you a mathematician?" he asked in a tone implying disbelief.

"No."

"Are you afraid of numbers?"

"No."

He smiled, then stepped aside so she could precede him through the gateway in the fieldstone wall that separated the park from the sidewalk on Central Park West. "I have to tell you before you tell me, is that it?" he guessed.

"It would be fair," she asserted, her voice surprisingly breezy.

"I work in video," he informed her. "I make videotapes. Commercials and the like."

"Commercials? You're in advertising?" She didn't bother to contain her surprise. She'd never met anyone in advertising who looked so scruffy.

"From nine to five," he allowed. "Your turn. Are you a computer buff? A bookkeeper? A teacher of remedial arithmetic?"

"I'm...in business," she answered carefully. Somehow she couldn't bring herself to tell him she was a corporate tax specialist at one of the city's major accounting firms. It sounded so insufferably boring to her. But since she was already acting so out of character today, she decided she ought to play the part to the hilt.

Sky's skeptical glance told her that he considered her answer inadequate. "I counsel businesses on strategies," she elaborated. It wasn't a lie, and it sounded almost glamorous.

"A consultant?" he mused.

"Close enough."

He led her across the street to one of the charming older apartment buildings overlooking the park. "Here already," he told her. "This won't take long, and when I'm done I'll reward you with some real wine."

In the ornate elevator Brooke entertained second thoughts. She was truly out of her element, not because she had found herself in an elegant and expensive apartment building, but because she didn't usually go off with strangers. Nancy should have gone to Corny Cobb's party in Brooke's place, she contemplated. Nancy was forever running off with strangers and becoming intimate friends with them. Brooke frequently entered the apartment she and Nancy shared to discover the living room swarming with unfamiliar people Nancy invariably introduced as "My dear friend So-and so, whom I met yesterday in the produce section at Gristede's," or "My *dahling* friend Such-and-such who held the bus for me on Fifty-ninth Street." It made for an interesting life, and Brooke didn't mind as long as she had the haven of her bedroom to escape to.

What would Nancy think if Brooke brought Sky Blue home with her? She'd probably congratulate her. That thought made Brooke cringe.

She wondered who the famous client Sky was taking her to visit would be. Most of the people who acted in commercials weren't that famous, but maybe this was some renowned star who had been hired to endorse a product. An ex-athlete flacking for dietetic beer, perhaps, or a Broadway star pushing photocopy machines on an unsuspecting public. The name Sky had given to the doorman sounded like "Willa Something-or-other." Brooke hadn't recognized it.

The elevator stopped on the twelfth floor and they stepped out into the luxuriously decorated hallway.

Brooke waited for Sky to indicate which direction they were to walk in.

Instead, he turned her to face him and reached for her name sticker. "You don't need this anymore," he observed as he gently peeled it from the gauzy blue-green fabric.

She fleetingly recalled the sight of Joy Foy peeling Sky's tag off his chest, but that memory was replaced by the present reality of Sky's fingers on her upper chest. He had lovely fingers, she noticed, long and golden, with clean, round nails. He seemed to be taking more time than necessary for the simple task, but Brooke couldn't think of a tactful way to request that he speed things along and yank the damned tag off. For some reason, she liked watching Sky's fingers on her, moving across the blouse, brushing subtly against the skin beneath it. It occurred to her that Sky Blue was definitely a sensual man.

She wasn't sure what about him gave her that impression, but as soon as it lodged within her she couldn't shake it. She glanced nervously at his eyes, which were focused on her name tag, their lids lowered. His brow and upper cheeks were the same golden color as his hands, and his lips—what she could see of them through the shrubbery of his beard—looked strong and forceful. She had never kissed a man with a beard before.

What in the world was she thinking of? What was she doing here with him? Logic reined in her imagination and she took a tense step backward. His hands dropped from her, his fingers pinching the sticker. He studied it for a long moment, then folded it once, pressing its gummed surface together, and dropped it into his shirt pocket.

"Look," she said, suddenly anxious about her predicament. Nancy would feel at home in such a situation; Nancy would welcome it. But wearing Nancy's clothing didn't magically make Brooke turn into her roommate. "Look. This is silly."

His eyes lifted to hers. "What's silly?"

"My being here with you."

"It'll only take a few minutes," he said, misunderstanding the cause of her apprehension.

"Sky, I don't even know you. If you think I'm the sort of woman who waltzes off with a man just because she met him at a party and—"

"Talk, talk, talk. Yaketa-yaketa," he teased, his lips skewing into a grin. "Relax." His tone was stern, though his eyes sparkled with amusement. "I'm not the bogeyman."

"Who are you?"

He studied her reflectively, his smile fading. "I'm someone who showed up at a social gig, took a look around and discovered a beautiful woman with a beautiful name, and I invited her out for dinner. Where's the crime in that?"

"I didn't say you were a criminal," Brooke defended herself.

"Then what?"

She faltered. Her fingers fidgeted with one of the oversized hoop earrings, which had somehow gotten tangled in her hair. "I'm not all that beautiful, Sky," she commented softly, "and my name is laughable. If you want me to believe you, you'll have to come up with something better."

He continued to scrutinize her, his gaze intensifying as he examined her upturned face. Her eyes were wide and glittering with something he could interpret as panic, and her lips were clenched in a taut frown. It was an amazing face, he thought, so animated, so expressive; its striking geometry danced through her emotions in a way she seemed totally unaware of. "Maybe you're not all that beautiful," he conceded. "Maybe I'm crazy. But I like looking at you. How's that?"

If anything, it made Brooke more uncomfortable. She didn't know how she felt about his looking at her. His eyes seemed to see much more than her mere features. They seemed to penetrate her skin, searching for something underneath it. She had no idea what.

She realized that she had to say something. "I just feel a little strange, Sky. I don't know what in the world I'm doing here." She hadn't expected to be that honest, but what she'd said was the truth.

"You're fleeing from the horrible music Corny Cobb had on his stereo," Sky suggested. "You're enjoying my company. You're looking for a free feed. What does it matter? Relax and have a good time. There's no crime in that."

He sounded more than a little like Nancy, Brooke mused. Nancy was always urging Brooke to relax and have a good time. Brooke knew she wasn't a very relaxed person, though she wasn't exactly high-strung. It was more a matter of her feeling out of place in situations this impromptu, and out of her depth with men as virile as Sky Blue.

He *was* virile, she admitted. And sensual. Big and magnificently built, with piercing eyes and gentle hands and a beard that Brooke was dangerously curious about. If she *really* wanted to be honest about things, she had to concede that she had spotted Sky before he had spotted her at Corny Cobb's party. And once she'd spotted him, she hadn't been able to keep herself from looking at him again and again. She liked looking at him, too. Perhaps he wasn't conventionally handsome, but she liked looking at him.

Maybe she was as crazy as he was.

"Okay," she yielded in a near-whisper. "I'm going to relax." Simply hearing herself say such a thing caused her anxiety to increase a notch, but she compelled herself to smile and waited for him to lead the way.

His grin was much more natural than hers, and when he folded his hand around hers she couldn't find the voice to protest. His hand was warm, hers icy, but he didn't comment on it.

They strolled down the hall, their steps noiseless on the plush burgundy carpeting. Sky drew to a stop by a door and depressed its buzzer. "This will only take a few minutes," he reminded her. "Having you with me gives me a good excuse to cut out fast."

She nodded. Possibly that was why he'd brought her with him.

She heard a sound emerging through the thick door, the whine of an ailing cat. Then the door swung open to reveal a tall, pencil-thin woman wearing a garish red silk kimono. Her fingernails were long, filed to points, and painted the same gruesome crimson hue of her kimono. Brooke raised her eyes to discover that the woman had an attractive, youthful face and straight platinum hair that dropped to her waist. The sound of the whining cat blasted through the open doorway, but now Brooke realized that it wasn't a cat at all. It was a woman's voice, singing—or, rather, screeching—accompanied by twangy electric guitars and a pulsing drum.

"Sky!" The woman wrapped her arms around Sky and planted a kiss on his bearded cheek. "Hello, honey, come on in. Hi!" she added, turning her neon-bright smile to Brooke.

On closer examination, Brooke realized that the woman's hair wasn't platinum at all. It was a pale, metallic green.

She felt Sky's hand at the small of her back, nudging her through the doorway. And abruptly she understood how Lewis Carroll's Alice must have felt when she fell down the rabbit hole.

Chapter Two

The apartment's foyer was cluttered with plants. They stood in pots on the foor, in rows on shelves along the walls; they hung from the ceiling. Brooke briefly considered whether the woman's hair only appeared to be green because she was surrounded by so much greenery. But the music was so raucous that Brooke had difficulty thinking at all.

"Brooke, this is Willow," Sky introduced the two women. "Willow, Brooke."

"Hi!" the green-haired woman yelled above the music. She shut the door, then took Sky's hand and wove gracefully through the foliage into a living room that might have been spacious—it was crammed with so many plants that Brooke couldn't estimate its size. Overgrown spider plants and asparagus ferns hung in multicolored macramé webs from the ceiling, not just by the window but throughout the room. Avocado trees and rubber plants rose from wicker baskets scattered haphazardly across the parquet floor. The windowsill was bedecked with more flora. Brooke wondered why anyone who lived in an apartment with a spectacular view of Central Park would want to obscure that view with houseplants.

"Where's Michael?" Sky asked Willow.

"Oh, he's around here somewhere." Willow waved vaguely about the room. Brooke imagined that a person could disappear into the indoor jungle and never be found again.

Sky smiled and touched Brooke's arm reassuringly. "This won't take long," he promised before picking his way through a copse of what appeared to be miniature palm trees and vanishing down a hallway.

"So," Willow said, turning to Brooke. "You're a friend of Sky's?"

Brooke could scarcely hear the woman, though she certainly seemed friendly enough. "Could you turn down the music a little?" she requested.

"Huh?" Evidently Willow couldn't hear her, either.

"The music!" Brooke hollered at the green-haired woman. Under normal conditions, Brooke would never refer to such strident caterwauling as music, but she didn't want to insult her hostess. "Could you turn it down?"

"Oh! Sure!" Willow forged her way through the underbrush to reach a well-camouflaged stereo and adjusted its volume half a decibel lower. When she emerged from the jungle, Brooke scrutinized her more carefully. Willow was barefoot and, from the looks of the clinging silk kimono, naked beneath the robe. "Would you like some wine or something?" she offered.

Why not? Brooke shrugged. This, like Corny Cobb's party, seemed a perfect occasion to get drunk. "Thank you," she said with a nod.

Willow led her to a small kitchen, which featured merely a countable number of plants, and Brooke dropped weakly onto a chair beside the tiny table.

Willow glided to the refrigerator and pulled out an enormous green jug of rosé. Brooke tried not to grimace as Willow filled two glasses that had begun their life as jelly jars.

"Don't your neighbors complain about the loud music?" Brooke asked.

Willow grinned. "Uh-uh," she replied. "What can they expect from someone like me?" She took a long swig of her wine. .

Brooke accepted Willow's comment, although she didn't exactly understand it. She tasted the wine, found it offensively sweet and lowered her glass.

Willow plopped onto a facing chair and crossed her legs Indian-style on the upholstered seat. "So you're a friend of Sky's?" she asked.

Brooke decided that the safest answer was a noncommittal nod.

"You know him long?"

"Not very," Brooke replied truthfully. She was eager to check her wristwatch and calculate precisely how long she'd known Sky, but she couldn't do that discreetly since her watch was hidden under the sleeve of her tunic.

"I love that man," Willow effused without prompting. "I'm absolutely in love with him. Isn't he something else?"

"Something else, yes," Brooke concurred faintly. She wondered whether Sky and Willow were in fact lovers. Given the way her afternoon was progressing, nothing would surprise her.

"I mean, I love him. God, I love that man. He's a rock, you know what I mean? Like, he's a rock. I mean, his eyes, you know? They're the sweetest eyes ever to walk the earth."

Brooke mulled over whether eyes could walk the earth, or, for that matter, whether someone named Sky could be a rock. But she tactfully chose not to pursue the thought with Willow. Now just didn't seem the appropriate time to discuss mixed metaphors with the green-haired woman facing her across the table. "He mentioned that you were a client of his," Brooke remarked.

Willow screwed her girlish face into a scowl. "Yeeeech. I hate when he talks like that. A *client*. Yeeeech! It's, like, so *business*, you know?"

Brooke scrutinized her hostess. Willow seemed much too flaky to appear in television commercials, and while Brooke didn't watch television very often, she was certain that if she'd ever seen a green-haired woman in a commercial she'd remember.

"I love that bracelet," Willow commented, gazing longingly at the silver snake manacling Brooke's wrist. *You would,* Brooke muttered silently. "Your name, too. Brooke. Like Sky. I love it."

"Willow's an unusual name," Brooke courteously observed.

Willow rolled her eyes. "I wish," she grumbled.

Brooke frowned. She'd never met a woman named Willow before, not even at Corny Cobb's gathering. "It is," she maintained. "Very unusual."

"I mean, I wish it was my name," Willow explained. "I mean, it *is* my name, you know? But not my real name." She leaned forward conspiratorially. "My real name," she murmured, her tiny nose wrinkling, "is Norma. *Norma*. Honestly. Isn't that disgusting?"

Actually, Brooke would kill for a name like Norma. "I think Norma is beautiful," she asserted.

"Yeah, for someone's next-door neighbor, maybe," Willow argued. "But I mean, honestly, do you think anyone would pay attention to me in my line if I was Norma? Yeeeech!"

Why not, Brooke wondered. Who cared what television commercial performers' names were? "What line are you in?" she asked politely.

Willow fell back in her chair, her small lips agape in astonishment. "Huh?"

"What line of work are you in?" Brooke repeated more loudly.

Willow suddenly appeared furious. "Don't you know who I am? I'm *Willow*!" she sputtered, as if that was supposed to mean something to Brooke. She hurled herself from her chair, pacing indignantly back and forth through the compact kitchen. "I'm *Willow*! Don't you know anything?"

Sure, I know some things, Brooke answered silently. *Ask me anything about the tax code. Anything at all.* But she said nothing as she tried to fathom Willow's unexpected irascibility.

Willow gestured toward the doorway to the living room. "*That*, you turkey, is who I am," she said meaningfully. "And if you don't know that, you don't deserve to be Sky's friend." She stormed from the room.

Brooke sat alone for a minute, treasuring her temporary solitude. Even here, away from the stereo, the music was far too loud, grating on her eardrums and aggravating her incipient headache. She stared at her jelly glass of wine and pushed it away. Absolutely ridiculous, she appraised her situation. Totally bizarre.

She couldn't sit alone in the kitchen forever. In fact, she didn't want to. If Sky wasn't going to come and fetch her, she'd leave without him. This stupid business trip had nothing to do with her, anyway. If he was rude enough to abandon her to a temperamental half-naked green-haired woman, Brooke might just as well abandon him. This wasn't exactly her idea of a good time.

She stood up resolutely and exited the kitchen. Willow didn't seem to be in the living room, although she could have been lurking beneath the hedge of blossoming begonias bordering the wall. Brooke tried to wend her way through the jungle toward the foyer, but when she accidently kicked over a bonsai orange tree in her path, she paused and stooped to gather up the strewn soil and replace it in the pot. Her cleaning efforts brought her to the hallway, and she was able to hear Sky's voice filtering through an open door, barely audible, given the cacophony of music.

She ought to say good-bye to him, she realized. Not that she owed him anything, but she really ought to. She was well-bred, up on her etiquette. She had no call to match his rudeness with her own.

The hall was devoid of plants, which Brooke found soothing. She tiptoed to the open door and peered in.

Sky and another man were sitting on the floor, surrounded by more plants. Willow was curled up in a corner, sulking. The man with Sky looked fairly ordinary, with wavy brown hair and a clean-shaven jaw, though he was smoking a pink cigarette. The men glanced up, and Sky smiled. "We're just about done here," he told her as he rose to his feet.

The other man extended the pink cigarette toward Brooke, and she instantly recognized that it wasn't a cigarette at all. Its acrid smoke stung her nostrils, and she hastily shook her head and turned away. "I'm leaving," she announced.

"Yes," Sky quickly agreed. "We're on our way. Michael," he addressed the man on the floor. "Just give it some thought. I think you'll see I'm right. Willow, good seeing you," he called to the contorted woman in the corner as he strolled to Brooke's side.

"Yeeeech," Willow grumbled petulantly. "A client? Is that how you think of me, Sky? A *client*?"

Sky laughed in response. He cupped his fingers about Brooke's elbow and escorted her down the short hall, working his way deftly around the plants to the foyer and out of the apartment.

As soon as the door was shut, smothering the hideous wailing music, Brooke spun around and glared at him. "How dare you bring me here!" she raged.

The color in his eyes seemed impossibly to darken, though they were still—yes—the gentlest eyes ever to walk the earth. "What happened between you and Willow? She stormed into the bedroom like a typhoon."

"Oh, the bedroom?" Brooke sniffed. "Was that a bedroom? I didn't notice a bed."

"The apartment *is* a little strange," Sky amiably agreed.

Brooke curled her lip and started briskly toward the elevator. Sky quickened his pace to keep up with her. He waited for her to explain her dudgeon. "That man," she muttered, "was smoking marijuana."

Sky studied her for a couple of seconds and then guffawed. "No kidding," he said, chuckling sarcastically.

"Sky, that's against the law!"

"Oh," he said, feigning shock. "Maybe we ought to go straight to the police station and report him."

"I'm not joking," she grumbled. "I want to go home." As if on cue, the elevator door slid open and she stalked into the car.

Sky followed her and pressed the first-floor button. "Brooke, what's the big deal? You've been drinking wine all day. Michael prefers a different poison."

"Wine is legal," she snapped, then simmered, eyeing Sky surreptitiously, surveying his scruffy hair and beard. "Were you smoking that stuff, too?"

"No," he told her. "I was discussing business."

"Oh, so if you weren't conducting business you would have been getting stoned, too?"

"No," he reiterated in a softer tone. "I don't enjoy it. It only muddles my mind, and I don't like being muddled." His somber manner convinced Brooke that he was telling the truth.

They emerged on the first floor and left the building. Brooke turned south in the direction of her apartment. She hadn't been lying when she told Sky she wanted to go home. She'd had enough of this weird day, with people named Orlando Florida and women with green hair and vile wine.

But Sky reached out and tightly gripped her elbow, holding her immobile. He gazed down at her, curiosity and confusion blending in his expression. "What happened in there?" he asked. "Why was Willow so sore?"

"I didn't know who she was," Brooke explained. "Was I supposed to?"

He seemed astonished. "You've never heard of Willow before? She's pretty famous."

"Not in the circles in which I usually travel," Brooke retorted.

He assessed her with his dark, probing gaze. "You were listening to her," he told Brooke.

"Well, yes, we talked for a while—"

"No, the music. That was Willow."

"Music?" Brooke sniffed. "You mean that woebegone ululating? You call that music?"

Sky's scrutiny deepened. "You don't like rock music?"

"Despise it," Brooke declared frostily. "In all honesty, I'd rather listen to Montavani sticking it to the Beatles than that grotesque banshee screeching."

"Hmm." That was all Sky said. "Hmm." Then he began sauntering toward the corner, Brooke in tow.

"I want to go home," she remininded him tartly.

"After dinner," Sky promised. "I'm starved."

"I'm not," Brooke protested just to be contrary. In fact, she was reasonably hungry.

Sky ignored her claim. "There's a good Spanish restaurant on Seventy-second Street. Do you like Spanish food?"

"Look." She refused to leave the corner, and Sky obediently remained by the curb with her. "I don't like you making assumptions about me, Sky. First you dragged me away from Corny Cobb's little fete—"

"You said you were ready to leave," he argued in his own defense.

"And then you dragged me to some green-haired twit's botanical garden," Brooke plowed ahead. "And now you're dragging me to dinner. Maybe you mountain men think macho is acceptable, but—"

"Mountain men?" His eyebrows lifted in surprise.

"That's what you look like," she insisted. "A mountain man."

A low laugh escaped him. "I'm not," he told her. "I grew up in Portland, Oregon, and now I live in Manhattan. I like the mountains, Brooke, but I'm not *of* them." His smile became gentle. "Looks can be deceiving."

"Yes," Brooke agreed in a muted voice. "I'm not what I look like, either."

"Hmm," he grunted again. His eyes coursed over her, and once again she couldn't help sensing that he was trying to see something beyond her face, beneath her porcelain skin. "You look like a reserved, uptight lady who could be incredibly happy if she'd let herself learn to go with the flow. I'd be delighted to find out that that's not what you are."

But that was exactly what she was, Brooke noted morosely. Whatever Sky had been searching for in her face, he'd apparently discovered the truth. "I'm happy," she murmured, averting her eyes.

"Maybe, but not incredibly happy."

"And what gives you the right to hang out a shingle, Dr. Blue? Do you engage in amateur psychoanalysis when you aren't making television commercials starring green-haired rock stars named Norma?"

No, he wasn't an amateur psychoanalyst, he almost replied. Though he might as well be one. His own brief experience in analysis had proved to him that he could analyze himself as well as a professional could. But that wasn't a subject he cared to discuss with Brooke. He was too puzzled by something else she'd said. "Norma?"

"That's Willow's real name," Brooke informed him. At his perplexed expression, she added, "Have I spilled the beans about something you didn't know?"

His lips spread in a grin. "As a matter of fact, you have," he answered, urging Brooke across the street and taking heart in her failure to resist him. "Norma, huh?" He laughed quietly.

"Did you know she's in love with you?" Brooke continued, amazed to find herself playing the amateur analyst's role and enjoying it.

"Willow? In love with me?" The idea seemed inconceivable to Sky. "Not a chance. She and Michael have been together since the start."

"Since the start of what?"

"Since the start of her career. He's her manager."

"Is he responsible for her dying her hair green?" Brooke asked, willingly matching Sky's leisurely gait as they turned onto Seventy-second Street.

"I don't know whose idea that was," Sky responded. "My only concern is how the video comes together."

"What video?" Brooke asked. Her fascination would have surprised her if she'd given it any thought.

"Rock videos. Have you ever seen them on television?"

Brooke shook her head. She'd read about them in the newspapers, but she certainly had better things to do with her life than watch rock videos on TV. "Is that what you do? You make rock videos?"

"I'm just getting into it," Sky told her. "Willow's first video was also my first video. I saw her performing one night at the Ritz, and afterward we got to talking. I don't know why she approached me—maybe

I looked like someone who knew how to use a videocam.''

"Maybe you looked like someone she could fall in love with," Brooke suggested.

Sky considered this, then shook his head. "Nah. Michael was there with her. She wasn't looking for action, just conversation. Anyway, one thing led to another, and she asked me to do a video for her. We were both just starting out, and we figured what the hell, we'd give it a shot. It was a big hit and it boosted both our careers. So now I'm making a second one for her new record, as well as a couple of others I've got lined up.''

"I thought you were in advertising.''

"I am. Advertising pays the bills until I establish myself more firmly in rock videos," Sky told her. "Anyway, rock videos are just another kind of advertisement. Promoting rock stars.'' He leaned against the glass door of a restaurant on the ground floor of an apartment building. Brooke entered, Sky following her.

The restaurant was notably elegant, its walls a comforting dark maroon color and its tables set with linen and crystal. Brooke wondered whether Sky would be seated, dressed as casually as he was, but the maître d' said nothing as he escorted them to a table for two. The refined decor of the place was a delightful change after Corny Cobb's party and Willow's apartment, and Brooke permitted herself to relax slightly. Very slightly. She still wasn't good at relaxing.

"Do you eat here often?'' she asked Sky as she surveyed the other diners. Every other man in the room was wearing a necktie.

"Not very," he answered. "I live downtown, so it's a bit out of my way."

Brooke experienced an unexpected pang at the thought that Sky didn't live in her Upper West Side neighborhood. She didn't know why such news should disappoint her, and she covered her distraction by studying the menu for several minutes. She and Sky both decided on paella, and Sky ordered a red Spanish wine whose name Brooke didn't recognize. Once the waiter had taken their order and departed, Sky's eyes narrowed on Brooke. "What makes you think Willow is in love with me?

"She told me she was," Brooke replied. "She said she loved you."

"That's just the way she talks," he said, brushing off Brooke's observation.

Brooke shook her head and smiled, for some reason eager to goad Sky. "She told me her name was Norma," she reminded him. "Why don't you think she'd be telling me the truth about you, too?"

He thought about this for a long moment. "Nah," he decided. "She's not my type."

"What's your type?"

"Stuffed shirts from *Bwah-ston*," he teased.

Brooke felt her cheeks color. She said nothing as the waiter approached with their wine and, after obtaining Sky's approval, filled two goblets for them. Sky lifted his glass in a silent toast, and Brooke mirrored him before sipping the wine. It was deliciously dry and subtle after all the revolting wine she'd consumed during the afternoon.

Lowering her glass, she matched his steady gaze. "That's a pretty good description of me," she allowed. "But you're wrong—I'm not your type."

"Oh? And why might that be?"

"You aren't a stuffed shirt."

He conceded with a warm smile. "No, I'm not. But few things thrill me as much as finding out what a woman's shirt is stuffed with."

Brooke bristled slightly at the lewd remark. "This isn't even my shirt," she heard herself retort. "If you saw me in my own clothes, you probably wouldn't even recognize me."

"Oh, I would," he asserted with quiet force. "I'm not really into shirts, Brooke. I'm into faces."

"Do I have a stuffed face?"

He refused to rise to the bait. "You have..." He paused to consider his words. "You have a fascinating face."

"Uh-huh," she grunted dubiously. "I have the face of someone who's not incredibly happy?"

"You have the face of someone who could be incredibly happy if she let herself," Sky corrected her. He rested his elbow on the table and propped his bearded chin in his hand, examining her face thoughtfully. "You have the sort of face I'd give my left arm to see lit up with joy."

She fumbled with her napkin, taking the time to smooth it neatly across her lap. She didn't think she cared for Sky's brand of honesty. Even though she was certain that she was fully capable of attaining some degree of joy, she couldn't deny that what Sky had implied was very close to the mark. Brooke wasn't a particularly joyful person. "Your left arm?" She laughed tensely. "Surely you exaggerate."

"Okay," he relented. "My left pinkie."

"I really have a pretty ordinary face," she pointed out.

"There's no such thing as an ordinary face," Sky disputed. "Every face is unique." Nearly every face, anyway, he added silently. "You just have to know how to look at them."

"Oh? Does that require a special talent?"

"I believe it does," he claimed. He removed his elbow from the table when the waiter arrived with their salads. Sky stirred the dressing into his greens, though his eyes never left Brooke. "You've probably seen some of my ads on the tube," he said. "Rickler's Candies, Culpepper Tools, the National Association of Florists. I specialize in faces."

Brooke tried to recall if she had seen any advertisements for those products on television. She rarely watched TV without a book on her lap, and read during the commercial breaks. "I'm afraid I don't remember those ads," she apologized. "I'm not a carpenter, and I don't care much for candy."

"Do you like flowers?" he asked.

"Yes," she allowed, "but I never buy them."

"Afraid they might make you incredibly happy?" Sky inquired, his smile not at all mocking. "Or is it just that you have dozens of male admirers sending them to you?"

She couldn't remember the last time anyone, male or female, friend or lover, had sent her flowers. But she wasn't about to reveal that to Sky. "I like live flowers," she maintained primly. "Florists cut flowers and then they die."

"The flowers florists cut would have died anyway," Sky commented. "They're raised for the sole purpose of being cut."

"Don't you think that's a waste?"

The waiter arrived carrying a double-sized covered dish of spicy rice-and-seafood stew. He spooned a portion onto Brooke's plate, then onto Sky's. Sky nodded at him, and he left the table.

Without lifting his fork, Sky leaned toward Brooke, bearing down on her with his piercing eyes. "Life," he said with understated intensity, "is for enjoying. For having fun. Lots of fun things are a waste, but who cares? Drinking wine is a waste because in the morning the high is gone. Going to work is a waste because you wind up spending all the money you've earned. Buying flowers is a waste because after a while they die." His gaze remained locked onto her, transfixing in its power. "Life is a waste because no matter how you live it you're going to wind up dead. If you're going to bother at all, you may as well make the most of it."

His philosophical speech stunned Brooke. She simply hadn't expected it. Sky was apparently quite carefree in his approach to the world, and his verbal essay proved as much. Yet she was surprised that he'd thought the philosophy through, that he'd reached his carefree state through a process of intellectual reasoning.

If she agreed with his view—and quite possibly she did, she privately conceded—she'd be incredibly depressed by it. But Sky seemed not at all depressed. He was smiling, although his eyes continued to caress her with their searing darkness. His beard reshaped itself about his grin, thickening at the areas on his cheeks where dimples were supposed to be. "Is that what you believe?" she probed. "That life is futile?"

"What I believe," he clarified, "is that life is futile, so you might as well have a ball while you're passing through. Important distinction, Brooke."

"And why are you trying to convert me?" she challenged him.

Because...because of what he saw in her face, he almost said. Because he saw in it the resentment and hurt he'd once suffered himself. He saw sadness in it, and withdrawal. Because her eyes were so lovely, so delicate in color, and her lips seemed to beg to be softened by a kiss. Because while he had no idea what had made Brooke Waters the way she was, he understood certain things about her, and he wanted to see her face lit up with joy. He wanted that.

But she was resisting him as much as she resisted all of life's frivolous pleasures. He resolved to buy her flowers. A big, gaudy, extravagant bouquet. So what if in a few days it would shrivel up? Brooke definitely needed flowers.

She was awaiting an answer from him, and he belatedly supplied a joking one. "Call me an unfulfilled evangelist. I can't resist a soul in need of saving."

"I'm a Methodist," she informed him dryly. "I'm sure my soul has already been saved many times over."

"I also can't resist a soul in need of sinning," he teased. "Brooke Waters—whosoever shirt you're wearing, you need it unstuffed."

She coughed to cover her embarrassment. She replayed mentally the several unnecessarily long minutes Sky had spent removing her name tag from the tunic, and the way his hand had felt on her shoulder, on her arm, wrapped around her own small hand. The way he had stared at her at the party in the park. The way her attention had been inexplicably drawn to the denim covering the fly of his jeans.

Honest to goodness, she muttered inwardly. How in the world had she managed to get into this situation? It wasn't like her, not like her at all. She liked situations in which she was in control, in which she felt competent and capable. She liked situations in which people weren't poking around in her soul looking for secrets to investigate.

She didn't like situations in which a man could exert such power over her. At least it certainly seemed as if Sky was exerting that kind of power. Why else would she have left the party with him, and gone to Willow's place and now to dinner? Why else would she have let Sky rearrange her afternoon and evening around him?

She honestly didn't like feeling so out of control.

She picked at her paella, which was spiced deliciously, the shrimps firm, the rice moist but not sticky, the peas obviously cooked fresh. But her nerves stifled her appetite, and she was able to force down only a couple of forkfuls before balancing her silverware on the edge of her plate and sighing.

Sky was consuming his portion with gusto; he had a big body to fill, Brooke reminded herself. But his attention was on her, and as soon as he read her discomfort he lowered his fork. "What's the problem?"

"I told you I wasn't hungry," she managed.

"You're angry with me?"

"Yes," she bluntly told him.

He weighed that information, not terribly startled by it. There had been a time in his life when he also resented people who tried to loosen him up. But that time had been just a blip in his lifeline. He'd been loose before, and he became loose again afterward. He wasn't sure whether Brooke had ever been loose.

Still, he wasn't ready to give up on her, not yet. He wanted to see the magic her eyes could perform when they glowed with pleasure. He wanted to hear her laugh, really laugh, laughter that spread up from the tips of her toes through her body before filling the air with a music more beautiful than anything ever recorded.

All he said was "Would you like me to get the check?"

"Yes."

"They've got terrific desserts here," he noted.

"I rarely eat dessert."

Of course she'd say that, he realized. She undoubtedly considered desserts a waste. He knew she didn't avoid desserts to preserve her figure; if anything, she could use a few more pounds on her lean frame.

He signaled the waiter and then requested both the check and a doggy bag for the significant amount of paella still left in the covered dish. "A doggy bag?" Brooke chided him once the waiter had removed the dish from the table and carried it back to the kitchen. The restaurant seemed much too classy for doggy bags.

"Sure, why not?" Sky said with a shrug. "If we don't take it, they'll just throw it in the garbage. You're the one who doesn't like waste."

"Yes, but still...." She couldn't recall a single time in her life, either as a child or as an adult, that she'd been at a restaurant with someone who requested a doggy bag. It wasn't that the Waters family was snobbish. It was just that asking for a doggy bag wasn't what proper Boston Methodists did.

The waiter didn't seem at all disturbed by Sky's request, however. He returned to the table to deliver the check and a brown paper bag that held a foil container of the leftover paella. Sky produced a credit card, and within several minutes, the bill had been settled.

Sky stood, lifted the bag and pulled out Brooke's chair for her. The gesture seemed oddly chivalrous, but it had a placating effect on Brooke. She smiled her thanks as she rose from the chair.

The evening air had grown cool, the sun having sunk below the New Jersey skyline during their dinner. Seventy-second Street was swarming with people enjoying a Saturday night out on the town, and Brooke almost suggested that they not call it a night yet. But then she glimpsed the doggy bag and it reminded her of the effect Sky had had on her appetite. She really needed to get away from him, from the virile stranger with the weird name. If she'd gone directly home from Corny Cobb's party three hours ago, she would have had a tranquil, untroubling afternoon reading the tax code and learning something useful, instead of letting this bearded man sweep her into the world of green-haired rock stars.

Sky considerately didn't take her elbow or her hand as he studied the crowded sidewalk and then the traffic-clogged street. "Should I find us a cab?" he asked.

"No, I live just a few blocks from here," Brooke told him, moving in a brisk stride toward Broadway. Sky fell into step beside her.

"It's a bustling neighborhood, isn't it," he observed.

What a safe, dull thing for him to say, Brooke
mused, after he'd spent their dinner criticizing her for
her alleged failure to be incredibly happy and medi-
tating on the substance with which she presumably
stuffed her shirt. Why couldn't he have chatted about
the neighborhood's bustle during their meal? Then she
might not have lost her appetite, and he wouldn't be
lugging a doggy bag now. "Yes," she responded in-
anely. "Especially around Broadway. Lincoln Center
is just a few blocks down. It always draws the crowds
on the weekends."

"Are we that close to Lincoln Center?" He
frowned, then glanced down Broadway, spotting the
performing arts center's white buildings not far to the
south.

Brooke frowned as well. She realized that if Sky
didn't know where Lincoln Center was, it was probably because he never went there. But why should he?
He was a rock fan. Brooke was a classical music dev-
otee. The reason she hadn't cared for "Montavani
sticking it to Lennon and McCartney" that afternoon
was that the strings were too syrupy, the orchestra-
tions too sentimental. She'd much prefer to listen to an
orchestra performing music that had been conceived
and written for orchestra. And Sky had probably
hated the music not because of the sentimental or-
chestrations but because they were a bastardization of
rock music, a transgression against the demigod
Beatles.

She and Sky continued their stroll in silence, at last
arriving at a monolithic complex of rent-stablized
apartments bordering the Hudson River. Brooke followed a twisting path through the complex to her
building, which was identical to every other one in the

complex. The buildings were a bit too characterless for her taste, but the rent was well below the going rate. She knew that if she and Nancy ever moved out of their comfortable two-bedroom apartment, thousands of people would line up for the opportunity to move in, even if the management doubled the rent.

Sky accompanied her through the revolving door into the stark lobby. She wasn't sure exactly how to say good-bye to him, so she stalled by striding to the alcove containing the tenants' mailboxes. She unlocked hers and found it empty. Nancy must have picked up the mail earlier. Brooke wondered whether she received any more unwanted invitations to appalling-appellation parties. She'd have to start beating Nancy to the mailbox.

She clicked the small brass door shut and turned to find Sky standing close to her. He'd set the doggy bag on a ledge where flyers and misplaced letters were left, and he was watching Brooke with interest. "I guess it's time to say good-bye," she said limply.

"Now it's time to say good-bye," Sky sang softly. At Brooke's puzzled frown, he continued the tune, which she realized was the "Mickey Mouse Club" theme song. She had watched a typical amount of television as a child, and had for a time been a regular viewer of the "Mickey Mouse Club"—until her older brothers had bought her her own set of Mouseketeer ears and scrawled "Wet Stuff" with an indelible purple crayon across Mickey's face on the front of the cap.

"M-O-U-S-E," she spelled out without bothering to sing the melody. The memory of her brothers' constant taunting vexed her. "That wasn't the best song you could have come up with," she mumbled grimly.

"Oh? What's the best song I could have come up with? Something by Willow, perhaps?" Sky's smile was teasing but friendly.

"Anything that wouldn't remind me that I'm stuck with a dumb name," she snapped. "But I suppose any tune would do that if you were singing it. You're doomed to be a reminder, Sky. If it weren't for my name, I never would have met you."

"I like your name," he argued gently. "I think it's lovely."

"You didn't go through life being called Drip," she pointed out.

He chuckled. "I've been called worse things more than once," he commented. "But when I was a kid I was bigger than most of the other kids, so that didn't last long. One or two fistfights were all it took." He raised his hand to her cheek, brushing back a strand of her dark blond hair that had gotten caught on her earring. His fingers paused, then stroked the smoothly chiseled line of her cheekbone. "It's a lovely name, Brooke," he whispered, his hand moving to her ear. "It makes me think of water."

"Funny thing about that," she said and laughed in spite of herself. But the warmth Sky's hand imparted to her skin wasn't at all funny. It radiated downward to her throat, to her chest, and she knew that if she didn't do something quickly she'd have her first opportunity to find out what it was like to kiss a man with a beard.

She didn't want to kiss him. The entire afternoon had been like something out of—no, not out of *Alice's Adventures in Wonderland* but out of Kafka. Too much weirdness for a prim accountant to handle. She ought to thank Sky for dinner, excuse herself, say she had a headache, which wasn't a total falsehood, and make a mad dash for the elevator.

Yet like the moment in Central Park earlier that afternoon, when Sky had approached her just as she was about to leave the gathering, she found herself unable to excuse herself from him. "A forest stream," he murmured, elaborating on her name. "Clean, crystalline water rushing through a forest, flowing over rocks and twigs and bubbling with laughter. That's what Brooke Waters makes me think of."

His lips were closer to hers now, but he was still offering her the chance to stop him. "Willow said you were a rock," she interjected in a soft voice.

"How can a sky be a rock?" he wondered aloud.

"That was my thought exactly."

That she had the same thought as he did pleased him. He smiled. "If you were a forest stream, I'd love to be a rock," he said. "I'd love to have your cool sweet water flowing around me."

It was a stunningly sensual thing to say, Brooke mused vaguely. But she'd known from the first that Sky was a stunningly sensual man. And when he finally lowered his mouth to hers, she didn't pull away.

His beard *was* soft, softer than she'd imagined. The silky hair stroked against her chin as his lips covered hers. He let his hand slide to the back of her head and held her close.

She felt his tongue against her lips, drawing a gentle moist line over the sensitive flesh. His kiss made her feel like cool sweet water, and she wanted to flow over him.

Her mouth opened, and he deepened the kiss. Brooke was having difficulty supporting herself as her legs went weak beneath her. She reached for Sky's shoulders to hold herself up.

She'd kissed men before. But never had she kissed a man whose body felt as firm and as steady as a rock, yet whose eyes seemed as endlessly dark as the midnight sky. Warm yet mysterious, stretching to infinity. Her own eyes closed as her body flowed toward his, as yielding as water against stone.

Water yielded to stone, yes, but it also eroded stone. Sky was aware of his body changing, giving in to Brooke. She was cool, fresh, pure, sweet. But surprisingly strong. He felt the current in her surging against him, spilling over him, altering him. He wanted much more than to look at her.

But suddenly she was pulling back. Her eyes drifted uncertainly from his face to the mail table behind him. "I'm not going to stand and neck with you in the lobby of my building." She breathed unevenly, her voice cracking to a whisper.

He watched her face, the nervous flicking of her tongue over her lips, the slight tremble in her hands as she withdrew them from his shoulders. "What are you going to do?" he asked.

"I'm going to thank you for dinner and say goodnight," she addressed the floor.

He slipped his hand beneath her chin and lifted her face to his again. One final look, he thought, one final look until he saw her again, one final look to last him through the night. "Can I call you?" he asked.

"I don't know."

He easily comprehended her edginess. She was frightened. Frightened of giving herself over to incredible happiness. He understood, but if he told her he did he'd sound condescending, and she probably wouldn't believe him anyway. "Will you give me your number?" he asked.

She shook her head.

"You're not in the telephone book?"

"Being unlisted does serve its purpose," she muttered.

He inched back a step, giving her the space she seemed to need. Then he reached for the doggy bag and pressed it into her fisted hands. "You'll probably get hungry later," he remarked in an even voice. "You'll be thankful for this." He touched his mouth to the lovely plane of her cheek, then pivoted and walked away from the mailbox alcove, his relaxed stride belying his disappointment.

He was disappointed, but not despondent. He'd see Brooke Waters again. He was certain of it.

Chapter Three

"Who died?" Brooke asked.

It was a justifiable question, given the size of the floral arrangement sitting on the dining table. Nancy had returned from work before Brooke and had not only emptied their mailbox but also retrieved from the building's doorman the massive bouquet that had been delivered to the building for Brooke. Nancy had been itching with curiosity, waiting for Brooke to arrive home and open the card.

Brooke stepped out of her spectator pumps and loosened the collar bow of her blouse as she circled the table, studying the flowers. The bouquet was motley, blossoms jammed chaotically into a tacky ceramic pot shaped to resemble a worn brown boot. The daisies clashed with the pink baby roses; the daffodils seemed awkwardly stalky despite the ferns bunched about their rigid stems. Two sprigs of baby's breath covered the tongue of the boot. A branch of pussy willows sprang out of nowhere to contribute its puffy gray nubs to the array. A scarlet bird of paradise loomed above the mess. The effect of the disorderly bouquet was just short of nauseating.

Brooke had seen bouquets this large at funerals, but she'd never seen a bouquet so utterly tasteless in her life.

"Who's it from?" Nancy demanded to know. She tugged off the rectangular white envelope taped to the toe of the boot and shoved it into Brooke's hand. Sighing, Brooke set down her attaché case and opened the envelope.

Okay, you call me, the card read. *Sky Blue.* And then a phone number.

Nancy nosily read the card over Brooke's shoulder. "Sky Blue?" she asked. "What's that supposed to mean?"

"I told you about him," Brooke muttered, dropping the card to the table.

Actually, Brooke had related to Nancy only a little bit about Sky. When she'd gotten to the apartment Saturday evening she'd found it empty. Nancy had left a note saying, "I went to a gala, *dahling,* for a Hungarian folk dance troupe. Will be home late if ever." She'd come home "ever," Sunday morning, to discover Brooke nibbling on cold paella and solving the crossword puzzle in the Sunday *Times* magazine. They'd had a minor altercation about the puzzle, since both Nancy and Brooke were crossword puzzle fiends.

Brooke had considered going to church Sunday morning, but had decided to do the puzzle instead. Sky had been correct in claiming that her soul needed more sinning than saving, and she simply hadn't had the energy to go to church. Nor had she had the heart to prepare a decent breakfast for herself. The cold paella had been just the thing to fill her stomach.

Once Nancy had announced that if Brooke made so much as a single pencil mark on the magazine's

acrostic puzzle she'd be booted out of the apartment
and left to sleep on subway grates in the Bowery, she'd
cheered up considerably and spent hours describing to
Brooke a dancer named Bogdan Hordak whom she'd
met at the gala. The cold war could be ended if people from opposite sides of the iron curtain learned to
love each other, Nancy had asserted.

Eventually she'd remembered to ask Brooke about
Corny Cobb's party. Although Brooke had mentioned that she'd wound up having dinner with one of
the other guests, Nancy had been much more interested in hearing all the odd names Brooke had encountered at the affair. Throughout dinner that night
she regaled Brooke with a series of "If So-and-so
married Such-and-such" jokes. "If Wanda Lan-
dowska married Howard Hughes and then divorced
him and married Henry Kissinger, she'd be Wanda
Hughes Kissinger now," Nancy said, giggling. "If
Leslie Caron married Elvis Presley, she'd be Leslie
Presley." Brooke cringed. She detested those jokes.
The one time she'd seriously contemplated getting
married, it had been because the man's name was Joseph Anderson. In retrospect, she realized that Joe
had had little other than his name to recommend him
as a husband.

"Sky," she told Nancy as she slumped into one of
the chairs by the table, "was the man with whom I had
dinner Saturday night."

Nancy's eyes shifted from the card to the bouquet
and then to Brooke. "Those flowers must have cost a
fortune," she murmured contemplatively.

"So much money and so little to show for it."
Brooke sniffed, eyeing the ugly bouquet and grimac-

ing. "Not to imply that this is little. But I imagine he can afford it. He works in advertising."

"That wasn't what I was getting at," Nancy said, shoving a thick lock of frizzy hair back from her face. "Obviously you haven't told me everything."

"What am I supposed to tell you?" Brooke asked innocently.

"You're suppose to tell me why a man would spend all that loot to send you flowers. What happened after dinner?"

"I said thank you and good night," Brooke claimed.

Nancy studied her roommate doubtfully. "Oh, come on, Splash. I'm a big girl. You won't shock me. After the night I spent with Bogdan nothing would shock me. Those Eastern bloc fellows..."

Brooke pressed her hands to her ears in mock horror. "I don't want to hear about it!" she protested, then relented with a sheepish smile. "I bet in Budapest Bogdan is a very common name."

"Brooke!" Nancy groaned impatiently. "Come on! Why did he send you all these flowers? Is it the real thing or what?"

"More likely it's 'what,'" Brooke replied calmly. "During dinner I told him I didn't think much of cut flowers. Apparently he saw that as a challenge." She scrutinized the atrocious bouquet one last time and shuddered. "If anything, this...this thing he sent me only proves my point. It's really gross, don't you think?"

Nancy planted her hands on her hips. She was wearing a baggy pants suit of wrinkled off-white linen, with a silver ring resembling an eyeball on her left index finger and four silver necklaces displaying a variety of link widths about her throat. The ensemble suited her perfectly, Brooke decided. "What I think, Brooke, is that you ought to telephone the man and thank him."

"Thank him? For making fun of me?"

"You *are* a drip," Nancy denounced her. She strode into the kitchen with the card, dialed a series of numbers on the wall phone and returned to the dining area carrying the receiver, which she thrust at Brooke.

Hearing the first ring, Brooke hastily stood up and started toward the kitchen, hoping to hang up the phone before Sky answered. But Nancy blocked the doorway, and before Brooke could shove past her roommate she heard Sky's husky voice through the receiver. "Hello?"

Exhaling, she glowered at Nancy and then turned her back on her. "Hello, Sky," she mumbled.

"Brooke! You got the flowers, did you?"

"Yes," she replied. "They had to knock out a portion of the outer wall to get them into the building."

"Big, huh?" Sky said, not at all irked by Brooke's negative tone. "Well, you know what they say: You can bring a horse to water, but you can't bring a horticulture."

"That's totally uncalled for," Brooke muttered, though she didn't know why his silly joke should embarrass her. She could feel her cheeks heating with a blush, and she stretched the extra-long telephone cord to the window in order to put some distance between Nancy and herself. "I didn't even want to phone you."

"Then why did you?"

"My roommate made me," she complained, shooting Nancy a quick, fierce glare. Nancy grinned.

"The same roommate who made you go to Corny Cobb's party?" Sky asked. "I've never even met her, and already I like her."

"You would," Brooke said seriously. "She's much more your type."

"Another stuffed shirt from *Bwah-ston*?" he teased. "How many of you are there running around Manhattan, anyway?"

"She's the opposite of me," Brooke corrected him. She didn't dare look at Nancy; she was certain that her end of the conversation must be sounding much too intriguing to her roommate. "She's a free spirit, Sky. Go with the flow and all that garbage."

"The only flow I'm interested in is Brooke Waters," he punned. "Can I see you?"

"Oh, Sky..." She sighed. It wasn't that she didn't want to see him. Far from it. In all honesty, she did. But she was shocked by the way he'd taken over an afternoon and evening of her life, whisking her away, bringing her here and there and to dinner and blithely ignoring her every attempt to resist him. She was even more shocked that she hadn't done much to resist. She was shocked that she'd let him kiss her—and that she'd enjoyed the kiss immensely. The entire episode had left her confused and mildly resentful, and she didn't see why she should subject herself to another go-round with him.

"What if I told you I didn't want to see you?" she hedged, shocking herself once again. She ought to have simply said no and been done with him.

"I wouldn't believe you," Sky responded.

"Then you're a fool."

"I won't argue the point. When can we get together?"

"Sky!" Her exasperation blended with a grudging admiration for him. He certainly was tenacious, and tenacity was a trait she held in high esteem.

"How about lunch?" he suggested. "That's nice and safe and properly stuffy, isn't it?"

"Lunch?"

"Great," he sped along, choosing to take Brooke's feeble echo as an acceptance of his invitation. "Are you free tomorrow?"

"Don't you think you're rushing things?" she reproached him.

"Hey, if I don't see you very soon the flowers are going to wilt and die. And then that chip on your shoulder might swell to the proportions of a redwood. We can't let that happen," he maintained. "Tomorrow it is."

Tomorrow. If they had a business lunch, Sky would see the real Brooke Waters—Brooke Waters the accountant. Maybe then he'd know what he was getting himself into, and he'd rethink his opinion of her. "Fine," she said brightly. "At least I think fine. I haven't got my appointment calendar with me."

"I can phone you at work tomorrow morning to confirm," Sky resolved. "Why don't you give me the number?"

Her defenses automatically rose. She'd been smart not to give him her home telephone number Saturday night. The flowers were ridiculous enough. What if he'd had the opportunity to augment them with a telephone campaign? "My work number, you mean?" she asked cautiously.

He had no difficulty interpreting her hesitancy. "If we're going to get together for lunch, I'd like to pick you up at your office. If you're going to give me your work address you may as well give me your work number, too.''

"Well..." She chuckled. "Only if you promise that you'll never send a bouquet as hideous as this to my office. It's bad enough my roommate has to know about this. If my colleagues did, too, I'd be mortified."

Sky erupted in a robust laugh. "Brooke, as soon as I'm finished unstuffing your shirt, the next thing on the agenda is mortifying you.'' Before she could object, he curbed his laughter. "Okay, okay, no mortification. Just an occasional humiliation now and again, maybe a bimonthly abashment."

"Is this your idea of incredible happiness?" she mused, unable to stifle her own laughter.

He sounded solemn when he answered. "Incredible happiness is a topic we ought to discuss in person. Can I have your office number?"

Reluctantly she gave it to him.

"Great," he said briskly, affording her no opportunity to change her mind. "I'll call you nine-thirty, ten or so." Then he hung up.

She didn't deliberately choose her pin-striped gray suit to wear to work the following day. Brooke was organized to the extent that she carefully rotated her suits and dresses, wearing them according to a precise schedule so she wouldn't grow sick of them. The suit she donned was arguably the stodgiest outfit she owned, featuring a nearly masculine blazer, with notched lapels and two unobtrusive buttons trimming each sleeve, and a straight skirt. She also wore an eggshell-white silk shirt with a high mandarin collar and her brushed-gold stud earrings. Her shoes were classic cordovan pumps. She filled a matching envelope purse with a lipstick and comb, and placed it inside her attaché case.

Nancy recoiled from her as she entered the kitchen and helped herself to a cup of coffee. "You're not wearing that!" she hooted.

Brooke inspected her roommate, who was dressed in something that resembled a stretched-out T-shirt, with broad pink and orange horizontal stripes. Then she lowered her eyes to her own apparel. She smiled whimsically. "It sure *looks* as if I'm wearing it," she commented lightly.

"Brooke, you've got a lunch date," Nancy unnecessarily reminded her.

They leaned against the counter to drink their coffee. There wasn't enough room at the dining table to eat; they'd discovered that last night. The flowers Sky had sent took up nearly the entire surface of the table.

"I frequently have lunch dates," Brooke calmly reminded her roommate.

"Not with men who send you bouquets in ceramic boots."

"If he wants to pursue me," Brooke commented, "he ought to know the real me. Tell me the truth, Nancy, isn't this suit the real me?"

"That suit," Nancy remonstrated, "looks like something female members of the Politburo wear."

"Oh, did you and Bogdan discuss Warsaw Pact fashions when he wasn't teaching you the polka?"

"The Hungarian dance troupe didn't dance the polka," Nancy retorted in a testy voice. "But I wore the dress that's made of two dozen silk scarves knotted together, and he adored it. If you'd like to borrow it—"

"Nancy! It's Tuesday. Tuesday at Benson and Broderick. I'm going to spend the morning collecting data for Chumley Car Rental's quarterly earnings statement, and I'm going to spend the afternoon hunting for loopholes for a very profitable robotics firm that is looking for an equally *un*profitable company to rent its tax credits to. People don't do those sorts of things wearing two dozen silk scarves knotted together." She paused to sip her coffee. "Besides, I've never cared for that garment," she added, unable to call it a dress. "It always makes me think of sneezing. Everytime you sneeze, you could untie one of the scarves and blow your nose on it. In the hay fever season you would wind up stark naked before noon."

"And have a fine time in the process," Nancy argued. "Everybody should wind up stark naked before noon at least once in their lives." She guzzled her coffee and slammed her empty mug into the sink. "We're both late, Splash. Time to make like a sheep."

And get the flock out of here, Brooke silently completed one of Nancy's pet sayings. Nancy was a fount of such slightly off-color expressions and Brooke actually found them amusing. She didn't even mind when Nancy called her Splash. From Nancy, such utterances seemed wonderfully in character and were never intended as insults. It wasn't the same thing as being called Drip by one's brothers, brothers who had grown up feeling rejected by their parents because they hadn't been girls and therefore hadn't collected their grandmother's bounty. Brooke's brothers had always been cruel in their treatment of their younger sister because they believed that she was worth thousands of dollars in their parents' eyes, while they were worth only a modest smattering of savings bonds apiece. It hadn't been Brooke's fault that she was female any more than it had been her fault that her mother's siblings had borne a statistically astonishing number of male progeny, leaving Brooke Jennings's promised donation untouched until Brooke arrived to collect it.

Of course, the money had gone to Brooke's parents, not to her. They'd been the ones to name her Brooke, after all. But if the money *had* gone to Brooke herself, the unlucky girl who had to go through life with such a ghastly name, she would have refused it. The politics of the Jennings clan sickened her.

As a rule, she tried not to think about it. She managed a cordial but distant relationship with her namesake grandmother, as well as with her parents. Her brothers she rarely spoke to at all. Both of them were married, and each had sired a son who was named after his father! Egos! Brooke moaned whenever she thought about her nephews' names. Not that Andrew Waters or Lawrence Waters were especially bad; it was just that neither of those hapless boys was given a name that a parent might have chosen simply because it sounded melodious or because the initials would look good on a monogrammed sweater or because the boys themselves *seemed* like an Andy or a Larry. If Brooke ever had children—and given that she was already thirty and not at all close to getting married, that wasn't too likely—she'd give her children the names she found in their eyes. She would lift her newborn baby into her arms and peer into its sweet, tiny face and know, instinctively know, that this precious little person was a Susan or a Patricia, a James or a Henry. That was the way children ought to be given names.

Riding the subway to her office on Park Avenue South, Brooke found herself wondering whether Sky had been named that way, whether his mother had cuddled him in her arms and gazed into his eyes and thought of the sky. But his eyes wouldn't have been sky blue. Brooke knew that sometimes babies were born with light eyes that gradually darkened over the first several months, but she simply couldn't imagine Sky's eyes ever being anything but strikingly dark. Maybe his mother had looked at him and thought of midnight. In any case, Brooke couldn't believe that Sky was named after a grandfather named Sky.

At a quarter to ten, Sky phoned her. She ascertained from Carol, the secretary she shared with several other accountants, that she was free for lunch and then told Sky that he could pick her up at noon. Carol had originally answered the call and had expressed doubt about Sky's name. "Some guy on the phone for you," she had announced the call, "but I think he's a phony. Says his name is—are you ready for this?—Sky Blue." It occurred to Brooke that Sky might have endured much more ribbing about his name than she ever had.

A few minutes before noon she visited the ladies' room to freshen her lipstick and brush her hair. As she examined herself in the mirror above the sink, she tried to imagine how Sky would look in a business suit. Advertising was undoubtedly a bit looser as a profession than tax accounting, but still...She didn't suppose he could show up at his advertising agency dressed in logger togs. Yet given his unruly hair and his beard, she couldn't conceive of him looking like a proper businessman.

She returned to her office, clicked on her computer monitor and ran through the Chumley figures one more time while she waited for Sky to arrive. He was only a couple of minutes late, and when Carol announced him she couldn't keep herself from snickering as she spoke his name. "This guy's for real, huh?" Carol whispered into the phone. "I thought it was a joke."

"It's not a joke," Brooke snapped in Sky's defense. Carol was so obtuse she had never recognized the absurdity of Brooke's name, though most of Brooke's associates had commented on it when Brooke joined the firm. Carol was also obtuse enough to ridicule a visitor while the visitor was still within earshot. On the other hand, Carol was gorgeous. Brooke's male colleagues generously forgave the woman for being a dimwit.

After saving her data, Brooke clicked off the computer, pulled her purse from the desk drawer where she'd stored it, and left her small, tidy office for the reception area at the end of the hall. Benson & Broderick, a gargantuan tax firm, occupied several floors of the building, and its employees were organized into work cells arranged according to the employees' functions in the company. Brooke's office, not surprisingly, was located along a corridor of corporate accounting offices.

Sky was seated on one of the sleek Naugahyde sofas across from Carol's desk in the reception area. He rose as soon as Brooke entered, and neither spoke as they surveyed each other. Brooke oughtn't to have been surprised to find Sky dressed in tailored corduroy slacks, a button-down shirt and a narrow necktie loosened at the throat. He'd already removed his jacket and slung it casually over his shoulder. His attire dampened the overaged-hippy effect of the beard and long hair. He looked, Brooke decided, like a college kid on a job interview—not yet groomed for the business world, but trying his best to appear neat and earnest nonetheless.

Except, of course, that a college kid on a job interview would look nervous, and Sky looked utterly confident and serene—and maybe just a touch bemused by Brooke's appearance, she discerned. His gaze slid slowly from her face to her prim suit, to the envelope purse she had wedged beneath her arm, to her slender, stockinged legs, to her classic burgundy pumps.

She looked to him like someone who'd appear in an aspirin advertisement, one that went "In an important, high-pressure job like mine, I get tension headaches *this* big" while not a hair is out of place, not a trace of pain marks her smooth brow. The thought amused him, even though he prided himself on producing commercials far less clichéd than that. If he were going to use Brooke in a commercial right now, he'd probably replace her prissy little purse with a Culpepper power saw and have her say, "Whenever I get a tension headache from my important, high-pressure job, I unwind by building bookcases."

His private chuckle caused Brooke to eye him quizzically, but he didn't bother to explain. "Let's go," he suggested, angling his head toward the door leading to the elevator bank. "I'm starved."

Brooke nodded and let him hold the door open for her. Nobody else was waiting for the elevator on their floor, and the broad vestibule onto which the elevators opened was empty. Its dim lighting gave the area a feeling of privacy. Almost before Brooke could press the summoning button, Sky had his hand on her shoulder, rotating her to face him, lowering his mouth to hers.

Again she knew that she could stop Sky's kiss before it started—if she wanted to. But she didn't want to. Something about his midnight-dark eyes, his delectably soft beard made her forget that she was a stodgy accountant whose personality seemed the very antithesis of Sky's. Something about the crisp, clean smell of him, and the heady flavor of his lips and tongue, made her want to kiss him as much as he wanted to kiss her.

His hand drifted from her shoulder to her chin, holding her mouth gently against his. It wasn't exactly a passionate kiss, yet it went beyond mere friendship, and Brooke felt her body softening as she had felt it soften in the lobby of her apartment building the last time Sky had kissed her.

She recalled that kiss as she experienced this one, and when she considered that Sky's kissing her in public places seemed to be becoming a habit, she edged her lips away from his. "You know, Sky," she murmured, slightly breathless, "I'm beginning to think you've got a touch of the exhibitionist in you."

His eyebrows arched at her unexpected observation, but his beard gave way to a warm smile. "Oh? Do I look like the sort of guy who drops his trousers on street corners?"

"I only meant...you're always kissing me in public."

"I'd much rather kiss you in private," he assured her, though she wasn't at all placated by the comment. She inched a step back from him. Before anything more could be said, the elevator arrived, already fairly crowded with workers heading for lunch.

Sky and Brooke jammed themselves into the car and fell silent. While they descended to the ground floor, Sky's eyes were on her, inspecting her thoughtfully. As soon as the elevator disgorged its passengers on the ground floor, Sky slipped his fingers through Brooke's and ushered her toward the doors leading to the street. "So you really are an accountant, huh?" he asked.

She peered up at him, but was unable to decipher his cryptic smile. "How did you know?"

"I asked around at work this morning. I guess I was the only person within the Greater Metropolitan Area who'd never heard of Benson and Broderick before."

"Just because I work for Benson and Broderick doesn't mean I'm an accountant," she pointed out. "I could be a secretary, a data processor, a personnel director—"

He shook his head. "I thought of all those things," he interrupted. "But now that I see you, I know you've got to be an accountant. Look at you!" His smile expanded. "All that's missing is a little tattoo on your forehead reading 'C.P.A.'"

Brooke said nothing. She ought to have been pleased; after all, she did want Sky to know who and what she was. But maybe she'd hoped that he had taken at least a few minutes to figure it out, or acted just a touch surprised by the realization. Maybe she'd hoped that he would have commented, "All that's missing is a little tattoo of a daisy on your left—"

No, she chided herself. It was just as well that Sky know the truth about her. It was only fair for him to know exactly who she was.

They entered a restaurant with a short line of people waiting to be seated and took their place at the end of the line. "So," Sky commented pleasantly, "you're an accountant."

"Yes."

"What flavor?"

"Flavor?"

"What's your specialty?" Sky clarified. "What do you do?"

"Taxes," she told him.

"Ah. Then you must be coasting right now."

"Coasting?" she asked.

"Well, April fifteenth has come and gone. It must be a light time for you at work."

"Oh, no," she corrected him with a smile. "I do taxes for businesses. They don't have to file by the April fifteenth deadline. That's only for individual taxpayers."

"It is?" Sky seemed astonished. "How come they get such a break?"

"They don't get a break," Brooke asserted, still smiling at Sky's ignorance. "They pay their taxes just like you and me. They just pay at a different time of the year, that's all."

"Why?" he asked.

Brooke hesitated. Why indeed? She'd never really given that question much thought. She contemplated it as a hostess led them to a cozy table against a wall and left them with two menus. When Brooke turned her attention to Sky she saw him watching her, waiting for an answer.

"Well," she replied, trying to sound authoritative, "in some cases, the companies work on their own fiscal year—for instance, June to May or September to

August—and their records are set up for that fiscal year, so it's easier to assemble the tax information around that. Or maybe it's just to make sure their returns don't get lost in the shuffle on April fifteenth. The IRS has enough on its hands in mid-April. A company might prefer to file at a different time to make sure its return isn't lost or buried.''

"I'd just as soon my return got lost and buried," Sky said, chuckling. "Who wants the IRS giving a return their undivided attention?"

Brooke grinned indulgently and turned her attention to the menu. She decided on a spinach-and-bacon salad, and Sky ordered a bleu-cheese burger and fries. When the waitress removed their menus and departed, Sky focused his attention back on Brooke. He'd already noticed that her makeup was very subtle, and he wasn't sure he liked the effect. Her eyes were more visible with the muted shadow and mascara, but he preferred them when they were recessive, requiring the viewer's full attention to absorb their understated beauty. Her lipstick…well, it wasn't really lipstick, more just a glossy tint, and Sky had kissed most of it off.

He was more aware of makeup than most men, and more critical of it, not only because of his fascination with faces but because as someone who filmed television commercials he was particularly knowledgeable about the professional uses of face paint. He examined Brooke's face and decided that she looked a bit more suave and professional than she'd looked on Saturday, a bit more mature. But on Saturday her cheeks had been pinker, their color heightened not by rouge but by the sun and the spring breeze and—he wanted to think—the pleasure she had taken in his company.

She was fighting that pleasure, Sky suspected. She was just the sort who would, one of those contained puritan types who were afraid to admit openly that they were having a good time. But he read beyond her show of resistance and knew that she liked him. Her mouth wouldn't have softened so readily against his if she didn't. She wouldn't have let him kiss her; she wouldn't have felt so good, tasted so good, looked so good being kissed if she didn't.

But all right, she wanted to play the puritan, the proper prig. She had her reasons, and he didn't want to rush her. He ought to make some effort to get to know her better, he resolved, even if she was—ugh!— an accountant.

The waitress delivered their food, and Sky waited for her to leave the table before speaking. "What exactly does a tax accountant do?" he asked.

Brooke glanced at him, her hazel eyes twinkling at his solemn expression. He appeared far more interested in her answer than any sane person ought to be, she mused. He was doing his best to come to terms with the real Brooke Waters, she realized, and she was oddly touched by his effort. "The same thing you do on April fourteenth, only at a more complicated level," she told him. "I collect all the available financial data from a client, figure out how much he's earned, what write-offs he's entitled to, how much I can reduce his tax burden. I give advice on ways to cut his taxes further, suggestions about how to reduce the tax bite in subsequent years. That's about it."

"Is that what I do on April fourteenth?" Sky asked, then laughed. He dabbed some ketchup onto his burger. "Actually, what I do on April fourteenth is curse a lot, drink heavily and lift a few numbers from some nearly unreadable little slip of paper that the ad agency sent me three months earlier. Then I write a check and drop the damned thing in the mail and drink some more and feel very sorry for myself." His eyes narrowed slightly as he added, "I also expend a great deal of energy berating the corporations whose taxes people like you figure out, because the corporations wind up paying zilch and I wind up paying some staggering amount that brings tears to my eyes."

Brooke grinned. "If you had to pay a single dollar it would bring tears to your eyes," she hazarded. "That's the way it is with taxes."

"Come, now," Sky challenged her, his good-natured tone contradicting his argumentative words. "You and I both know that thanks to magicians like you, Corporate America never pays its fair share of taxes. It's the little guys like me who pay the lion's share."

"That may be," Brooke allowed. "But I didn't write the tax laws, Sky. All I do is find ways for my clients to comply with those laws to their best advantage. I might be able to reduce a firm's tax bite to zero, but it's all within the bounds of legality. If the system's inequitable, it isn't my fault." She nibbled a forkful of spinach, swallowed and continued, "Many individuals wind up paying more than they have to because the tax laws are so convoluted and arcane that taxpayers aren't aware of all the write-offs they're entitled to. People like me get paid a great deal for our expertise, but we deserve it. We know those tax laws in a way the lay person doesn't."

"Uh-huh," Sky grunted. "In other words, I'm a bozo and I should be paying someone like you two thousand dollars in order to find out that Uncle Sam should be refunding me fifty cents."

"I don't charge individuals that much," Brooke assured him. "In fact, I rarely do individual returns—only for my roommate and people like that. I tend to find individual returns pretty boring. Unless, of course, they've got something interesting going on—some fancy stock manipulations, maybe, or an in-home business or something."

"An in-home business?" Sky asked, perking up.

"You know what an in-home business is, don't you?" Sky's sudden interest surprised Brooke. "You know, someone who runs a mail-order business out of her living room, or an artist with a studio in the den, perhaps."

"Or a drug dealer?" Sky teased. "A bored housewife who turns tricks for pin money?"

"Of course," Brooke played along in a dry tone. "According to the law, income from drug dealing and prostitution is fully subject to taxation."

Sky laughed briefly, then grew serious again. "I find this very intriguing, Brooke," he confessed.

"You don't have to say that," Brooke refuted him. "It really isn't very intriguing at all."

"It is to someone who runs a business out of his home," said Sky. He chewed on a wedge of fried potato, his eyes impaling Brooke with their constant darkness. "You know I make rock videos on the side. I earned a bit of money doing it last year, and I declared it on my ten-forty like a genuine, law-abiding citizen, but now I wonder if someone like you couldn't have found all kinds of legal ways to ease the tax crunch for me.''

"I'm sure I could," Brooke asserted.

"But it's too late," Sky grumbled. "I filed two weeks ago.''

"You could file an amended return.''

"What's that?''

"An amended return? You're allowed to file a form amending the figures on your original tax return for up to three years following that year's return. If you think you've got write-offs you haven't used, you ought to consider that option. It could be worth a lot of money to you.''

He leaned forward. "Would you help me?" he asked. "I mean, I'd pay you. I'm really an ignoramus about this stuff—as I'm sure you've gathered by now." Brooke opened her mouth, but Sky forged ahead before she could speak. "I know, you find individual returns boring. But I've never gone to an accountant in my life, Brooke. Would you help me out? As a friend?''

Much to her amazement, Brooke heard herself agreeing to help Sky out. She mentioned her standard hourly rate, which didn't faze him in the least, and described the sort of records she'd need to see, which, he claimed, he had dumped in a carton and stored in a closet. She hesitantly noted that if he was working out of his home it might be useful for her to see his apartment, and he immediately invited her to visit his place, where he'd be able to supply her with all his papers and an unending supply of decent wine if she liked.

They made a date for Saturday afternoon at one, and Sky wrote his address on the back of his advertising agency's business card and gave it to Brooke. "By Saturday the flowers should be dead," Sky noted with a sly grin. "Do you want me to send you some more? Are tax accountants allowed to accept bribes?"

"If you send me flowers like that ever again," Brooke warned him, "I'll charge you twice as much to do your taxes."

But what she was actually thinking, as they conversed about inconsequential matters during the remainder of their lunch, was that she'd succeeded with Sky far beyond her expectations. She had wanted him to know the real her, and not only did he now know the real her, but he was eager to exploit the real her. Well, not literally exploit her, she allowed; he was willing to pay for her time and knowledge.

But he didn't take her hand when they left the restaurant, and after walking her back to her office building he bade her good-bye with a simple "See you Saturday afternoon"; not even a kiss on the cheek. Brooke didn't like the feeling. All of a sudden, she *didn't* want him to think of her only as an accountant—*his* accountant. Now he was hiring her, now she'd be working for him, and one didn't kiss an employee, did one?

Apparently Sky didn't. And Brooke didn't like it. Her disappointment took her by surprise, but as she rode the elevator up to her office she felt dejected, deflated, not at all satisfied with the impression she'd made on Sky. Now he saw her not as a woman with a bizarre name who reminded him of a forest stream flowing over a rock, but as an accountant who could save him some money.

And in all honestly, she didn't like the change at all.

Chapter Four

Sky had his door open when the elevator let Brooke off on his floor of an aged, slightly seedy apartment building in the Murray Hill neighborhood, a few blocks from the United Nations. She wasn't at all surprised to see him wearing his snug, evenly faded jeans. He also wore a white T-shirt with a record album's jacket reproduced across the chest. Approaching him, Brooke was able to make out Willow, the green-haired rock star, on the T-shirt. The album's title was "Weeping Willow," and when Brooke recalled the howling music she'd heard at Willow's apartment, she decided that "Weeping" was appropriate.

"Come on in." Sky greeted Brooke with a light kiss on the cheek. Better than nothing, she reassured herself as she stepped inside his large studio apartment.

It wasn't exactly messy, but it was cluttered and disorganized. A double bed protruded from one wall, a bureau from another. An enormous desk blanketed with papers partially blocked a closet door. A broad sheet of white oaktag consumed much of the circular dining table's top, with a collection of pens beside it. Videotapes and magazines were stacked in piles atop a bookshelf. Electronically distorted music boomed from a stereo. Brooke had no difficulty identifying the whiny voice. "That's Willow, isn't it?" she muttered.

Sky laughed. "I'll turn it down," he offered, then strode across the room to his stereo and adjusted the volume lower. "I was just listening to a tape of her new album to get in the mood."

The mood for what, Brooke wondered. Suicide? Or maybe homicide?

"Can I get you something to drink? Some wine? Real stuff, out of a corked bottle instead of a screw-topped jug."

"No, thanks," she said, surveying the apartment one more time. "Given that you're paying good money for my services, I ought to stay sober."

"Okay. We'll open the wine after you're done, when we've got something to celebrate. I hope," he added. "Ever since we had lunch the other day I've been dreaming of the yacht I'm going to buy with the tax refund you wrangle for me."

Was that what he'd been dreaming of? Brooke had been dreaming of finding the right clothing to wear while doing his taxes. She'd wound up borrowing Nancy's off-white linen pants suit. All of her own clothing had seemed too dowdy and grim. She had been vaguely surprised by her concern about looking just right for Sky—looking like herself, only a bit more womanly than professional. Ever since they'd set up this visit on Tuesday, she'd been dreaming of clothing.

And his beard. She'd been dreaming of the way it caressed her chin when they kissed.

Thinking about that made her cheeks flush with color, and she determinedly pushed the idea from her mind. "I may as well get started," she announced.

"Okay." He waved toward his bed. "If you want, you can spread out there," he suggested, without any indication that his invitation for her to settle on his bed might have implications totally unrelated to the IRS. "Or you can use the dining table, but you've got more room on the bed."

"Whatever," she said with a shrug. "You're using the dining table yourself, aren't you?"

She glanced at the white oaktag on the table. It had been marked with a series of framelike boxes, the first few containing crude drawings of stick figures and trees. "Storyboard," he said in answer to the question in Brooke's eyes. "I'm trying to map out Willow's new video." Brooke's quizzical expression caused him to explain further. "You organize the main shots this way, by drawing them in the series you'll follow when you shoot. I'm not too good with pen and ink, as you can see. At the ad agency, we've got people who know how to draw doing the storyboards."

"It looks almost like a comic strip," Brooke commented.

"It does, sort of," Sky agreed. "I'm hoping that when Michael—Willow's manager—sees this he'll stop badgering me. He's got a ridiculous notion that we should do Willow's video kind of like a concert film, just showing her standing there, singing and wiggling her kazongers and what have you. Frankly, I think that's boring, but when I told Michael that, he got all uppity, as if I'd personally insulted his beloved lady."

"What's your idea for the video?" Brooke asked, unable to make sense of the rudimentary drawings on the storyboard.

"I thought something surreal and outdoorsy, having her moving through the trees. I mean, with her green hair and all—"

"To say nothing of her name," Brooke remarked. "Maybe you could clothe her in bark and have her do an impersonation of a willow tree."

Sky laughed appreciatively. "Now that would be funny. But Willow would hate it. She doesn't have much of a sense of humor when it comes to herself." He abandoned the table for the closet. Because of his desk's location, he couldn't open the door completely, and it took him a while to unwedge and remove a large carton, which he hoisted onto the bed. "Here's last year's life story," he announced. "Anything else you might need?"

"I brought what I need with me," Brooke answered, patting her attaché case. It contained pens, pencils, a calculator, scrap paper and all the tax forms she thought she might have use for.

She arranged herself comfortably on the bed, then opened the carton and cringed. It was crammed with loose papers. She overturned the carton, set aside Sky's copy of his return, and then bent to the chore of sorting all the scraps and scribblings.

It was tedious work, perhaps, but in its own way satisfying. Brooke had become an accountant because she liked sorting and organizing things. She viewed doing tax returns as something akin to solving a challenging high-stakes crossword puzzle. The work was frequently intellectually stimulating, and being able to save a client money was always a pleasure.

But Brooke had also chosen to become an accountant because it suited her temperament. It was dry, unobtrusive work. People took accountants seriously. Anyone who could take a disorderly heap of records like Sky's and make sense of it was deserving of respect, and Brooke happily immersed herself in the task of finding some tax savings for Sky.

He settled at the table and examined his storyboard for a while. Then he turned his gaze to Brooke. He watched her pull off her shoes and tuck one foot beneath the other thigh. Her legs delighted him. He'd never seen her sit except at a table, where he'd been unable to view her legs. He couldn't keep himself from suspecting that she ordinarily crossed her legs at the ankle and pressed her knees tightly together when she sat. It was a ladylike way to sit, the way little girls were taught in convent schools.

Of course, Brooke hadn't gone to a convent school; she was a Methodist. But he suspected that her primness had been ingrained early. She'd probably never dared to wear patent leather shoes as a child, believing the myth that boys could see up a girl's dress by studying the reflection in the patent leather.

Sky's attempt to picture Brooke as a girl was thwarted by the reality of her presence as a woman on his bed. Her legs were lovely, yes, and her arms, her slender body. He liked the loose folds of the white linen covering her, the rounded scoop of her blouse's neckline, the cuffs of her blazer rolled up to display her delicate wrists. He liked her face, devoid of makeup, her long, pale lashes resembling curling filaments of sunshine as they caught the light of his bedside lamp. He liked the sharp angles of her profile, the soft fall of her hair across her brow.

Her appearance was informal, and Sky wasn't quite sure what message she was trying to give him with it. When he'd last seen her, she'd looked perhaps three steps removed from a Salvation Army major. Maybe he shouldn't have kissed her at all, but he'd acted impulsively, so glad to see her at first that he'd ignored the vibrations she'd been emanating with her clothing and her attitude. But clearly she'd wanted him to back off. So he had.

His fascination with her puzzled him. It transcended the intriguing structure of her face, the genuine physical attraction he felt for her. Sky harbored a strange yearning to get to her, to insinuate himself under her skin. He wanted to make her laugh. That was why he'd sent those horrendous flowers, and he was pretty certain they'd been a success. She had laughed about them. He wanted her to laugh some more.

Brooke was becoming a compulsion with him. If he wanted to be logical about things, he'd be appalled by the hold she was developing over him without even trying. But Sky didn't care much for logic. As he'd told her at dinner that day they'd met, you only go around once in life, so you might as well have fun and not tangle yourself up in rationality. If his attraction to Brooke was unfounded, unreasonable, unrequited, so what? Sky had been rejected before in his life; it didn't bother him. As far as Brooke was concerned, he had nothing to lose, everything to gain. The whys weren't important.

Sky observed the appealing way she thought with her mouth. She drew her lips into a tense line of concentration, then moved them soundlessly as she conversed with herself, then relaxed them and whistled softly through her teeth. He wondered if she was at all aware of the things she did with her mouth while she worked. He wished he had a videocam available so he could tape her. Except that as soon as she saw the camera she'd become acutely self-conscious and stop moving her mouth.

She glanced up suddenly and caught him staring at her. One thing Sky wasn't was self-conscious, and rather than pretend that he hadn't been watching her, he merely leaned back in his chair and greeted her with a smiling nod.

Well, she thought. *That's a new one.* Before she'd gotten her M.B.A., she'd worked for one of the store-front tax preparation chains. People would enter with their annual records in a shopping bag, empty them onto her desk, and then gaze past Brooke at the clock on the rear wall, at the scattered receipts on her desk, at their hands. Brooke figured that they were shy about having someone paw through their financial affairs, or that they wanted to remain aloof from the nitty-gritty of adding up the pluses and minuses and measuring the pinch Uncle Sam was going to give their bank accounts. Or maybe they were embarrassed that a stranger was going to know their age, their social security number, the sum they spent that year on medication, their failure to donate to charity, their having fudged a bit on child support.

But Sky was freely staring at her, not at all embarrassed by having his financial secrets exposed. Brooke now knew that he was thirty-three, that his ad agency paid him handsomely, that he didn't exert himself much when it came to financial planning, and that, judging from a first perusal, he'd apparently over-paid his taxes. She found his candor amazing. Most people were incredibly private about their finances. They'd rather discuss their neuroses, their sexual pro-clivities, their political affiliations and childhood diseases than how much they earned and how much they'd declared on their tax returns.

Sky clearly expected her to ask him something, and when she didn't, he prodded her, "Fire away."

"Where do you usually work?" she asked.

"You mean at the agency?"

She shook her head. "On your rock videos. Do you usually work at the dining table?"

"Oh." He glimpsed his half-finished storyboard, then shrugged. "Sometimes. Sometimes on the floor, sometimes on the bed. No particular place."

Brooke adopted a lecturing tone. "Sky, what you want to do is establish an in-home business. But the IRS rule is that the portion of your home you write off as a place of business has to be used exclusively and regularly for that purpose. I assume you must use your table for dining at least as often as you do for working."

Sky considered, then grinned slyly. "And I can assure you I don't use my bed exclusively for work, either."

Brooke pursed her lips. "I'm sure," she mumbled, then reverted to her professional manner. "Do you ever use your desk for work?"

"When I go to the trouble of clearing it off," he replied.

"From here on in, I want you to use your desk for business, Sky. Either that or buy a drafting table. Set it up in a corner of the room and call it your office. I admit it's kind of difficult to have an office in a one-room apartment, but a lot of people do that in New York. At least we can deduct a portion of your rent as a business expense."

"No kidding?" Sky tossed down his pen and approached the bed. "What else have you got up your sleeve?"

"Well, let's assume you're going to write off one-third of your rent. Let's assume that your desk plus, oh, a hundred square feet of floor space is your office—a third of the apartment. Then we can also write off a third of your utilities."

"Really? The tax man is going to believe this?"

She scanned the room and smiled wryly. "If you got audited, he wouldn't. He'd come to see your office and find you working amid the salt and pepper shakers on your dining table and disallow the entire write-off. But if you legitimately established a working place here, one portion of the room devoted exclusively and regularly to your rock video enterprise, then he'd accept it. There are other ways of legitimizing your business in the government's eyes, too."

Sky lowered himself onto the mattress a discreet distance from Brooke. He examined the neat piles into which she'd assorted his papers, and her equally neat figures on her scrap paper. She wrote her numbers in precise columns, tidily labeled. Her handwriting was impeccable. "What other ways?" he asked.

"Business cards, for one thing."

"I've got business cards," Sky said, reaching for his wallet. Then he let his hand drop from his hip pocket. "I already gave you one."

"Those were cards for the ad agency you work for," she explained. "You need cards for yourself. 'Sky Blue, Maker of Rock Videos' or something along those lines. With your home address and your home number. Stationery, too, if you want to go all out."

Sky examined her face thoughtfully. "Do you think I should go all out?"

"Well, I'm not going to give you business advice, Sky. I don't know anything about the rock video business. I've never even seen one of those things. But—" she inhaled "—you earned a fair amount of money on the video you made for Willow last year, and you've got several projects lined up for this year, so you may as well start thinking of this as a genuine enterprise, not just something you're doing as a hobby. These things obviously pay well," she added, trying not to sound too surprised. Given what she'd seen of Sky's records, he wasn't wanting for money. Even as a novice in the rock video business he'd been paid a great deal for directing Willow's first tape, and he collected a royalty whenever the tape was aired on one of the rock video television stations. "If you're serious about entering the business in a big way, you ought to start thinking like an entrepreneur."

"Meaning my own fancy-dancy business cards," He chuckled. "Yes, ma'am. Anything else?"

"You've got to start keeping neater records," she reproached him. "You've got to save every receipt. Studio rentals, equipment rentals, everything. It took me all this time just to sort through your papers here and get them in order. Every expense you incur in making a rock video can be deducted from your earnings."

He inspected his tax return, then Brooke's scratch paper. "If you add up all these legitimate expenses, one hot-shot entrepreneur named Sky Blue probably lost money last year on his rock videos. Rookie season and all."

"Fine. Then we'll deduct your loss from your income from the ad agency."

"We can do that?"

"Of course."

He eyed the papers again, shaking his head in astonishment. His gaze rose to Brooke's face, his eyes dark upon her. "No kidding," he murmured appreciatively. "You really are going to save me money, aren't you."

"Not a yacht's worth, but yes, I'll get you a refund."

"I'm awed."

She shifted uneasily beneath his steady scrutiny. She wasn't sure she wanted him to be in awe of her. Awe implied fear, distance, detachment. Respect. One didn't kiss a woman one awed, any more than one kissed one's personal accountant. Particularly when the two things overlapped.

Her vision dropped to his beard, to the strong yet gentle lips she knew were lurking within the dense black curls that covered his jaw. She was glad to be saving Sky money, glad to be helping him. But she was unnerved by the understanding that that wasn't all she wanted with him.

"What?" He detected the discomfort in her averted eyes, her taut lips. "What's the matter?"

"Nothing," she mumbled, fidgeting with the papers spread between them on the blanket. "I should get back to work."

"No rush. Didn't you say I had three years to file an amended return?"

"Oh, so you were paying attention the other day." She laughed nervously.

"Hanging on your every word," he said with mock seriousness. He reached for her face and lifted a silky strand of hair away from her cheek. She flinched. "Feel awkward sharing the bed with me?" he asked.

"Surrounded by all these vital documents, I doubt you'll risk anything," she joked. "You could lose an invaluable receipt in the process."

"Sinking my yacht before I've even had a chance to buy it." He twirled his fingers through her hair. She stared at the papers. "Help me out, Brooke," he implored her. "Do you want me to keep my hands to myself? Give me a hint."

"I don't know," she answered honestly, still not brave enough to meet his eyes with hers.

"Hmm." He nodded, having expected as much. "You've been sending me so many contradictory messages, I'm a bit confused myself." He let his hand fall from her hair as he stretched out on the mattress, propping one pillow against the wall to cushion his shoulders. "Okay, Brooke Waters. I'm going to be a good boy and not touch you, despite the fact that you're voluntarily sitting on my bed."

"Voluntarily?" She snorted.

"All right. You're sitting on my bed because I agreed to pay you twenty-five bucks an hour."

"That sounds even worse," she complained, though she was smiling.

He laughed softly, then reached for her hand and clasped it. "For twenty-five bucks an hour, I get to hold your hand. How's that?"

"Still pretty insulting," she maintained, unable to suppress her grin.

"Now." He studied her hand, admiring the evenly filed ovals of her fingernails. "A week ago I tried to bulldoze you and you reacted by getting all huffy and puffy and thanks-for-dinner-good-night. The next time I saw you, you were Ms Ramrod Proper, as tense as a tuned piano wire. And now...now you look absolutely beautiful, soft and welcoming and intelligent. I know if I kissed you, you'd enjoy it, but I don't know if I should."

"Because you're in awe of me?"

"Because I'm confused."

"I'm confused, too," she admitted. Sky pulled her alongside himself, arranging the other pillow behind her head. She extended her legs carefully so as not to disturb the stacks of paper she had painstakingly organized.

"Why are you confused?" Sky asked.

"Well, for one thing, I don't think I ever met anyone so straightforward in my life," she confessed with a feeble laugh. She found strength in Sky's undemanding grip on her hand, and she took a deep breath. "I've never met anyone at all like you, Sky, and I don't know what to think."

"Then why not stop thinking?"

She groaned. "That's not the way I am."

"It's the way you could be, if you let yourself," he contended gently. "But we'll get back to that. First tell me why you don't know what to think about me."

She reflected for a moment. "It's not just what you do, Sky, though that's a good part of it. I hate rock music. In my opinion, popular music reached its peak in the early eighteenth century, and it's been going downhill ever since."

"Okay," he replied noncommittally. "It's not just what I do. Keep going."

"Well..." She studied him intently. He looked un-
kempt to her. Not that his jeans and T-shirt were dirty
or torn, but they were so unlike the genteel grooming
she favored in men. And his hair really was a bit too
long for her conservative tastes. And his beard..."I've
never even known a man with a beard before," she
said.

"You haven't? What about Abe Lincoln?"

"Never met him," she solemnly pointed out.

"Santa Claus?"

"That's a fake."

"Santa Claus is a fake?" Sky seemed outraged.

Brooke laughed. "I'm not sure, but his beard is. At
least it's a fake on all those impersonators in the department stores—and that's as close as I've ever gotten to the man." She dared to lift her fingers to Sky's
beard and combed them through it. It felt soft and
slightly springy. "When did you grow it?"

"Seven years ago," Sky replied.

"How come?"

He fell silent for a minute. "I guess I got tired of
looking at my face."

"I bet your face is very nice," Brooke argued.
"What I can see of it is nice. I bet beneath all that hair
you're very handsome."

"You don't think I'm very handsome now?" he
asked, again pretending to be outraged.

"I think you might be handsomer if you shaved,"
she told him unflinchingly. If he could be forthright,
so could she.

"Well, I won't," he said firmly. "I like the beard. I
think it gives me an aura."

"An aura of hair."

He chuckled, then captured her hand and pulled it from his beard, drawing it comfortably to his lap. "Okay. My career and my beard. What else?"

Brooke ruminated. She liked the way his hand made hers seem tiny, almost fragile. His fingers were long, the bones thick, the palm lightly calloused. She ran her thumb thoughtfully across his hand and it reflexively curled around hers. "I don't know, Sky," she murmured. "You don't seem to have any of the things I consider important in a man."

"And what might they be?" he asked, genuinely interested.

"You aren't all that neat," she observed, scanning the room and scowling. "I like neat men. Clean-cut. Serious. Cultured."

"Who says I'm not cultured," he protested.

"Rock music isn't cultured," Brooke earnestly explained. "Classical music is cultured."

"I like classical music," Sky said.

"You didn't know where Lincoln Center was."

He shrugged. "I don't go to recitals. I'm sure if I did I'd think they were swell, but I just never get around to it." He considered her words. "It sounds to me as if you're looking for an A-one bore. The city is filled with them, Brooke. Why haven't you nailed one down by now?"

"I'm not looking to nail down a man," she declared. "If one should happen along, fine. If not, fine. It isn't a big thing in my life."

"Why not?"

"You know, you're awfully nosy," she complained, though for some reason she really didn't mind his probing. She felt too relaxed, stretched out beside him, her feet surrounded by his tax information, to be offended by his questioning.

"Awfully," he agreed. He examined her knuckles as he thought. "Here's the way I see it, Brooke. We're not as different as you make us out to be. I think we've got a lot in common."

"Sure," she scoffed. "We've both got peculiar names."

"Beyond that. We're both honest; we're both professionally successful. We enjoy kissing each other—although you keep backing off like an overgrown virgin on that issue." Before Brooke could object, he continued. "We both think green hair on a woman is stinko. We both know the right time to leave a party."

"Are these the traits by which you judge people?" Brooke asked, amused by the trivial things that seemed to matter to Sky.

Undeterred, he forged ahead. "We both thought those flowers I sent you were repulsive. We both derive pleasure from reducing my taxes."

"So do a million other people...derive pleasure from reducing their own taxes, anyway," Brooke maintained. "And I'm sure a million other people would also find those flowers repulsive." She exhaled, her mind struggling to come up with the more substantial differences that separated her and Sky. "Admit it, Sky," she pressed him. "You're a much warmer person than I am."

"Sure, I'll admit that," he amiably agreed.

"Then why? Why me? Why don't you find some warmer woman to chase after?"

He eyed her pensively, his lips curved in a cryptic smile. "I haven't always been so warm, Brooke. I've had my cold days, too. It's much nicer to be warm than cold." His smile expanded slightly. "What all that special could I offer to someone who already knows that? It's more of a challenge to try to warm you up."

"Oh, I'm a challenge?" Brooke posed, oddly disappointed. "Is that all? You're intrigued by me because you think I'm hard to get?"

He weighed his words before speaking. "Do you know the principle behind the electric light bulb?"

His digression took Brooke by surprise, but she played along. "I know the basic theory."

"What old Tommy Edison figured out," Sky explained, "was that the more resistant the metal, the brighter the light it gives off when you force energy through it. The path of least resistance may be easier, Brooke, but I'm going for the brighter light."

She considered his metaphor and found it touching. But it also unnerved her. Evidently Sky wasn't going to give up on her until he saw her glowing like a two-hundred-watt bulb. The more she resisted him, the harder he'd try.

"Tell me," he urged her. "Tell me what it was that made you freeze up."

"I'm not frozen up," she asserted, once more unable to take offense at a remark she could have construed as an insult. "I'm reserved. I've always been reserved."

"Why?"

"Why is the sky blue?" she countered, then caught Sky's eye and laughed at her unintended pun. "Oh, Sky, I don't know. This is just the way I am," she insisted, mildly impatient. "Maybe it's what happens when you grow up in Boston."

"Have you got a lot of Puritan in your background?" he asked.

"As a matter of fact, Grandmother Brooke has the family tree charted back to the Mayflower."

"Who?" Sky asked, pouncing on the name.

"My grandmother...Brooke," she replied uncertainly. Why was he staring at her like that? Why did she feel as if he were trying to dissect her?

"You've got a grandmother named Brooke?"

"Yes. I was named after her."

"And you hate her?" he queried.

"We're not particularly close. Why do you ask?"

"Because I think you've got one of the most enchanting names I've ever heard, and you act as if the very sound of it is poison."

Uncomfortable, she shifted on the bed and wriggled her hand free from his. She generally didn't discuss the origin of her name; it only made her angry. But there was no point in hiding the fact from Sky. They'd already been too honest with each other for her to retreat from him at this point. "Maybe we would have been closer if I hadn't been named after her," Brooke allowed hesitantly. She toyed with one of her earrings, twirling it nervously between her thumb and index finger. "I was named after her for money, Sky. My parents didn't even want me. All they wanted was a daughter they could name after Grandmother Brooke because she promised money to the first of her children who named a granddaughter after her."

Sky frowned in bewilderment. "I don't get it."

"What don't you get?" she asked. "Money. My mother and her sister and brother went on a baby-making binge, trying to win my grandmother's contest. I was the first girl born. My birth brought fifty thousand dollars to my parents, which was a lot of money thirty years ago."

"It's a lot of money now," Sky commented, inspecting her face as if searching it for clarification of her unusual story. "Just because they collected some eccentric old lady's dough at your birth doesn't mean they didn't want you."

"They didn't," she repeated dryly. "They didn't really want my brothers, either. If Larry had been a girl, they never would have had Andy and me." She curled her lip as she thought about her childhood. "I hardly saw my parents at all when I was growing up. I was raised by a nanny."

"If your parents could afford a nanny, what did they need fifty thousand dollars for?" Sky asked.

"They didn't *need* it," Brooke corrected him. "They *wanted* it. It was play money for them. A competition they wanted to win." She sighed dismally. "My mother wanted to keep her siblings from getting the money. A power grab, I suppose. If my parents truly cared about me, Sky, they would have realized that Brooke Waters just didn't work as a name. They didn't, though. They never bothered to think about what I'd have to go through with a name like that." She turned her large, pale eyes on him. "Surely you can understand that. You had to fight kids because of your name."

"Maybe you should have fought kids, too," Sky mused.

"Come, now. I was a girl. A *lady*. Well-bred. Besides, my brothers were bigger than me. By the time I started school, my brothers had already ragged me to death about my name. On the rare occasions I can't avoid seeing them, they still call me 'Drip'." She shook her head. "What would have been the point of getting into fistfights? It wouldn't have changed my name."

"Have you ever thought about changing your name legally?" Sky asked.

She nodded. "Yes, but I couldn't bring myself to go through with it. You grow up with a name and it becomes your identity, a part of you. I couldn't have legally changed my name until I turned eighteen, and by then it was too late. I was already Brooke Waters. There didn't seem to be much point to changing it at that stage."

Sky said nothing. His gaze coursed over her face, and then he looped his arm around her and tucked her head into his shoulder. His fingers drifted through her hair, but there was nothing sensual about his stroking. It was a gesture of friendship and camaraderie.

"Did you ever think of changing your name?" she asked him.

"Never. As you said, it becomes a part of you. You accept it...you learn to enjoy it if you can. I can," he added. "I like to see the reactions of people when I introduce myself. I like to watch them squirm and squint at me and try to figure out if I'm pulling their leg. It's kind of a game with me. If I like their reaction, I decide I like them. If I don't like their reaction..." He poked his thumb downward and wrinkled his nose in disapproval.

"Wasn't my reaction that it was an awful name?"

Sky grinned. "But you looked so cute when you said it," he teased.

Brooke smiled as well. "Why did your parents do it to you?" she asked. "Not for money, I hope."

"No, not for money. For fun," he said, which didn't surprise Brooke. She imagined that the sort of parents who would produce a son like Sky would probably be a lot like him. "My father's name is Melvin Irwin Blue. Everyone calls him M.I. As in 'M.I. Blue'." He hummed a few bars of "Am I Blue," and Brooke giggled. "Well, I guess he figured, when you've got a name like Blue, you may as well make the most of it."

"So he named you Sky."

"Yes." Sky followed his own thoughts for a long moment, his grin softening. "There are advantages to being called Sky. I was always the only Sky in my classes. And it had a kind of hip organic appeal to it. Maybe you were considering changing your name, but when I was in college, I knew lots of people who were changing their names from Mary to Anemone and from William to Shabazz. A name like Sky fit right in."

Brooke digested what he'd said. It seemed to her that Sky's name suited him in a way she couldn't exactly identify. Maybe it was that he'd made his peace with it.

In a curious way he seemed like the sky to her, a spring sky, big and protective, clear and warm. She thought of the sky when it was at its most beautiful—during a vibrant sunset, or filled with mist before dawn, or blue, an unbroken blue expanse spreading its canopy over the earth. Those were the things Sky made her think of. Even if his name weren't Sky, she'd think of such things.

"Do you want to get back to my taxes?" he asked, breaking into her reverie.

The question startled her. "Do you want me to?"

"Not really," he confessed. "But I've got work to do, too. I've got to finish the storyboard so that tomorrow I can convince Michael I'm right about the video he wants me to make for Willow."

"You're the video artist," Brooke pointed out. "Michael shouldn't have hired you to do it if he didn't trust you."

"I like the way you think," Sky commented cheerfully. "Maybe you should be my manager."

"You could use one," she muttered, surveying his papers and then his jumbled desktop.

He eased her head from his shoudler and gazed at her. "Watch your step, Brooke, or I may hire you." He brushed his lips over her brow in a light kiss, then swung his long legs off the bed and stood up. "Are you busy tomorrow?"

"What did you have in mind?"

"You could come with me to Willow's place and help me sell my concept to Michael."

"Oh, I couldn't," Brooke demurred. "I don't know the first thing about rock videos."

He waved toward the assorted papers on the foot of the bed. "By the time you finish plowing through those, you'll know a whole lot about rock videos," he told her. "Come along with me. It'll be fun."

Brooke pictured herself prowling through Willow's jungle and shuddered. "Fun?" she grumbled.

"Ah, do I sense resistance?" he teased. "You're beginning to glow like a light bulb already."

"And if I stop resisting, you'll stop trying to force energy through me?" she shot back.

He smiled slyly. "Stop resisting and find out."

"You're incorrigible, Sky," she scolded, folding her legs as she sat up and reached for her calculator.

"I'll take that as a yes," he declared as he strode back to his storyboard. He lifted his pen and bowed over the oaktag, engrossing himself in his drawing.

Brooke scrutinized him for several minutes. His eyes were fixed on his work, his pen moving animatedly as he sketched his scenes. But he was smiling. Not quite a smug smile, not quite a complacent one, but a definite smile.

Chapter Five

"Make yourself comfortable," Sky suggested, waving toward the bed. He had picked Brooke up at her office and brought her home with him to watch rock videos.

She smoothed out the rumpled blanket before sitting. She tugged off her shoes and then adjusted one of the pillows behind her head. After carefully arranging the accordion pleats of her shirtwaist dress beneath her hips, she extended her legs comfortably toward the foot of the bed. He wheeled his portable color television set over, then turned it on and pressed the button on his cable channel control box to the station that broadcast rock videos exclusively. Brooke and Nancy didn't subscribe to cable television so Brooke had never watched the station before.

"Study up," Sky ordered her before vanishing into the kitchen. "You've got lots of learning to do."

She did. She wasn't sure how Sky had managed to get her involved in his enterprise, or why—except for the fact that she had better business sense than he did. But he'd been astonished by her performance with Michael and Willow, and he was already declaring her indispensable.

SHE'D GONE WITH HIM to Willow's apartment Sunday afternoon, feeling utterly ignorant and out of place. They settled on the floor of the room Sky had once identified as a bedroom. It contained fewer plants than the living room, so all four of them could sit on the woven straw mat covering the floor in the center of the room and see each other without having to peek around branches and leaves.

Willow was dismayed by Sky's having brought Brooke along. She alternately glared at Brooke and pouted or sidled kittenishly up to Sky while he defended his storyboard to Michael. Out of deference to Brooke, Michael refrained from smoking marijuana during the meeting, but there his deference ended. He didn't care at all for Sky's concept of the video. "If the viewer can't see Willow, they're going to listen to her singing, and that could be trouble," Michael claimed. Brooke found herself agreeing.

"They're going to see Willow," Sky insisted. "They'll see her surrounded by foliage. What could be more in character?"

"Come on, she's a singer," Michael argued. "Let 'em see her sing. Why not?"

"They'll see her sing. We'll do lip-sync, like we did with the first video. It worked well," Sky reminded Michael.

"Look. This is the budget the record company gave us," Michael outlined. "You wanna drag a dozen folks with weirdo faces out to some park and have them squirm around the trees? Man...do you have any idea what that's gonna cost?"

"Do you have any idea what it's going to cost if we have to rent a studio? I can get a park permit for peanuts. Money isn't the issue here, Michael."

And so they debated, Brooke listening and trying to imagine what one of these videos looked like. She was totally unprepared when Sky suddenly turned to her and said, "Explain to Michael why I'm right."

Nonplussed, she flexed her jaw a few times before speaking. "Sky's an artist," she attempted. "You've got to trust him." Michael sneered, and much to her amazement, she heard herself say, "If you just tape her standing at a microphone and singing, her fans won't bother going to her concerts. They can stay home and watch her for free on television. Don't you think you ought to offer them something they can't see anywhere else?" Where had she come up with such a superb argument, she wondered. How in heaven did she dare sound so completely authoritative on a subject about which she knew absolutely nothing?

Michael appeared mildly persuaded, but Willow wasn't convinced. "Don't listen to her, Michael," she whined. "She doesn't even know who I am."

I know you're Norma, Brooke thought, though she respectfully remained silent.

The discussion dragged on for hours, and the foursome retired to a restaurant to continue the debate over dinner. Willow insisted that they go to a vegetarian place in the neighborhood, and then requested just a salad, claiming she wasn't hungry. She could have eaten a salad anywhere, Brooke fumed as she forced herself to order something that turned out to be quite green and pasty. But she remembered to instruct Sky to make a note, as he picked up his receipt for the dinner tab, of who had been at dinner and what they'd talked about. "It's deductible," she reminded him.

There were two more such dinners during the week, which Sky insisted Brooke attend with him. At those meals she once again asserted that if Sky taped Willow performing as if she were in concert he might be jeopardizing her ticket sales at real concerts. Whether or not her position was valid, it seemed to sway Michael, and at Thursday night's dinner he reluctantly agreed to go along with Sky's concept.

"I feel like an idiot," Brooke told Sky after they'd said good-night to Willow and Michael and were walking to her apartment building. "I was just talking through my hat. I have no idea what these films even look like."

"But you said everything so definitively," Sky pointed out. "Nobody dared to argue with you. Accountants speak with the voice of God," he added teasingly. "You don't argue with someone who's managed to make sense of the tax code."

"Willow does," Brooke noted. "She can see right through me. She's probably figured out that when it comes to music I'm about three centuries behind the times."

"The fact is, everything you said about the video was right," Sky bolstered her. "And Michael finally realized it. Willow can choose to believe that or not, but Michael makes the ultimate decisions when it comes to her career."

"I imagine she would have taken it better if you'd been the one to convince him," Brooke commented as they reached the revolving door leading into her building. "She loathes me, I think. She'll never forgive me for not knowing who she was the first time we met."

"Maybe she's just jealous of you," Sky suggested.

"Jealous? Why?"

"*You* were the one who said she was in love with me," he reminded her. Then he leaned over, kissed Brooke's cheek and said, "I'll pick you up at your office tomorrow. It's about time you saw a few rock videos and backed up your innate brilliance with some concrete knowledge." He pivoted on his heel and strolled away from the building.

It had been a downright peculiar week, Brooke decided as she settled back against the pillow and stared at the screen of Sky's television. Chaste kisses on the cheek but nothing more, no attempt to force energy through her resistance, to turn her on like a light bulb. A warm compatibility, a focus on business and tickly kisses on the cheek, beard to skin. Except for that offhand remark the previous night about Willow's being jealous of Brooke because Willow was in love with Sky.... What was that supposed to mean? Sky couldn't be in love with Brooke. If he was, he wouldn't have kept kissing her on the cheek, would he?

They were friends, she'd grant that. Quickly becoming close friends. They were learning from each other. Sky was learning that one was supposed to save receipts from business dinners, and now Brooke was learning what people under the age of twenty watched on television. A strange friendship, but an interesting one. Much to her surprise, Brooke found herself willing to flow with it for the time being.

Sky appeared in the kitchen doorway, twisting a corkscrew into the cork of a wine bottle. "Mouton Cadet," he told her. "Do you want to get drunk so you can truly appreciate the spectacle you're viewing?"

"It couldn't hurt," Brooke said with a laugh.

She watched him wrench the cork from the bottle, sniff it and roll his eyes. "I tend to judge wines by price," he explained sheepishly. "And this, by that particular standard, is a super wine."

"Deductible, too," Brooke pointed out. "After all, I'm here on business. You didn't get a receipt from the cabdriver, did you?"

"Uh-oh," he groaned. "You should have reminded me. I still haven't got the hang of this." He set down the bottle and rummaged through the mess on his desk until he unearthed a clean sheet of paper. "Three-twenty, wasn't it?" he asked as he jotted down the price, the date, the people present. "A cheapie. We should have walked."

"Walking isn't deductible," Brooke quipped. She continued to watch him as he produced a wineglass, poured some white wine into it and carried it to the night table beside the bed for her.

"Okay," he said, loosening his tie as he strode back to the kitchen. "I'm going to make dinner. You watch the tube and become an expert."

"Yes, boss," Brooke said obediently.

She reached for the wine and sipped. She didn't care what the wine had cost; it was excellent. Lowering the glass to the table, she turned her attention to the television. A young man with his hair shaved into a Mohawk was hanging by gravity boots from a horizontal pipe and wailing about how some woman had turned his world upside down. Brooke scowled and took another sip of wine.

The upside-down man disappeared, and another video began, this one featuring a cast of actors and musicians well beyond their teens dressed as children and romping around a kindergarten classroom. The women in the tape wore fluffy crinoline petticoats that propped up their skirts to reveal inordinate amounts of leg. It struck Brooke as sexist, and she scowled again.

In the compact efficiency kitchen, Sky set about preparing dinner. He wasn't a great cook, but he was creative, and he figured he could find enough interesting ingredients in his refrigerator and cabinets to concoct something edible. He'd originally considered taking Brooke out for dinner, but he wanted her to see some videos, so eating in seemed a smarter idea.

He set a large skillet on the stove and assorted a bunch of vegetables to toss into it. A green pepper, some mushrooms, a quarter of a cauliflower, an onion. Soy sauce, sherry. Two cans of "mixin' chicken." It would all go together somehow, especially with rice. He measured some water into a pot and set it to boil.

He hummed along with the rock music emanating from the other room while he worked. He was familiar with many of the videos that accompanied the music, having studied the form for a long time before embarking on his first venture in the field. Instead of trying to picture the visuals, he tried to picture Brooke watching them.

He'd known she was special from the moment he saw her, but he'd never guessed how useful she could be to him in his business. It wasn't just the tax savings, or even her willingness to put his enterprise into some sort of order. She had good instincts. Her intelligence enabled her to deal sensibly and successfully in a business she didn't know a thing about. There was something to be said for organization, after all, he mused. Brooke had a very organized brain.

He liked the dress she was wearing tonight. It fit her well, flattering her slender figure in a way her suits didn't. And she wasn't wearing much makeup. She looked beautiful.

The vegetables began to simmer in their sauce, and he lowered the heat beneath the skillet and set its lid in place. Then he filled a glass of wine for himself and leaned against the counter, watching the stove. He could join Brooke in the other room if he wanted, but he decided not to. Right now he preferred only to think about her.

She'd really loosened up this past week. By last night, she didn't even seem to be noticing Willow's hair anymore. But Brooke's transformation went well beyond being able to talk shop with a green-haired rock singer. It had to do with her exposing herself to an alien world. It had to do with her opening up, not shrinking away. She seemed confident, even courageous. She was turning out to be much more than Sky had bargained for, and he wasn't sorry.

Still, he was acting with restraint around her. He didn't want to rush her, to force things. He would accept her friendship until she was ready to offer him more than that. It was difficult holding back. Those little pecks he'd been giving her on the cheek in farewell... He cursed softly as he contemplated his willpower. Kissing Brooke on the cheek was like savoring a microscopic taste of chocolate mousse and then shoving the bowl away. He wanted so much, but he had to wait for her.

It wasn't like him to be this patient. But then, it wasn't like him to try his luck with a woman like Brooke. She'd been pretty accurate when she had claimed that she wasn't his type—at least, she wasn't at all similar to the women he'd known in the past. When she had accused him of chasing her just because she was a challenge, she'd been pretty accurate, too. She *was* a challenge.

Yet she was more than just a challenge. She mattered to Sky—she was mattering more and more to him. The closer he got to breaking through to her, the stronger his desire to break through to her became. Once or twice, engaged in a heated argument with Michael, she'd become so uncharacteristically passionate that Sky had had to stifle the urge to make love to her right at the restaurant table. He'd seen the promise of incredible happiness in her eyes. He'd felt it. It made him ache with longing.

Such a strong desire didn't bother him, even if it was out of the ordinary for him. He found it kind of amusing, actually, rather delightful. He wasn't satisfied by it, but satisfaction didn't count for much in Sky's scheme of things. Satisfaction implied a conclusion to him. One was satisfied by results, not processes. Sky was the sort of person who took much greater pleasure in traveling than in reaching a destination. He appreciated the means far more than the ends. The ultimate destination, the ultimate end was death, so there was no point in racing toward destinations and ends, as far as he was concerned.

He lifted the lid of the skillet to check his stew, stirred the stew perfunctorily and lowered the lid again. He listened to the music and tried to guess what Brooke was thinking.

He heard her laughing. At first just a soft chuckle, then a higher-pitched giggle. Her rare laughter, he'd learned this past week, was usually constrained and quiet, poised and ladylike.

But not now. The giggle bubbled over into a full-fledged bellylaugh, a body-shaking guffaw. He set down his wineglass and moved to the doorway.

She was bent forward, practically doubled over with laughter. One hand gripped her abdomen, and the other was clapped over her mouth, as if she were trying to stuff the gales of laughter back into her body. Her eyes were closed, and tears leaked through her long lashes onto her flushed cheeks. God, she was beautiful, he thought. This was the laughter he'd been waiting for since the first moment he saw her: laughter that rose from her soul, laughter that shattered her prim facade and energized her spirit, laughter that made her glow.

"What's so funny?" he asked, venturing into the room.

She glanced up at him, then erupted in a fresh spate of giggles. "This—this thing they just showed," she stammered, waving at the television. Glimpsing the television set, she succumbed to more laughter. She was laughing so hard she started to cough.

He turned to the screen and shrugged. The video being shown wasn't that comical.

"Not this one," she clarified, reading his puzzled expression. "The last one." She sniffled and dabbed at her damp eyes. "They had these singers frolicking on a beach, dancing in the sand and all, splashing in the surf. And then suddenly—"she had to stop speaking as another series of giggles wracked her "—suddenly they were buried in the sand, Sky, just up to their necks, so all you could see was their heads. Just four disembodied heads—and they were singing. Sky, it was hilarious, just these heads sitting in the sand singing...." Her voice dissolved into more laughter.

He nodded, recalling the video she described. He'd found it hilarious the first time he'd seen it, too.

But he was more interested in Brooke than in the video. He moved to the bed, studying her streaming eyes, her glistening teeth, the faint dimples denting the smooth hollows of her cheeks. She still clung to her stomach, apparently suffering a stitch from having laughed too hard.

He'd never seen her looking so alive, so lovely. Her laughter seemed to have released her from herself, draining her of her reticence, her sense of propriety. It had liberated her, and he was stunned by the transformation in her. So stunned he couldn't keep himself from sitting on the edge of the mattress beside her and touching his mouth to hers.

His kiss seemed to startle her at first. She hadn't stopped smiling, and her lips didn't immediately fit themselves to his. He cupped his hands about her head to steady it, then continued kissing her until her mouth molded to his, until she gradually began to return the kiss. As soon as he sensed her submission to it, he filled her mouth with his tongue.

She tasted warm and sweet, deliciously feminine. Her laughter melted into a soft moan in her throat, and her fingers reached up to comb through his thick dark hair. *Yes,* he thought, *yes, she's ready, she's finally ready.* He would indeed have given his left arm to have her so ready for him, to have her so receptive to the joy he knew they could discover together.

He shifted on the bed, extending his legs beside hers, covering her chest with his. Their mouths were moving as one now, hungrily consuming, devouring, sharing. Her foot brushed along his shin and she moaned again. Her hips twisted on the mattress.

His mouth left hers to taste her chin, her throat. He let one hand drop to her shoulder, feeling the narrow bone through the crisp cotton of her dress. "Sky," she whispered, her breasts rising against him, her hips twisting again.

He groaned. She felt good, indescribably good, better than any other woman he'd ever known. The skin of her neck was as smooth and silky as the skin of her face. Cool and dry, blessed by a distant scent of lilac.

Her hands trembled in his hair. She whispered his name again, and the sound worked on him like an aphrodisiac. "Sky..." as if she were breathing him, thriving on him. He wanted her so much.

His hand slid across the front of her dress to her breast. She gasped at his touch, then spoke his name again. He heard a plea in it, a question. "Yes," he murmured, hoping that would be enough of an answer for her.

It wasn't. "Why?" she asked. "Why are you doing this?"

He lifted his head from the base of her throat and stared at her, astonished. Why was he doing this? Wasn't it obvious? Did she need a diagram to make things clear for her? "What do you mean?" he asked, hoping he didn't sound too exasperated.

Her eyes met his. They were still moist, a pale green-gray, her curling lashes glimmering with residual tears. She didn't look sad, or, for that matter, happy. Only confused. "All week long, Sky..." she began, then faltered. She appeared so vulnerable all of a sudden that he berated himself for his impatience. He lifted his hand to her hair and stroked it tenderly.

"All week long what?" he prodded her.

"You've been kissing me on the cheek," she managed.

He smiled tenuously. "I like your cheek," he explained. "It's a very pretty cheek. I also like the rest of you, so I've decided to move on."

"Sky." Her voice emerged stronger now. "Why all of a sudden?"

"All of a sudden?" he blurted out, then laughed. "I've been waiting for a green light from you, a go-ahead, any sort of sign. All week long I've been kissing you on the cheek and then racing home and taking a cold shower. What did you think?"

"Did I give you a sign?" she asked. She didn't sound forbidding or disapproving, merely perplexed. "Just now? I gave you a sign?"

He leaned back to examine her face. She was frowning slightly, her brow marked by a crease, as if she honestly didn't understand how alluring she was, how sexy he found her, as if she was totally unaware of what she was doing in his arms. She *was* like an overgrown virgin, he pondered. "You kissed me back," he pointed out.

"Yes, but..." She closed her eyes, awash in bewilderment. She had kissed him, she had practically lost all sense of herself in his kiss. Sky's kisses were so overpowering that she'd eagerly submitted to them. She thirsted for more. She wanted him, suddenly, crazily. Yet after a week of business dinners and chilly farewells, his new approach to her seemed terribly abrupt. She hadn't been prepared for it, and certainly not prepared for her own reaction.

"But what?" he asked.

She said nothing. She was too addled to think straight.

"Brooke," he murmured, bowing to graze her forehead, brushing back her thin bangs with his lips. "Brooke, I've spent this week falling in love with you. Why are you so surprised?"

"Falling in love with me?" she echoed vaguely.

He answered by covering her mouth with his again. She surrendered momentarily to his searing kiss, her tongue meeting his, her hands relaxing against the back of his head. Then she turned away, another surge of bewilderment coursing through her.

"How can you be falling in love with me?"

"How can I help myself?" he returned. Her mouth was no longer available to him, so he kissed her ear instead.

He felt her shuddering beneath him. Her breath caught in her throat, and her thighs grew tense against his. "Sky." She sighed weakly. "It doesn't make sense."

"It doesn't have to," he reminded her, then twirled his tongue around her earring.

Not to him, perhaps, but to her it had to. She was losing control again, losing control of herself, to Sky. Maybe he did love her, or at least he thought he did. And that was sufficient as far as he was concerned. But what about her? Was she falling in love with Sky?

He wasn't her type, she tried to convince herself. But that argument didn't seem to carry much weight when her entire body was responding so vividly to his sensual overture. A churning warmth in the pit of her stomach informed her that physically he was very much her type.

Physical attraction wasn't the issue. It wasn't that she didn't want to have sex with him. It was love they were talking about, and that was where she was having difficulties. "Sky," she insisted, fighting herself more than him. "Please, Sky, we have to discuss this."

He inhaled sharply, then pulled himself up from her. "You know what your problem is, Brooke?" he chided her, trying to keep his tone calm. "You analyze too much. That's fine in business, but not in love. Just quit analyzing so much and go with the flow."

Go with the flow, she contemplated. No. Not when it came to love, not when it came to her heart. That was the most dangerous way to approach love, she thought. It was the surest route to heartbreak.

She couldn't help but analyze. She knew Sky well enough by now to understand that he was playing life's game for the fun of it, having himself a ball on his way to the grave. He'd told her as much the first evening they'd spent together. She admired his philosophy, maybe even envied it. But it wasn't hers. She was too serious, too earnest, too reserved. She couldn't simply transform herself into a forest stream, rippling beautifully along its weaving course to wherever. She just wasn't constructed that way. She couldn't do it.

It didn't matter that right now she wanted Sky, that right now her entire body throbbed with yearning. Sky Blue could break her heart. She knew it. He could make her lose control, and if she lost control she'd be left with nothing.

She rolled out from under him and stood up. Her shoulders were shaking, and she occupied herself by straightening out her dress. "I'm sorry," she whispered tremulously.

He fell heavily onto the bed and peered up at her. He did nothing to conceal his disappointment. His breath was ragged, his legs bent at the knees, his hands curled into fists. "Oh, Brooke," he muttered hoarsely. "So am I."

Bravely she gazed at him. His hair was disheveled, his eyes nearly opaque. Looking at his beard, she relived the feel of its texture against her chin, against her throat. She realized with a pang that he was quite possibly the most attractive man she'd ever known, beard and all. "Do you want me to leave?" she asked meekly.

"Hell, no. If you leave, how am I going to convince you you're wrong?" he posed with a wry smile.

His ability to joke about what was obviously a frustrating situation for him heartened her. She struggled to match his smile, but she felt sick inside, her own frustration welling up, bickering with her brain for having been too sensible at a time when she ought to have gone with the flow.

She thought she ought to say something, but she wasn't sure what. Before she could come up with an idea, Sky heaved himself off the bed. He shrugged his shoulders in an exaggerated movement to work out his tension, then sniffed. "Something's burning," he mumbled, striding briskly into the kitchen.

She remained standing where she was for several moments, surveying the windows that extended along one wall. They were filled with the muted lavender light of dusk. Her gaze wandered to his sloppy desk and then to his bed. She grimaced and stalked to the kitchen.

Sky seemed to have come to grips with himself, because he offered her a big smile when she entered. "Just the rice," he informed her. "Sticking at the bottom. Most of it's salvageable."

"Good," she said.

She stood out of his way as he gathered dishes, silverware and paper napkins and haphazardly set the dining table. He tossed the several pens that had been sitting there onto his desk. One rolled off but Brooke didn't bother retrieving it from the floor. That would be much too prim and proper a thing to do, she decided.

He carried the wine bottle to the table, and Brooke fetched her glass from the night table before joining him. He refilled their glasses, then served up the stew. They sat facing each other, pretending to be interested in their food. "Very tasty," Brooke critiqued.

"Okay. That ought to do it for courtesy," he cut her off with a grin. "Let's talk like real people now."

She sucked in her breath, then mirrored his smile. "Be my guest," she invited him.

"Ever been in love?" he asked.

Jump right in, why don't you, she muttered under her breath. "If you're asking me if I'm a virgin—"

"No, I'm not," he interrupted. "I'm asking if you've ever been in love. Although that's a reasonable question, too. Are you a virgin?"

"No," she said curtly.

He faked enormous relief. "Thank heavens! I've only offended you emotionally, then, not physically."

"You didn't offend me," she stated, reaching for her wine. She took a long sip, then lowered it. "I suppose I should be flattered."

"Flattered?" He considered the word, then nodded. "Yeah, I guess it must be flattering when a man tells you he's in love with you. Have you ever told a man you were in love with him?"

"You're unbelievably pushy," she reproached him.

"That should come as no revelation by now," he mocked himself. "I've been unbelievably pushy since Corny Cobb's party. Are you going to answer my question or play games all night?"

She fidgeted with her fork, then sighed. "I almost got married once," she said.

His eyebrows arched slightly as he digested this information. "What happened?"

"I didn't," she replied.

"Why not?"

"I..." She didn't love Joe, that was why not. "It wasn't going to work out," she answered evasively. "We met in business school in Chicago. Upon graduating, he decided to take a job in Boston. I decided to take a job with Benson and Broderick in New York. So we split up."

"You couldn't find a job in the same city as him?"

"He couldn't find a job in the same city as me," Brooke corrected Sky. "I didn't want to go back to Boston. The farther I get from my family, the happier I am." She sighed again. "I guess if we had wanted to we could have found work in the same city, but we didn't want to. Obviously it wouldn't have made much of a marriage."

"But you must have loved him if you even considered it."

"I loved his name," she confessed. "I think that was the thing I loved best about him."

"What was his name?"

"Joseph Anderson."

"Joseph Anderson?" Sky hooted. "What a horrible name."

"Horrible? I think it's a wonderful name." She bristled. "My big dream was to become Brooke Anderson. Brooke Anderson," she repeated. "A completely meaningless name."

"Meaningless," Sky scoffed. "That's exactly what it is." He ate in silence, collecting his thoughts. "So," he confronted her. "Back to question one: Have you ever been in love?"

"No." There was no point in lying. Sky would continue to badger her until she told him the truth. But before he could capitalize on it, she decided to give him a dose of his own medicine. "Have you ever been in love?"

"Oh, sure," he said decisively.

"Good Lord, the way you say that I'm almost afraid to ask how many times."

"Hey, I'm not the accountant here," he protested with a laugh. "I don't keep records."

She lowered her fork and bit her lip. Sky sounded dreadfully cavalier about love. She supposed she should have expected as much. Falling in love was undoubtedly an integral aspect of having a ball while one was passing through life. She didn't like the notion that Sky considered love so trivial that he could fall in and out of it with all the commitment of the proverbial bumblebee flitting from flower to flower. "I take it you've been in love enough times to consider yourself an expert on the subject," she muttered tartly.

"I'm not an expert," he murmured, becoming earnest. He drained his wineglass, then leaned back in his chair and appraised her. "I like women. And yes, I've been in love a few times." He paused to replenish his glass, then dribbled the remaining drops of wine into Brooke's still half-full goblet. "The first time was when I was in high school. We were kids. We swore undying love, then went off to college and promptly forgot about each other.''

"I don't think that counts as love," she argued.

"Of course it counts," Sky insisted. "It was very real. Immature love, granted, but love just the same." He eyed Brooke critically. ''There isn't a gauge you have to measure love against, you know, and say, 'Well, this love counts because it ended in marriage, but that love doesn't count because they grew apart after a couple of years.' There are different kinds of love, Brooke, for different people at different stages of their lives. No one kind of love is more legitimate than another."

"You don't think lasting love is more valuable than passing love?" she asked, pleased that the discussion seemed to have veered into the abstract.

"More valuable, yes. More legitimate, no."

"So you've had a number of legitimate but not very valuable love affairs," Brook summarized.

Sky chuckled. "You like belittling love, don't you?"

Quite the contrary, she silently disagreed. It seemed to her that Sky was the one belittling love. The more times one was in love, she believed, the less important love must be. In her mind, love was so special, so precious, that she was unable to consider the man she nearly married as someone she loved.

She wanted to fall in love. But she hadn't. She wouldn't label the occasional friendships she had with men love; calling them love wouldn't magically *make* them love. She had tried to be in love with Joe, and after knowing him for three years, talking marriage, meeting his family and introducing him to hers, she ended up convinced that she didn't love him. If she had loved him, she would have known it.

She wasn't in love with Sky, either. She enjoyed his company and treasured the time they spent together. She liked looking at him, spending time with him, even arguing with him. But if she loved him, wouldn't she know it? She wasn't romantic enough to think she ought to hear bells ringing every time she gazed into the eyes of a man she loved, but she knew there had to be something more than respect, pleasure, sexual awareness and the mere fun of being friends.

She sipped her wine and thought about it. There *was* something more with Sky, she reflected. She did feel something besides friendship and attraction. She felt fear, the fear that he could break her heart. Wasn't that why she'd run from him when he began to make love to her?

Could it be love, then? No, she resolved. Self-protection wasn't love. A man could break a woman's heart in plenty of ways, and love didn't necessarily have to be a part of it.

Sky was waiting for her to speak. She drew in her breath and said, "I'm not belittling love, Sky. Just the opposite. I think love is such a rare, wonderful thing that I don't use the word lightly.

"You're saving the word for some clean-cut strait-laced fellow with a neat apartment, huh?" he needled her.

"I'm saving the word for someone I love," she parried.

"And I'm not him." He mused for a moment, scratching his beard thoughtfully, then shrugged again. "Okay, I'll bite. What do you feel for me?"

"You're pushy," she said quickly. "That you'd ask such a pushy question proves the point."

Sky laughed. "What else?"

Brooke moved her lips, then sighed. "I don't like baring my soul, Sky. I don't like talking about these things. I've already told you more than I usually tell people. Can't we change the subject?"

He laughed again, but he sensed her discomfort, and his laughter was soft and gentle. "Brooke, you've got so much locked up inside you," he chided her. "You've got it locked up so deep inside you that you can almost pretend it isn't there. But it is. You're as passionate as I am, only you don't know how to let it out."

"Look," she snapped. "I've been doing my damnedest to go with the flow for you, but I'm not in the market for therapy. Pushy is an understatement, Sky. You're irritating."

Something sparkled in his eyes. "Fantastic," he murmured. "It's fantastic when you let it show, Brooke."

Let what show? She reflexively glanced down to see if her dress was unbuttoned. Raising her eyes to his again, she frowned.

"It's all there inside you," he explained in a low voice. "I've been catching glimmers of it all week. You'd be presenting an argument to Michael, all sensible and rational, and then Willow would say something and you'd let loose with a flare of anger. Or earlier this evening, when you fell apart laughing. Or whenever you kiss me. It's all there, Brooke, and when you let a little of it out, you take my breath away." He reached across the table for her hand and covered it with his own. "That's why I'm falling in love with you, and I don't give a damn if it's logical. All that matters is that it's happening."

"What if it's not happening to me?" she asked dubiously.

"It would happen if you'd let it," Sky insisted.

She peered into his eyes. They were so dark, dark yet animated, like shadows in a dense forest. She discerned life in them, the life that lurked within shadows, not quite revealing itself but making its presence known. She longed to see the shape of it, to meet it. But even that desire wasn't love. Sky was wrong. She couldn't just go with the flow and call it love.

She dropped her gaze to her lap. "I like you, Sky. I do like you," she offered apologetically.

"But?"

"No buts," she said with a meek smile. "I even—" she forced her honesty into words "—I even would enjoy making love to you. But you want more from me than a roll in the hay, don't you?"

Sky was touched by her candor. His hand tightened around hers, and he lifted it to his lips to kiss her palm. "You aren't the sort of woman who rolls in the hay anyway," he joked, then grew solemn. "Yes, I want more from you. And now you'll say you can't give me anything more, and I'll say you're wrong."

"I'm so glad you've worked it all out," she said with a sniff. "You don't even need me here. You could have had this entire conversation by yourself."

He grinned briefly. "No, I do need you here. And I can wait until you're ready to admit you're wrong."

"You might have a very long wait."

"Fine. In the meantime you can help me make a fortune in the rock video business." He stood, stacked the dishes and carried them into the kitchen.

Brooke felt no relief that the troubling conversation had drawn to a close. Once again she found herself admiring Sky's tenacity, his willfulness, his stubbornness. All right. She'd add admiration to the list of things she felt for him: friendship...fascination...attraction...admiration. How many more items would the list have to contain before she could sum it up and call it love?

Maybe Sky was right. Maybe she was too analytical, although it struck her that he was doing as much analyzing as she was. Maybe he was right in asserting that she was too sensible about a feeling that by definition wasn't very sensible. Maybe she was too sensible ever to fall in love.

But to fall in love would mean more than to stop being sensible. It would mean relinquishing control. Brooke knew that instinctively. And she didn't think she could do it.

She couldn't expect Sky to understand. Sky "Happy-Go-Lucky" Blue was so different from her temperamentally that he couldn't possibly understand Brooke's need to feel in control of herself, in control of her life. The very first thing that had ever occurred in her life had been her naming, and she had had no control over that. Her conception, her birth, her name—-all part of a family contest with greed as the only rule and money as the prize. She'd been a victim of it.

So she clung to the things she did have control over. She had learned to check her emotions carefully. She had learned to be sensible and logical. It was the way she coped, the way she survived.

And no matter how seductive Sky was, she wasn't going to let him take her control away.

Chapter Six

Brooke hung up the telephone and groaned. "Hey, Splash," Nancy called to her. "Dinner's on the table."

Reluctantly she trudged to the table and dropped onto her chair. Nancy beamed a bright smile in Brooke's direction and shoved the platter of broiled chicken toward her. She took a leg quarter and groaned again.

"Why the long face?" Nancy asked.

"That was the box office at the Metropolitan Opera," Brooke grumbled, referring to her telephone conversation. "They're just as bad as Avery Fisher Hall and the State Theater. It seems that every seat to every performance at every theater in Lincoln Center is booked well into the twenty-first century."

"This is not what I consider a tragedy," Nancy chirped as she doused her salad with dressing. "As a matter of fact, I'd like to take some of the credit for it. The city's Department of Cultural Affairs has been striving to make all cultural facilities in the city profitable and enthusiastically supported. I'm proud of our efforts."

"Yes, you're doing a swell job," Brooke said mournfully. "That doesn't help me much."

"Why? What's the problem? You and I have tickets for several Mozart concerts this summer. Can't you wait till then?"

Brooke sighed and listlessly speared a tomato wedge with her fork. "Sky and I made a deal," she explained. "I'm supposed to go and watch him film his rock video on Long Island this coming Saturday, and in return he's supposed to attend a concert at Lincoln Center with me. We're trying to broaden each other."

Nancy studied her roommate and grinned slyly. "So buy a couple of tickets for something in the twenty-first century. Maybe the relationship will last."

Brooke exhaled. How could she think of a long future with Sky when she wasn't sure that she loved him or, for that matter, that he loved her? He hadn't breathed a mention of the word "love" since his abortive attempt to seduce her a week and a half ago. In fact, they hadn't even seen each other since that night.

They'd talked frequently on the telephone, but once he'd gotten the go-ahead from Michael on his concept for Willow's video, Sky had been swamped by the work entailed in organizing the taping. Because he couldn't work on the video during regular business hours, he'd had to commit his evenings and weekends to hiring the extra performers he needed, obtaining the proper permits for filming in a state park on Long Island, and renting vans and equipment. When he talked to Brooke, their conversations, while light and friendly, tended to center on business matters. It was simply a telephone version of getting kissed on the cheek, Brooke thought.

That shouldn't have bothered her. She'd been the one to back off from him, and she ought to have been pleased that he was respecting her reluctance to tumble into an affair with him.

But the truth was that she missed him. She missed seeing his warm eyes and his thick, unruly hair; his tall, well-proportioned body. She missed his gentle sense of humor. She missed his pushiness. She missed his kisses on her cheek.

All right, she mused. She'd add "missing him" to the list. It still didn't compute to love, but missing him was a major item. One didn't miss a person one didn't at least care for.

She cared for Sky, no doubt about it. She'd grown accustomed to seeing him, talking to him about deductibles over dinner, going with his flow. She admitted to herself in a moment of scathing honesty that she actually might have missed losing control to him that evening on his bed. Her life in the past week had consisted of her dressing in one of her perfectly pompous outfits, going to her office, manipulating data on her computer, reassuring clients, coming home, dining with Nancy and chatting with Sky on the telephone. She was so much in control of things that it was beginning to irk her.

She'd been hoping to buy some tickets to a concert so Sky would have to take a night off from work and see her. It wasn't just that she wanted to convert him to classical music. She wanted to see him, to see what would happen to her when she was with him again, to discover whether she'd be more able to loosen up now than she'd been the last time they were together. It was a hazardous curiosity, she knew, but she was willing to take the risk.

"How about folk dancing?" Nancy broke into her thoughts.

"Huh?"

"Bogdan's folk dance troupe is scheduled to return to New York for one more concert before they leave the States," said Nancy. "This Friday night. They'll be performing at Town Hall."

"The deal I made with Sky was for Lincoln Center," Brooke emphasized.

"So what? Town Hall's a nice theater."

"But Hungarian folk dances?"

"I'll grant you it isn't your beloved Bach," Nancy conceded. "But the music is lively and the dancing is really good."

Brooke curled her lip. "Hungarian folk dances," she muttered. "It's probably like watching a group of slightly drunk people performing the 'Alley Cat' at a wedding."

"It's nothing of the sort," Nancy protested. "It's balletic. The troupe has had classical training."

"If it's that good," Brooke mused, "then they're probably sold out, too."

Nancy shook her head. "Bogdan's supposed to call me tomorrow from Cincinnati. He's going to be reserving a house ticket for me for the farewell performance. I can ask him if he'll wrangle a pair of tickets for you guys, too."

Brooke didn't doubt for a minute that Bogdan would call Nancy. Nancy made friends in strange places, but the friends she made generally became friends for life. Brooke suspected that over the next few decades Nancy would be receiving countless long-winded aerograms from Budapest filled with charmingly jumbled English expressing Bogdan's great admiration for the beautiful American lady who had once showed him such a fine time in Manhattan.

"What do you say?" Nancy prodded her. "Town Hall Friday night."

"Friday night might be a problem," Brooke hedged. "We've got to get an early start Saturday morning. Sky said something about leaving the city by seven to be able to make the most of the daylight."

"So you can spend the night with him," Nancy pointed out. Before Brooke could object, she continued, "Hey, I'm dying to meet this man already. I'll be a good girl, I promise. I won't even wear my dress made of two dozen silk scarves. Bogdan's already seen it on me anyway."

"And off you, too," Brooke teased.

Nancy wasn't at all offended. "He liked it better on me than off me," she declared. "Of course, he liked *me* better when it was off me. But the dress really looks lousy on a hanger, and Bogdan was the first to comment on it."

"Of course it looks lousy on a hanger," Brooke snorted. "It belongs in a linen closet. Preferably hidden beneath the washcloths."

"So I'll get some tickets for you," Nancy resolved. "They'll probably be freebies. You can't knock that."

"Sure I can," Brooke argued, just to be ornery. "If I paid for them I could write them off as a business expense. Entertaining a client."

"If you're still thinking of Sky as a client, you've got a screw loose," Nancy chided her. "Wise up. If Sky was just a client you wouldn't have been mooning around the apartment these past how many days."

"I haven't been mooning!" Brooke shot back, bristling, but Nancy's knowing look silenced her. She *had* been mooning. *Add that to the list*, she admonished herself. Mooning and missing.

As promised, Nancy got Bogdan to agree to set aside two more tickets for his troupe's performance at Town Hall. "He was absolutely adorable," Nancy reported after hanging up the phone. "He said, 'Any friend yours of which is one of mine.' In his thick sultry accent...."

"Spare me the details," Brooke stifled her as she nudged her away from the telephone. "Now I've got to break the news to Sky that he's going to spend the evening with me watching a group of trained ballet dancers doing the hootchy-kootchy."

"Hungarian folk dances?" Sky roared when Brooke announced the plan to him. "What happened to classical music?"

"What happened is there isn't a ticket available for love or money," Brooke informed him. "This was the best I could do."

"Hungarian folk dances," he repeated. "I thought you were going to be trying to culture me."

"This is culture," she said, though her voice lacked conviction. "According to my roommate, the troupe is trained in ballet."

"Ballet?" Sky said with a groan. "It's sounding worse and worse."

"Look, Sky," Brooke argued grittily. "If I've got to get up at the crack of dawn to watch Willow cavorting through Bethpage State Park in time to some screeching and screaming, then you can watch a Hungarian dance troupe."

"If that's your idea of logic," Sky taunted her, "there's hope for you yet. Friday night, huh. We'll have to make it an early evening. Why don't I pick you up at work, we'll grab a bite to eat and then we'll meet your roommate at the theater."

MAIL THIS CARD TO RECEIVE 4 ROMANCE NOVELS PLUS A VALUABLE GIFT

FREE

▼ Tear off and mail this card today. ▼

EXTRAS:

- OUR FREE NEWSLETTER HEART TO HEART
- OUR FREE MAGAZINE ROMANCE DIGEST
- SPECIAL-EDITION HARLEQUIN BESTSELLERS TO PREVIEW FOR TEN DAYS
- NO OBLIGATION TO BUY EVER

SAVINGS:

$1.00 OFF THE TOTAL RETAIL PRICE. PAY NOTHING MORE FOR SHIPPING AND HANDLING.

SAVINGS DATA CARD

Notice: Mail this card today to get 4 Free Harlequin American Romance novels plus a FREE valuable gift. You'll get 4 brand-new American Romance novels every month as they come off the presses for only $2.25 each (a savings of $0.25 off the retail price) with no extra charges for shipping and handling. You can return a shipment and cancel anytime. The 4 FREE books and valuable gift are yours to keep!

154-CIA-NA3Y

☐ MS.
☐ MISS:
☐ MRS:

(Please PRINT in ink)

FIRST NAME   INITIAL   LAST NAME

ADDRESS   APT.

CITY OR TOWN   STATE   ZIP CODE

Offer limited to one household and not valid for present subscribers. Prices subject to change.

NOTE: IF YOU MAIL THIS CARD TODAY YOU'LL GET A SECOND MYSTERY GIFT FREE

"Fine," Brooke agreed. "Come by my office at five. I'll be waiting."

According to her schedule for rotating her work clothes, she was supposed to wear a starched cotton suit to work on Friday. But she decided to disrupt the schedule. She didn't want to look like a stuffed shirt when she saw Sky. She knew she couldn't borrow any of Nancy's outfits; she'd be dismissed in a trice if she showed up at Benson & Broderick's offices wearing anything that outlandish. She pawed through her closet until she found something she could pass muster in at work that looked remotely feminine: a slim-fitting sheath in a muted aquamarine shade that brought out the soft green color of her eyes. She could wear it buttoned up during the day, and with her beige blazer it looked fairly demure. Then when five o'clock rolled around, she could unbutton the collar, add a string of pearls, and dress it up.

Even with the blazer, the ensemble caused Brooke's secretary to bolt in her chair when Brooke entered the reception area for the corporate tax wing. Ever the diplomat, Carol blurted out, "Geez Louise, Brooke. How come you're dressed like a human being today?"

Brooke eyed the voluptuous blond secretary and decided not to make an issue of her tactlessness. "I bought it for Halloween," she replied crisply, then spun around before Carol's desk to model the dress for her. "Do you think anyone'll recognize me when I go trick-or-treating?"

"Probably not," Carol said thoughtlessly, handing Brooke a stack of papers. "Here are those letters you wanted me to type yesterday. I hope you don't mind the White-Out."

Brooke grimaced but thanked Carol before carrying the letters to her office to proofread. Counting the blobs of correction fluid speckling each letter, Brooke calculated that Carol had caught approximately forty percent of her errors. Brooke carefully penned in the rest of the corrections, and left the letters in her "out" basket.

Her day seemed to drag. She was amazed by how eager she was to see Sky, so eager that she checked her wristwatch every half hour, so eager that she wasn't able to eat lunch. She would have been just as anxious to see him tonight if they were planning to attend a rock concert, she realized. It no longer mattered that they were going to a performance neither of them had much interest in. All that mattered was that they were going to be together.

Maybe, she said to herself. *Maybe this is love.* The possibility rattled her, and as soon as she had stored in her computer the data she'd been fooling around with in search of juicy loopholes for one of her clients, she cleared the screen and typed a list. "Missing. Mooning. Eager to see him. Loss of appetite."

She paused, studying the brief list, tapping her fingernails against the edge of the computer's keyboard. What else?

"Kissing." Yes, there was definitely sexual magnetism between her and Sky. She deleted "Kissing" and replaced it with "Chemistry." "Sense of humor," she added. "Strong hands. Gorgeous eyes. Virile build."

The pluses were coming too easily to her. She hastily skipped several spaces to begin her list of minuses:

"Beard," she typed. She considered the word for several minutes, then sighed and deleted it. She added it to the first list. She'd grown to like his beard.

"Sloppy," she typed on her list of Sky's drawbacks. "Rock music. Disorganized. Lackadaisical about logistics of business. Pushy. His name."

She hesitated, deleted "His name" and typed "Sky Blue."

"Sky Blue," she whispered aloud. *Sky Blue.* Much as she hated to admit it, she had come to adore his name. When he'd asked her why she had never bothered to change her own name, she'd told him that her name was too much a part of her. In her own case, she considered that a misfortune, but in Sky's case...in his case the name fit. It was an integral element of him, his essence. He was Sky. She simply couldn't imagine calling him anything else.

With a deep sigh, she removed his name from the negative list and added it to the positive list.

She studied the two lists intently. The positive list seemed much more persuasive than the negative list. So why was she holding back? Why couldn't she just admit that she loved him?

"Me," she typed on the negative list. That was the big why. She was afraid, afraid of what loving someone like Sky could mean.

She wasn't casual when it came to her clothing, and she wasn't casual when it came to her heart. If she were ever to love a man, to love him enough to relinquish her precious self-control, such a love would imply a major commitment to Brooke. Maybe she was old-fashioned, but that was just the way she was.

She didn't condemn people like Nancy, who seemed to suffer no qualms about engaging in a brief fling with a touring foreign dancer. Nancy was much more well-adjusted, much more up-to-date than Brooke. This was how people were nowadays. They wore blue jeans; they enjoyed sex; they went with the flow. Sometimes Brooke wished she could be more like Nancy. She genuinely admired her roommate.

She genuinely admired Sky, too. But his attitude was more like Nancy's than like Brooke's. He'd been in love before, and he'd emerged from those affairs undaunted, unscarred. Perhaps Brooke would be just one more such love for him, a pleasant transient occurrence, someone he'd remember with fondness when he described his past love life to his next woman.

Was it possible that that was why she was holding back? She closed her eyes and relived mentally what had happened on his bed that last time she'd seen him. She hadn't stopped him because she was afraid of losing control. She had stopped him because she was afraid of having her heart broken.

It wasn't as if she were one of the walking wounded, some tattered soul who'd barely survived her last encounter with a man. When she and Joe had broken off their engagement, she hadn't been depressed about it in the least. Neither had he. She'd never lost control with him. She'd never given herself completely to him. They'd been compatible, they'd had similar tastes, and they'd both enjoyed their subscriptions to various classical music series. She'd been twenty-four when they met, twenty-six when they'd decided to get married. It had seemed like the right thing at the time, something she ought to do if she ever wanted to have children and settle down. Women were supposed to get married in their twenties, she thought.

But then he'd accepted a position with an insurance company in Boston, and Brooke had adamantly refused to look for work in that city. Nor would Joe consider turning down the job and looking for another. The management position at John Hancock was exactly the sort of job he'd been looking for, he had argued. So Brooke had ended the engagement. And Joe was no more crushed by her decision than she was. They were that alike.

Since coming to New York City, Brooke had dated on occasion. She went out for several months with a fellow she'd met through work, and Nancy had set her up a few times with men she knew—more than once with men she'd had amicable affairs with. None of the men Brooke had met in the city had ever put her in mind of things like heartbreak. None of them until Sky.

She checked her watch and switched off her computer. It was nearly five o'clock; Sky would be arriving soon. She had hoped she would be able to straighten out her troubling thoughts before he arrived, but she hadn't. Now there wasn't time.

She raced down the hall to the ladies' room to rearrange her dress. She opened two of the cloth-covered buttons at her throat, then strung her pearls about her neck and fastened the clasp. She gave her hair a vigorous brushing to bring out its blond highlights, freshened her lip gloss, dabbed cologne behind her ears and pinched her cheeks to imbue them with color. "Hungarian folk dances," she muttered at her reflection. She wondered if the evening would be a disaster, if by the finale Sky would request that she not bother accompanying him to the video shoot tomorrow.

Chastising herself for her defeatist attitude, she left the powder room for her office. Her telephone began to ring as she reached the doorway, and she stretched across her desk to answer it. "That guy, Sky Blue, is here again," Carol announced.

"Tell him I'm on my way," Brooke said quietly before hanging up. As she turned from the telephone, her vision caught on the monitor of her computer. In repose it was just a smooth green-gray rectangle, but her mind conjured up the image of the two lists she'd composed on it. She tried to recall everything she'd written on each list, but the only item that came back to her was "Sky Blue," an item she'd transferred from the minus column to the plus column. If only it were as easy to manipulate emotions as it was to manipulate figures for tax purposes, she thought, sighing, the world would be a much less complicated place.

Taking a deep breath for fortitude, she grabbed her purse and walked down the hall to the reception area. Sky was standing by the doorway, dressed in...a suit.

Brooke blinked twice to make certain she wasn't hallucinating. No, it really was a suit: a soft-shouldered blazer of beige summerweight wool and slim-fitting trousers of the same fabric.

She lifted her gaze to his face and found him chuckling softly at her astonished expression. "What's the matter?" he asked. "Did a dog mistake my leg for a fire hydrant?"

"I've never seen you dressed so...neatly," she managed.

He shrugged. "I wasn't sure what people are supposed to wear to Hungarian folk dance concerts. I figured I ought to play it safe."

Brooke steered him out of the reception area toward the elevator bank. Several other people were waiting for the elevator, and Sky didn't kiss her. "Since when are you the sort of person who plays it safe?" she posed in a soft voice.

"The last time I tried not playing it safe, the lady squirmed out from under me," he replied. He was smiling, but his eyes informed Brooke that he was serious.

She said nothing as they entered the elevator with the other waiting people. The car was jammed, and Sky's body was pressed up next to hers. She hadn't forgotten how attractive he was, but the heat that flushed through her at the intimate contact with him jolted her nonetheless. "Chemistry," she contemplated, recalling one of the items on her list.

Outside the building they started down a side street in search of a restaurant. Sky made no affectionate move, not even bothering to take her hand. Brooke suffered a twinge of disappointment, then took matters into her own hands. She slipped her fingers about the bend in his elbow and held herself close to him. He peered down at her and smiled, tucking his elbow firmly against his side to hold her hand securely in place.

They entered a small French restaurant, and because it was still early they were able to get a table. Sky explained to the waiter that they had theater tickets for seven-thirty, and the waiter assured them that they'd be served promptly. Brooke ordered poached salmon, Sky beef bourguignon and a bottle of Médoc. The waiter took their menus and departed.

"Is this a business dinner?" Sky asked ingenuously, though his eyes sparkled with mischief. "Should I save the receipt?"

"This," Brooke declared, "is a friendly dinner."

His smile grew warm and gentle. Brooke examined his face across the table. Pale shadows underlined his eyes. He looked tired, and she told him so.

"That's not surprising, considering the way I've been hustling, trying to get everything arranged in time for tomorrow," he noted. "Poor me, working myself to the bone," he added with mock self-pity.

"Have you ever thought about quitting the advertising business and doing rock videos full time?" she asked him.

"Constantly," he replied. The waiter brought their wine, and Sky waited until it was poured and he and Brooke were once again alone before continuing. "I've got two other videos lined up for taping this summer, and I've been in touch with the manager of another group—we're just in the early talking stage. If I can really get this thing going, I'll quit the advertising work for good. But until I'm sure this rock stuff is for real I can't afford to quit my regular job."

If he managed his savings better, he probably could, Brooke mused. But obviously he was concerned about his future earnings. He was still too new in the rock video field to be certain that he'd last in it. "You don't seem the type to play it safe, Sky," she remarked, sounding more critical than she intended.

He laughed, not at all minding her friendly scolding. "I'm not an idiot, Brooke," he defended himself. "The ad agency pays me more than a steady salary. If I left, I'd lose my insurance coverage, my pension plan, all those perks. I'll do it when I think I can afford it, but I'm not going to jump the gun."

She ought to have been mollified by his sensibility, but she wasn't. She'd grown too enamored of Sky's whimsical approach to life, his breezy unconcern about such things as job security and perquisites. He almost sounded like a stuffed shirt when he talked this way. He sounded uncomfortably like her.

She meant to say something along those lines, but the words that emerged were "I've missed you."

His eyes widened, and he shifted in his seat. He began to say something, then stopped himself. His beard parted as he smiled. "Good." he murmured.

Something clicked inside Brooke's skull, and she realized that, while she didn't doubt that he'd been working hard during the past two weeks, there was another reason why Sky hadn't seen her. It was the same reason he hadn't kissed her or taken her hand. He *wanted* her to miss him. He wanted her to learn for herself that she was growing dependent on his company.

She was slightly annoyed that he'd been testing her that way, yet she couldn't deny the success of his ploy. "This is not to say I'm in love with you," she hastened to add.

"It's not to say anything except that you've missed me." Sky concurred. "I've missed you, too. You're looking beautiful tonight."

"You're looking good, too," she said. "You've trimmed your beard, haven't you?"

"You can tell?" He laughed. "Nobody else noticed. I trim it twice a year, whether or not it needs it."

"Of course. You don't want anyone mistaking you for Santa Claus," she joked.

"Of course," he cheerfully agreed. "Given how fat and jolly I am." The waiter arrived with their salads, refilled their wineglasses and vanished from the table.

"Do you still think you're in love with me?" Brooke asked.

Sky toyed with his fork, then laughed. "You're much too analytical, Brooke," he reproached her. "Talk, talk, talk. Do you want a receipt, something on paper for your records?" At her stony glare, he conceded. "Yes, I'm still in love with you. After two weeks do you think I'd change my mind?"

"Who knows?" she said with a sniff. "You've been in love so many times before...."

"Not so many times," he argued. "Just enough to know that it's not the sort of thing you ought to talk about in great detail. You simply accept it and go with it."

"So you're still going with it," she mumbled, then nibbled on a chunk of lettuce to give herself a chance to think. "Where do you suppose it's going to take you?"

"I really don't care where it takes me," Sky maintained. "If you know where you're going, why bother taking the trip? It's much more fun to be surprised."

Brook shook her head but remained silent. It seemed to her that the surprises in such an event were more apt to be painful than pleasurable. Even knowing with Joe that they were going toward marriage, she hadn't been able to loosen up enough to love him.

Me, she reflected, recalling her lists once more. She was the stumbling block in her relationship with Sky.

She liked assurances, guarantees, the feeling that she was on top of things. When she began a tax return, she didn't know how much money she'd be able to save a client, but she knew enough to be reasonably certain that she'd come up with an economical solution to the client's financial situation. When she began a crossword puzzle, she didn't know what words would satisfy the clues, but she knew that when she was done every blank square would contain a letter, every letter would complete two words, everything would fit neatly and symmetrically. That was her nature. That was the way she approached life's problems.

She admitted to herself that tomorrow she would be traveling into the unknown. She had no idea what the filming of a rock video would be like, no idea whether she'd enjoy the experience. She could expend one day being daring, but not her entire life, not her soul. She wasn't that foolhardy.

That Sky *was* that foolhardy was part of his appeal, an important part. Perhaps his appeal in Brooke's eyes was directly related to the fact that his personality was antithetical to hers. He offered her a taste of the very things that were lacking in herself. But she wasn't sure whether that item belonged on the plus list or the minus list.

"Hungarian folk dances." Sky cut into her mental meandering. "Is there any reason in particular that we're going to see this thing?"

"My roommate has gone bonkers over one of the dancers," Brooke explained, then added, "She claims the troupe is splendid, but I don't know how objective she is. I suppose they wouldn't have been granted visas if they weren't talented. There are limits to détente, after all."

"Not in your roommate's eyes," Sky hazarded. Brooke laughed.

The remainder of their meal was accompanied by idle chatter, and the waiter had them out the door by ten past seven. They walked uptown through the balmy spring evening to Town Hall, a massive rococo theater with grandiose pillars adorning its front facade. The stairway leading to the doors was crowded with people conversing, searching their pockets for tickets, and savoring a final cigarette before curtain time. Maybe it was just Brooke's imagination, but it seemed to her that a large proportion of the crowd were speaking in a foreign language. Hungarian émigrés, she guessed, anxious for a reminder of the Old Country.

She and Sky found Nancy watching for them inside the lobby. Nancy was arrayed in a gaudy backless jumpsuit of mustard-colored chiffon, with an even gaudier purple feather boa slung around her neck. Brooke remembered the day Nancy had purchased the boa at a thrift shop on Broadway. "Isn't it kitsch?" Nancy had crowed. Brooke had gagged at the sight of it.

"Nancy, this is Sky Blue," she dutifully introduced the two. "Sky, my roommate, Nancy Carlin."

Nancy ran her eyes up Sky's long body to his face. "Well, it's about time," she declared. "I've heard a lot about you." Brooke winced.

Sky chuckled. "I'm not foolish enough to ask what you've heard," he said as he shook her hand. "I've heard a bit about you, too. I suppose thanks are in order."

"Thanks?" Nancy asked, puzzled.

"It's thanks to you Brooke attended Corny Cobb's party. Thanks to you again that she called me when I sent her those flowers."

"Oh, God, they were bodacious," Nancy said, groaning. "I'm surprised you look so normal. He looks like a Benson and Broderick numbers cruncher," she observed to Brooke.

Brooke winced again. "He does not," she argued.

"Too bad for Benson and Broderick," Nancy said with an exaggerated sigh. "I'm convinced that if more accountants were hipper and hairier, the budgets of the world would automatically come into balance."

"I'm not about to grow a beard," Brooke muttered.

The lobby's lights flickered, and Nancy handed Brooke two tickets. "I guess it's time to make like sheep," she said as she preceded them toward the auditorium.

"Make like sheep?" Sky whispered to Brooke.

"Don't ask," she whispered back. They trailed Nancy and an usher down the aisle to their orchestra seats.

Brooke positioned herself between Nancy and Sky. As the house lights dimmed, Nancy leaned over the arm of the chair and confided, "He's a fox, Brooke. I'd stop thinking of him as a client if I were you."

Brooke was glad for the auditorium's darkness. She felt her cheeks coloring, a deeper hue than she could ever produce by pinching them. Her blush intensified when Sky reached across the opposite arm of her seat to take her hand.

The curtain rose to reveal the dance troupe arranged in a dramatic tableau. The partisan audience burst into applause, but Brooke was unable to clap; Sky refused to release her hand. A small orchestra featuring guitars, accordions and clarinets began a boisterous tune, and the tableau dissolved as the festively clad dancers began their first number, a wheel-ing stomp that left Brooke mildly dizzy.

"Which one's Bogdan?" she murmured to Nancy, figuring she could regain her bearings if she had one dancer in particular to focus on in the dance's intri-cate pattern.

"Third from the left," Nancy answered, although the dancers suddenly reeled into a different forma-tion. "Sixth from the right," Nancy hastily amended.

The man she'd pointed out seemed nice-enough-looking, with blond hair and blue eyes and a broad, open face. His shirt, like those of the other men, was white and blousy, with a bright red-and-green ab-stract design embroidered across its upper half, and his trousers were black knickers. The women in the troupe wore embroidered black skirts, and both the men and women had on ballet slippers.

The music was sprightly, the dancers graceful. Al-though this was not the sort of performance Brooke usually went to, she found it enjoyable. She leaned toward Sky and whispered, "What do you think?"

"I'll reserve judgment," he responded.

She glanced at his face and found his expression one of forced tolerance. She imagined she'd probably look about as thrilled tomorrow when she watched the taping of Willow's video.

The dance ended, and a cute duet between a man and a woman ensued. Not quite ballet, Brooke con-ceded, but charming. It was followed by a rambunc-tious dance performed by a trio of men, one of whom was Bogdan. Nancy sat upright, staring unwaveringly at the stage, her face aglow with rapture.

After another group dance, the program broke for an intermission. Sky, Brooke and Nancy stood to stretch their legs. "What do you think?" Nancy crooned. "Isn't he something else?" Did you see how high he leaped? The man's an athlete, no question about it."

"Nancy," Brooke warned, "if he's planning to defect and hide out in our apartment, I want to know about it in advance."

"Oh, no," Nancy said with a giggle. "He adores Hungary. He's already invited me to visit him there. He says Budapest is very Western. Discos, boutiques and Rubik's Cubes everywhere you look."

"Gosh, it sounds irresistible," Brooke muttered sarcastically. "One of my life's goals is to be surrounded by Rubik's Cubes."

Ignoring Brooke, Nancy leaned past her to address Sky. "Enjoying it?" she asked.

"Trying," he managed gamely. Brook gave his hand a squeeze.

The lights flickered, and they resumed their seats for the second half of the concert. Sky tugged Brooke's arm across the armrest to his seat and clasped both his hands about her fingers. The troupe returned to the stage and filled it with their energetic dances, but when Brooke turned to Sky she discovered him ignoring the performers and studying her hand. His thumb moved slowly over her knuckles, tracing their angles, then delineating the narrow bones of her hand to her wrist.

"Chemistry," she thought again as his fingers imparted a sensuous warmth to her skin. It rose through her veins to her heart, like energy passing through a resistant wire. Though no light emanated from her, she knew she was glowing. Her pulse responded by racing, skewing slightly out of control. Her pulse and her mind both, she admitted. Losing control to Sky.

The knowledge that she was willingly losing control and not even fretting about it astonished her, but she accepted it. Sometimes at work she was handed figures that gave her difficulty, numbers that didn't add up, calculations that didn't result in the most beneficial bottom line. When that happened, she couldn't simply change the numbers. She had to accept them, work with them, do the best she could under adverse circumstances. Not everything in the universe could fall within Brooke's control, and she had to accept that.

So she would accept the obvious: She was falling in love with Sky. She was happier tonight with him than she'd been during the previous two weeks without him. She was glad he was beside her, holding her hand. She was grateful that he'd tested her, giving her the opportunity to discover for herself what was developing between them.

He wasn't the ideal man she'd pictured in her dreams. His hair was still too long, waving down to the collar of his jacket. But at least he had worn a suit. And trimmed his beard. And asked about saving the dinner receipt for tax purposes. He was learning from her and trying for her. And she in turn was permitting herself to lose control.

She watched the dancers, but her mind pursued its own thoughts. All right. The plus list was what counted, and Sky's pluses were valid. So was the shimmering warmth that continued to spread through her as his hands came to rest around hers. Maybe the possibility of future heartbreak wasn't as important as being herself and letting the forces of nature determine her course.

She would let Sky make love to her tonight, she decided. She would invite him back to the apartment; Nancy would probably be spending the night in Bogdan's hotel room, so Brooke and Sky would have the place to themselves. Or, if Sky preferred, she'd retire to his apartment. They could stop by her building so she could pick up some clothing for tomorrow, then cab downtown to his place for the night. Whatever he wanted. She was ready to love him.

The curtain fell on the final ensemble dance, and she turned to Sky to declare her intention. His head was bowed forward, his eyes closed in thought. She angled her head to see his face, to catch his attention and whisper to him that she loved him.

But she wound up saying nothing because he was fast asleep.

Chapter Seven

Brooke's gentle nudging, combined with the spirited applause that greeted the dancers as they took their curtain calls, roused Sky. He shook his head, dazed, and then smiled sheepishly as his eyes sharpened on her. "Oh," he said. "Sorry."

She grinned, forgiving him his faux pas. "You thought it was that boring, did you?"

He peeked over her shoulder at Nancy, who was on her feet, clapping wildly. Then he turned back to Brooke. "I hope Nancy didn't notice."

"I think she's conscious of only one man in the entire theater at the moment," Brooke reassured him. "It'll be our secret that you nodded off."

He yawned, then stood up and helped Brooke out of her seat. He forced himself to applaud, and Brooke appreciated his effort. He seemed almost too fatigued to move his arms.

When the curtain dropped for the final time, Nancy spun around to them. "What did I tell you?" she enthused. "Were they great or were they great?"

"Spellbinding," Sky lied. Brooke stifled a laugh.

"Well, listen, folks, I've got to run. I promised Bogdan I'd meet him backstage after the performance. Sky, nice meeting you," she said, briskly shaking his hand before she whipped her feather boa around her neck. "I'll see you around, Brooke." With that she disappeared down the aisle, masterfully elbowing a path through the surge of people in pursuit of her beloved.

Sky held Brooke's hand as they made their leisurely way toward the lobby. Peering up at him, she reconsidered her decision to spend the night with him. He looked utterly exhausted. He needed his rest more than they needed each other tonight. "Are you going to be able to function tomorrow?" she asked him.

"Three cups of coffee and I can function for a year," he boasted, though he didn't sound convincing.

They left the theater and ambled to the corner of the street. Sky scanned the avenue in search of a cab. Two were claimed by other audience members before he flagged one down for himself and Brooke.

He provided the driver with Brooke's address, and as the car headed uptown, Brooke contemplated one last time suggesting that they spend the night together. But Sky's eyelids were drooping in the shadowed rear of the cab; the mere rumble of the car's engine seemed to tranquilize him. Not tonight, she decided firmly, swallowing her disappointment. If she was really in love with him, she wouldn't change her mind in two weeks, just as he hadn't changed his mind about her. Sex could wait.

The cab drew to a halt by her apartment's entry, and Sky kissed her cheek. "I'll be by for you at seven tomorrow," he reminded her.

"I'll see you then." She resisted another surge of disappointment at his unromantic farewell before letting herself out of the cab.

"Am I supposed to get a receipt for this cab ride?" he called through the open window.

"No," she told him with a chuckle. "Tonight wasn't business."

"Whatever you say," he mumbled drowsily. "Sitting through that show felt like work to me. I'll see you in the morning." He leaned forward to direct the driver, and the cab pulled away from the curb.

Brooke felt surprisingly lighthearted as she entered her apartment. She was in love, out of control, and she didn't mind in the least. That Sky fell asleep during the performance didn't bother her one bit. He'd looked terribly sweet when he slept. Someday, she thought, someday soon she'd be waking up beside that sweet sleeping face. No matter where the flow she was going with ultimately carried her, she was certain that it would take her to Sky's bed before long.

Her restlessness when she climbed beneath the covers didn't trouble her. Ordinarily she was a sound sleeper, the sort of person who could sleep through a world war if one erupted outside her window overnight. But thinking about Sky kept her awake. She recalled the electric thrill that had coursed through her the last time she'd been with him, when he'd lain beside her and kissed her and caressed her through her dress. The response of her body to his touch had been immediate and powerful, and Sky had clearly been aware of it. She imagined that he would be a sublime lover, as full of humor and tenderness in his lovemaking as he was in everything else he did.

She tried to picture his body unclothed. She tried to visualize the long, lean lines of it. Good Lord, she chastised herself. She was beginning to behave the way Nancy did, thinking of a man as a sex object. Yet she was sure he'd be delighted if he knew the turn her thoughts had taken.

She finally managed to drop off to sleep around midnight, and when her alarm clock woke her at six-fifteen the following morning she felt surprisingly refreshed. She took a quick shower and dressed in a navy-blue blouse, a pair of pale blue corduroy slacks and her loafers. She downed a cup of coffee and a bagel, gathered up her purse and a white cardigan, and left the apartment to wait for Sky in the lobby.

He arrived in a rental car only a few minutes later. The backseat was occupied by two men and a woman. Brooke smiled politely at them as she took her place beside Sky in front.

He was already steering away from the building before he introduced them. "Brooke, this is Stan Levin, Julie Peterson and Ron Barlow. Guys, Brooke Waters."

"Brooke Waters?" the one named Ron said with a guffaw. "As in river?"

"As in shut up," Sky cheerfully silenced him.

Brooke appreciated Sky's intercession; she couldn't have been as blunt as he was, since Ron was a stranger to her. She twisted in her seat to study the three people in the rear. They were young, and although they were sitting she discerned that they were all slender in build. All three of them had straight black hair, and while none of them was classically handsome, they looked distinctive. The man named Stan had thick, bushy brows; Ron had a prominent beak nose and Julie's eyes were so large and round that they seemed to bulge slightly from her face. "Are you people going to be acting in the video?" she asked, remembering that Sky was enamored of unusual faces in his films.

"Aren't you?" Julie asked as the men nodded.

"Brooke's my business manager," Sky explained. Brooke didn't bother to correct him. If that was how he wanted his actors to think of her, she'd play along.

"Business manager?" Stan hooted. "Since when did you ever have a dime's worth of respect for business managers?" His dense brows furrowed as he eyed Brooke. "I've worked with Sky before," he informed her. "A Rickler's Candies gig last year. The man is downright disrespectful when it comes to business."

"Not disrespectful," Sky disagreed. "Simply ignorant. That's what Brooke is here for."

"You were very disrespectful to my agent," Stan claimed.

"Because your agent is a boob. Brooke is a genius," Sky replied. "How can I possibly disrespect someone who's actually saved me genuine money? Whereas whenever I talk to your agent, it winds up costing me money." Stan laughed.

Owing to the early hour, the parkway was fairly empty. Sky hummed an unfamiliar melody as he drove. Brooke snuck inconspicuous glimpses of him when she could. He wore his form-fitting jeans and a loose cotton shirt of sunshine yellow with the sleeves rolled to his elbows. His forearms were sinewy, strong and graceful. Simply looking at him reminded her of her love for him. She hoped he'd forgive her if she fell asleep while watching the filming today, though she hoped she wouldn't. She hoped today would end differently than last night.

"Are you well-rested?" she asked him softly at one point when the backseat passengers were engrossed in their own discussion.

"Sure," he swore with a broad smile. "That extra nap I had at the theater was all I needed."

"They really were quite good," she commented, referring to the dancers.

"If you like that sort of thing."

"I like it more than I like Willow's singing."

"Tit for tat, huh?" he said with a grunt. "The deal, Brooke, was that I'd go to your show if you'd go to mine. We didn't establish any rules about catching a few z's along the way."

"In that case, I should have brought my pillows along," Brooke teased. Sky caught her eye and they both laughed.

Several cars, a large truck and a trailer were already at the park when Sky cruised into the otherwise empty parking lot. A sprawling grove of trees beside a meadow was roped off, and a park ranger stood guard by the lot, eyeing the milling people distrustfully. "Sky to the rescue," Sky boomed as he coasted to a halt by the ranger.

He sprang from the car, tugging several folded permit papers from his hip pocket as he approached the ranger. The two of them bent their heads together to talk, and then the ranger nodded and stepped aside. Sky shouted, "Let's get moving!" and the dozens of people present shifted into high gear.

The actors who had accompanied Sky and Brooke vanished into the trailer, along with several other people who had arrived in another car. Technicians began to unload cameras and sound equipment from the truck's van and lug it into a clearing amid the trees. Brooke spotted Willow lounging on the bench of a picnic table, and since Sky was absorbed by his preparations, Brooke strolled over to the bench to greet the singer.

"He brought you along, did he?" Willow asked, running her talonlike fingernails haughtily through her green hair.

"So it seems," Brooke replied pleasantly.

"I still think this is a stupid idea for a video," Willow said, sulking, though she politely shifted on the bench to make room for Brooke. "They want me hanging from a branch or something."

"I'm sure there's a good reason for that," Brooke pointed out, though she couldn't for the life of her imagine what it might be.

"Well, I'll tell you," Willow conceded. "You were right about one thing—Sky's brilliant. I wish this was just going to be a straight concert shoot, but what the hell. He must know what he's doing."

"Of course he must," Brooke rapidly agreed.

"But you were wrong about everything else," Willow muttered. "My fans'll come to my concerts no matter what. I'm Willow, for crying out loud"

Indeed, Brooke mused. Crying out loud was a precise description of Willow's music. "What's the song the video's going to be based on about?" she asked courteously.

"It's called 'Out on a Limb.' That's why Sky wants me hanging from a damned branch when I sing it," Willow answered.

"'Out on a Limb,'" Brooke echoed, strill striving for congeniality. "Do the lyrics have anything to do with trees?"

Willow seemed to warm slightly to Brooke. She was obviously proud of her new song. "It goes 'Out on a limb/Because of him. He's gone *fern* other/And now he's in *clover*/I *axed* him to love me/But I'm afraid he'll shove me/He wants to *leaf*/And all I know is grief/His *bark's* worse than his bite/And I'm scared of this height/Out on a *limb*/Over him.'"

"That's very clever," Brooke managed, trying not to cringe.

"Isn't it?" Willow bragged. "I wrote the words myself."

"Willow!" a woman hollered from the doorway of the trailer. "Come on—costume time."

Willow rolled her eyes and sighed. "Show biz," she said with a disdainful groan as she rose from the bench and slunk toward the trailer.

Brooke settled comfortably on the bench and watched the activity unfolding before her. Several actors, all of them young and slender with straight black hair and riveting faces, emerged from the trailer clad in white leotards and matching tights, their faces powdered with a chalky white substance. They scouted the trees. A few adventurous ones started climbing them.

A chubby young man with a headset wrapped around his neck lugged a stereo tape player to the table and dropped it on the splintery wood surface with a thud. "I'm setting up here," he told Brooke.

"Am I in your way?" she asked.

"Not at all," he assured her as he plugged a thick extension cord running from the truck into the machine. He fastened a tape to one of the reels, slipped on his headset and ran the tape a few times to make sure he had set it up properly.

Two technicians carried ladders into the grove, and Sky involved himself in arranging his actors in and around the trees. Brooke quickly comprehended that the actors were going to impersonate animals. Some of them sat on their haunches, holding acorns in their fingers like squirrels. Two brave souls—Julie and a male actor with similarly buggy eyes—perched on a sturdy branch to imitate owls. Definitely surreal, Brook mused, remembering Sky's term for his concept of the video.

Her vision traveled to the park ranger, who stood by the truck, looking as bemused and out of place as Brooke. Surrounded by grubby technicians and actors in leotards, Brooke felt incredibly square in her staid outfit. With her cardigan tied by its sleeves about her neck, she resembled more a model for The Talbots than a participant in the circus swirling around her.

But this was the pact she'd made with Sky. He'd done his part last night, and now she had to reciprocate. As anomalous as she felt, she was honestly glad to be here. It was worth it to see him working, to observe his relaxed manner when he dealt with his subordinates, to hear his warm laughter whenever someone shouted something from a tree branch down to him.

It was a far cry from what Brooke did at work, sitting primly at her desk and doodling on her computer. But Sky had been right when he'd insisted that for all their differences, he and Brooke had some things in common. They were both good at what they did. They were both skilled and talented, successful in their professions, able to get things accomplished. That Sky could organize such a tangle of people and equipment awed Brooke, possibly even more than her ability to organize receipts and numbers awed him.

By nine-thirty Sky had arranged his actors and cameramen to his satisfaction. A ladder was set up beneath the thick limb of an oak tree where Willow was to be placed, and she emerged from the trailer, clad in a revealing leotard of puckered brown fabric. It almost looked like the bark of a tree, and Brooke wondered whether Sky had taken seriously her suggestion that he have Willow resemble a tree in the video.

Issuing a long string of curses and complaints, Willow allowed two assistants to help her up the ladder and onto the tree limb. "Sky, honey, this is creepy!" she shrieked from her precarious perch. "What if I fall?'

"Let's not find out what if," he yelled up to her, his smile easy and his tone confident. "Let's just shoot the tape and have fun."

"How can I have fun?" she wailed. "I think I'm gonna puke."

"Don't puke," he commanded her. "It won't film well." He gestured to the assistants to remove the ladder, and Willow began to keen.

"I hope he's got this gig insured," the sound technician muttered as he rewound the tape to the right spot. Brooke nodded in hearty agreement.

"Okay, everybody," Sky called out through cupped hands. "We'll walk it through once to the music and see how it looks. Jimmy?" he asked, turning to the sound man, who nodded and clicked on the tape, unplugging his headset so the music would feed through the speakers.

"Out on a li-i-i-mb!" Willow's voice screeched through the stereo, accompanied by a raucous rock combo. Willow didn't bother trying to mouth the words. She clung to the limb and glowered sullenly at Sky.

He ignored her, moving from camera to camera, checking angles, studying his actors. They were quite good. The actors playing squirrels fidgeted jerkily with their hands. The actors playing owls kept their eyes wide and round as they flicked their heads from side to side without moving their shoulders. Two tall actors portraying deer stood stone-still behind a tree, their slim legs slightly parted, their heads angled, their nostrils flared. Brooke was impressed.

She noticed a figure emerging from the trailer and approaching the table. She recognized Michael and waved to him. "How goes it?" he whispered as he joined her on the bench.

"This is interesting," she replied frankly.

"Willow's being such a prima donna about the whole thing," he commented. He reached into this shirt pocket, withdrew a box of cigarettes and lit one. It wasn't pink, and Brooke relaxed sightly as the familiar scent of tobacco smoke filled her nostrils. She should have known Michael wouldn't be so stupid as to smoke marijuana within view of a park ranger. Their several meetings had proved to her that he had a reasonably intelligent head on his shoulders.

"If I had to sit on a tree limb, I'd be pretty scared, too," Brooke said in Willow's defense.

"Scared? Hey, the lady's taken sky-diving lessons. Don't talk to me about scared. She's just doing her star number."

"What's your opinion?" Brooke asked. "Is this video going to be good?"

"I think so," Michael said with a nod. "I think it's gonna work. If Willow doesn't blow it. She won't," he decided, puffing on his cigarette. "If Sky says do it, she'll do it." He eyed Brooke curiously. "Do you and he have something going?" he asked.

Brooke crossed her ankles and swallowed. "We're friends," she mumbled evasively, fidgeting with one of the sweater sleeves dangling down her chest.

"Willow's got eyes for him, you know," Michael commented nonchalantly.

Brooke shot him a quick look. "I think she respects him," she allowed.

"Respects him? Give me a break. If he snapped his fingers she'd turn to mush for him."

"I thought—" Brooke moistened her lips, wondering why Michael was confiding in her this way "—I thought you and Willow were a couple."

"A couple of what?" he quipped. "Brooke," he murmured more softly, shoving a thick shock of his wavy brown hair from his brow. "You and I, we understand each other. We're business, am I right? They're artists," he said, waving toward Sky and Willow. "Willow and I have things figured out between us. We work together, we live together, we make a lot of money together. Extracurricularly speaking, what she does is her problem. I just don't want her getting hurt, you know?"

"I don't want her getting hurt, either," Brooke remarked, finding the statement ironic, given Willow's current precarious position, draped along the lofty tree branch.

"She gets hurt, she'll do a number on me, cancel a concert and crawl into a hole. That's why I'm asking. Are you and Sky tight? Is Willow setting herself up for something I ought to know about?"

This had to be one of the most peculiar conversations Brooke had ever had. She didn't want to be a part of Willow's and Michael's bizarre arrangement, whatever it entailed. She didn't even want to know about it. On the weird scale, Willow and Michael were probably two notches higher than Corny Cobb and Orlando Florida. "Why don't you discuss this with Sky?" she suggested.

"He's working. You're sitting. How come he brought you here, anyway?"

Brooke wasn't going to reveal to Michael the pact she and Sky had made. Even their inane bargain about swapping one Hungarian folk dance troupe for one rock videotaping seemed too personal to share with Michael. "He thought I should learn something about what he does," she replied vaguely.

"Oh, come on," Michael snorted in disbelief. "You already know plenty about what he does. You couldn't have sold me on his concept if you didn't know Sky's business."

Brooke gnawed her lip and twirled the ribbed cuff of her sweater sleeve through her fingers. If Michael learned how ignorant she'd been while persuading him to go along with Sky on this video, he might put a halt to the taping and swear never to use Sky's services again. She had to come up with a better answer. "Well, of course I know his business," she answered, which wasn't a total lie—she was on intimate terms with the financial aspects of it. "But I'd never seen an actual taping before. Sky thought I'd enjoy it."

Michael jumped to his own conclusion. "So you and he have something going, then, huh?"

"I really wish you'd discuss this with Sky instead of me," she said in a prickly voice.

Ignoring her comment, Michael nudged her in the ribs. "There. There she goes," he whispered and pointed. Brooke followed his extended finger toward Willow, expecting to see her tumbling out of the tree. But in fact, she appeared quite content dangling off the limb, one of her arms curled around Sky's neck as she murmured something into his ear.

Brooke didn't feel alarmed. She didn't feel even the slightest bit jealous. She had never been a particularly jealous person; the emotion struck her as a waste of energy. Besides, Sky had declared his love for her, and she trusted him. Two weeks ago, she wasn't sure she believed him when he had told her he loved her, but now she did. Now she knew that they weren't too different to become lovers, that Sky could learn to pay attention to finances and Brooke could learn to go with the flow. She loved him, and she had faith in his love for her. Willow could stroke the back of Sky's neck for as long as she wanted and it wouldn't change Sky's feelings one whit.

Discovering such abiding faith inside her, such unshakable trust, caused Brooke to giggle. She really must be in love with him, with his pushiness and his lousy taste in music. This must be what love is like, she contemplated, stunned by the sheer novelty of it. Brooke "Drip" Waters, stuffed shirt from Boston, at the age of thirty was crazy in love. Her giggling built into a full-bodied laugh, and Michael's perplexed frown only fed her laughter until she was nearly doubled over and gasping for breath.

Nobody else involved with the taping could have detected the sound of a woman's laughter above the cacophony of Willow's song on the tape, but Sky heard it at once. He turned so swiftly he almost dragged Willow off her limb.

She'd been purring to him about how uncomfortable she was in the tree, but how willing she was to endure such discomfort for him. Yet all he heard was the music of Brooke's laughter, music more beautiful than classical, than rock, far surpassing Hungarian folk tunes or Montavani. He'd heard it only once before, but it had transfixed him then, and it transfixed him now.

He fleetingly wondered what in the world Michael could have said to Brooke to set her off like that, but he didn't really care. All he cared about was that she was submerged in her lovely laughter, encompassed by it, dancing in her soul. The tape of Willow's song was winding down, the actors and cameramen were awaiting instructions, yet all Sky could do was stare at Brooke, mesmerized by the glorious sight of her.

She straightened up, slowly regaining her composure, and patted the moisture from her eyes. She blinked; her eyes locked into Sky's and her smile softened slightly. She seemed almost embarrassed by her hysterics, and if there hadn't been twenty-three other people to witness, Sky would have raced to her and dropped to his knees before her and begged her to laugh some more and never, ever, to be embarrassed by such a thing.

Instead, he did something equally impulsive: he yanked a camera from the cameraman nearest him, hoisted it onto his shoulder and began taping Brooke.

Her eyes widened in shock, and she shook her head and covered her face with her hands. And then...then she started laughing again, just as he'd hoped. "Stop!" she yelled between wrenching giggles and hiccups. "Sky! Don't!" She twisted sideways on the bench and turned her quaking shoulders to him.

"Okay. End of shoot," he announced, to the cheers and applause of the assembled actors. He took a bow, handed the camera back to his assistant, and shouted, "Set up. We'll put the next run-through on tape, boys and girls."

While the actors rearranged themselves and Willow pushed her lower lip forward in an exaggerated moue, Sky ambled across the grove to Brooke. "How—how could you do that?" she accused him, still sputtering with a residual chuckle.

"How could I not?" he countered, oblivious to Michael, to the sound technician, to everyone but Brooke. He bent over, angled her face up and planted a kiss on her lips. "You're beautiful," he declared softly. "I shouldn't have brought you here. You're quite a distraction." One more light kiss and then he swung around and loped back to his actors to make certain they were all set for the first take.

Taping a rock video was similar to taping a commercial; it had more in common with filmmaking than with television taping, where several cameras all fed into one central taping monitor and the director worked from a tech booth, switching from camera to camera, recording only the shots he wanted. It was more expensive to tape with three cameras simultaneously, and to splice the tapes into a whole in a lab after the shoot was completed. More expensive, but more flexible. Sky wanted miles of tape to play with. He'd put it all together like a mosaic when he was convinced he had enough material to work with.

He hadn't had much academic training in the art, just a couple of film courses in college for the heck of it while he was majoring in political science and contemplating law school. But fate had dealt him a hand he hadn't expected, and playing it out had led him to New York, to a journeyman's position with an ad agency where he could learn by watching others and, eventually, by doing. He'd been fortunate in finding himself working for an open-minded employer willing to take a chance on him. Sky's quirky, distinctive style, concentrating on strange, captivating faces, quickly marked him as a contender in the field. After the most devastating blow of his life, the few months of analysis, the decision to grow a beard and put Portland as far behind him as he could, he'd vowed to let fate take its course, and things had fallen serendipitously into place. His obsession with faces came to bear fruit, and Sky learned to relax and enjoy himself again.

Now even more wonderful luck had entered his life in the form of Brooke Waters. Not only was she a beautiful woman with an exotic, tantalizing face, not only was she knowledgeable enough to offer him the means to establish himself as an independent professional, but she had given him more, far more. He had recognized pain in her, a pain as real as the anguish he'd once known himself, the pain of believing that life was unfair and that even if you started out with love and warmth and family, as Sky had and Brooke apparently hadn't, you could find yourself suddenly without it, without the love of someone so important, so necessary to your life that you began to lose your grip on your own identity. He'd lived through such pain and conquered it, and now he was teaching Brooke to conquer it. Whenever she laughed, whenever she freed herself to experience happiness, he understood why she meant so much to him.

Pushing his thoughts about Brooke down into his heart, he cleared his mind and turned his attention back to the taping. He had Willow and the actors run through the video again, and then one of the actors reminded him that, per union rules, he had to give the performers a ten-minute break. They leaped from the trees and emerged from the shrubbery, some heading to the trailer for coffee and others engaging in loosening-up exercises on the grass. By the time they were ready for a third run-through, a small crowd of onlookers had gathered in the parking lot behind the rope. Sky ignored them as he assembled his cast for another take. Then they broke for lunch.

Sky drifted to the bench where Brooke was sitting and dropped down beside her. "You haven't fallen asleep yet," he observed playfully.

"I probably won't," she predicted, accepting the sandwich and coffee a technician brought her. Sky helped himself to a sandwich and a can of soda, and they swiveled on the bench to face the table while they ate.

"You're enjoying it?" he asked, obviously pleased.

"So far. If you keep doing the same thing over and over again this afternoon, I might begin to grow restless." She heard a petulant whimper in the distance behind her and glanced over her shoulder to see Michael conferring with Willow in the grove. Reflecting on her unnerving conversation with Michael, she asked warily, "How is Willow holding up?"

Sky grimaced. "She's messing up the lip sync," he complained. "She's hardly trying. I may have to do some close-up work with her next week to get it right. She's in a vile mood, for some reason."

"Michael told me she has the hots for you," Brooke mentioned lightly.

Sky eyed her, then chuckled. "This must be the big rumor of the year. I keep hearing it everywhere but from the source."

"Don't you think it's odd that Michael, of all people, would tell me such a thing?" Brooke asked.

"Michael and Willow are odd people," Sky said with a shrug.

"You don't seem to be taking this very seriously," Brooke commented. "If you break Willow's heart, she may never want to work with you again."

Sky considered the point, then shrugged again. "Willow's heart isn't my problem. Her video is. We'll make this one so fantastic that she'll gladly work with me again."

"You're very arrogant."

"One of my many admirable traits."

"Sky, you don't seem to comprehend the import of the situation. You're just starting out, and Willow's an essential client."

"And you're my business manager," Sky teased.

"As your *alleged* business manager," Brooke asserted, "I'm giving you a bit of sound advice. I'm not saying you have to return Willow's affection. I'm only saying you ought to be sensititve to her. She's essential to your business. It's important for you to keep that in mind."

Sky shrugged nonchalantly. "As my business manager, it's your job to worry about the import of the situation. It's my job to make a good video." He slugged down some soda straight from the can, then stood. "Back to work," he said with pretended dismay. "Catch you later."

Brooke watched him stroll back to his cameramen to talk about the afternoon's taping. The woman who had summoned Willow to the trailer for costuming moved among the actors, touching up their makeup with white powder and black eyeliner from a large case of face paint. The crowd of onlookers had swelled during the lunch break, and Willow was obliging her fans by autographing the pieces of paper they thrust at her over the rope.

Brooke wondered why she had badgered Sky about his failure to take Willow's attraction to him seriously. Brooke wasn't truly Sky's business manager, merely an occasional adviser. Whether or not Willow asked him to work with her again shouldn't matter so much to Brooke.

But she knew why she'd discussed Willow with Sky, and she knew why she felt strangely let down by his remarks on the subject. She'd been hoping to hear him swear that he loved her, and that Willow's attentions were doomed to remain unrequited. It wasn't jealousy on Brooke's part, but insecurity. Brooke wanted to hear Sky tell her he loved her. She wanted to hear him say it again.

Yet he *was* saying it, in his own way. His ridiculous antics with the camera that morning when she'd been laughing were just one of the ways he said it. His dazzling smile when he looked at her said it. The speed with which he hastened to her side for lunch said it. And since she still hadn't confessed her love to him, maybe he was holding back the words, continuing to test her, possibly even entertaining his own insecurities.

She would tell him tonight, she vowed. She would tell him with words, with actions, with her heart. And if he never made a third video for Willow, so be it. There would be other clients, other work, other successes.

The afternoon proceeded much like the morning, with run-throughs, shifting of cameras to accommodate the shifting sunlight, head shots, more run-throughs. Finally, at five-thirty, the shoot was wrapped and the technicians began to pack up.

Sky surprised Brooke by inviting the participants to join him at an Italian restaurant in Greenwich Village for dinner, and a number of them promised to meet him there. Brooke had been hoping to have time alone with him now that the taping was completed, but evidently she'd have to wait.

Naturally, she joined him for dinner. Fifteen of Sky's colleagues showed up at the small restaurant, taking up two tables in a partitioned back room, acting rowdy and flamboyant and utterly weird. Brooke managed to consume two glasses of Chianti and very little of her lasagna. The obstreperous artists seemed to her as bizarre as the peculiarly named people who had attended Corny Cobb's party several weeks earlier, and her impatience compelled her to rely on the tart, heady red wine to get her through the meal.

At last, sometime after nine, the festivities broke up. As they left the restaurant, Sky turned to Brooke and said, "Why don't we go back to my place for a quiet drink? I could use some unwinding."

"So could I," she quickly agreed. Her pulse sped slightly as they strolled toward Sixth Avenue in search of a cab.

Now she would tell him, she resolved as they rode in silence to his building. Now she would tell him what she'd never before told a man. Now she would tell him she was ready for whatever journey she and Sky were destined to travel together. She twisted her hands nervously in her lap and gnawed on her lower lip, praying for the courage to say what had to be said, to do what had to be done.

Wrapped up in her own emotions, she was completely unprepared for the sight that greeted her when Sky led her into his apartment. It was neat. Impeccably neat. Not only was the bed stringently tidy and the dining-room table devoid of pens and papers, but the desk was completely clear of rubbish. She hadn't even known that it was a rolltop style, it had been so cluttered the last few times she'd seen it. But now its surface was clean and dusted, a honey-colored stained wood, the polished narrow slats of its lid catching the light of his bedside lamp and shimmering. "It's beautiful," she gasped.

"My office?" Sky said with a chuckle. "Tell me I'm a shrewd businessman. I'm finally prepared to invite the taxman to come in and audit me."

"Good for you," she said, moving to the desk to admire it more closely. "It's really a lovely piece. You shouldn't have kept it hidden underneath all that trash."

"You like it?" he boasted, visibly gratified. "I picked it up years ago at a flea market and refinished it myself." He vanished into the kitchen, calling over his shoulder, "I've got another bottle of Mouton Cadet, if you're interested."

"I'm interested," Brooke responded, her gaze fastened to the desk. She fingered the small brass key inserted in the lock and twisted it. Hearing the latch of the rolltop give way, she wondered whether Sky had simply hidden the mess beneath the lid, and she nosily opened it up.

She shouldn't have been cynical, she reproached herself. The surface of the desk was spartan. Papers were sorted into the small cubbyholes at the back, and a freshly lined leather-trimmed blotter was centered in front of the chair. Tucked beneath the blotter was a bill from a stationery store, and when Brooke read it she realized that it was an order form for personalized business cards and letterhead paper.

Sky had taken all her advice to heart, she realized, and the comprehension warmed her greatly. Sloppiness and a lackadaisical attitude toward business practices had to be scratched from his list of minuses. If the lists weren't already weighted in favor of her loving him, the enormous change his desk had undergone would have made the difference.

She wedged the stationer's bill back under the blotter. As she reached for the lid to draw it down again, her attention was caught by a small framed photograph half hidden in one of the cubbyholes, and she pulled it out to look at it.

It was a photo of Sky. He was standing on a beach in a pair of shorts and a T-shirt, his hands on his hips and his smile radiant, his thick hair whipped back from his brow by the wind. He appeared much more youthful in the photograph, maybe because he was clean-shaven, yet he was hypnotically handsome.

She found it strange that he'd keep a photo of himself in a frame on his desk. Perhaps he just liked to have it handy to remind himself of how he looked without a beard.

She heard his footsteps and her cheeks reddened slightly as she set down the photo. "Caught in the act," she mumbled contritely.

Sky extended a glass of wine to her and said nothing. He was smiling tentatively, but his eyes were impenetrably dark.

"So that's what you'd look like if you shaved," she said.

"Something like that," he confirmed quietly.

"Isn't it a little conceited to keep a photo of yourself on your desk?"

He sipped his wine, then let out his breath. "That isn't me. It's a picture of my brother."

"Your brother?" she exclaimed, then covered her surprise by laughing. "I'm almost afraid to ask about his name."

"True," Sky told her. "True Blue."

"Oh, God," she said, a chuckle escaping from her throat. She reached for the photograph and studied it intensely. "True Blue. There's quite a resemblance between you and him."

"He was my twin," Sky told her, pulling the photograph from her hand and setting it in its place on the desk. He shut the desk and locked it.

"What do you mean, he *was* your twin?" she asked. "If he's your twin, he can't suddenly stop being your twin."

"He can if he's dead," Sky said bluntly.

Brooke felt the color drain from her face as she watched Sky roam to the window. He stared out at the night for several long minutes, then closed the drapes and turned back to her. "I'm so sorry," she said in a small voice.

"No need to be," he assured her with a gentle smile. "It isn't your fault."

He drifted to the bed and stretched out on it. Brooke swiftly crossed the room and sat beside him on the mattress. She took a bracing sip of wine, then set the glass down on the night table and faced Sky. "When did it happen?"

"Almost eight years ago."

"Oh, Sky...I'm sorry," she repeated.

He forced his grin wider. "It's history, Brooke. I've come to terms with it. These things happen."

He'd accepted it, she knew. Maybe that was a sane thing to do in such a circumstance. As alienated as she was from her brothers, she couldn't begin to imagine how she would feel if one of them died. But to lose a twin—it must be like losing half of oneself. "Do you want to talk about it?" she asked.

"Do you?" he countered.

She tried to interpret his enigmatic expression. His eyes seemed impossibly deep to her, their profound darkness glimmering with a pensive sadness despite his smile. "How did he die?" she asked.

"He was hit by a car while bicycling," Sky informed her. "It was a foggy, drizzly day. He probably shouldn't have been out on his bike, but...well, that's the way the Blue boys were. Forever throwing caution to the wind."

"Does..." She paused, uncertain of whether she had the right to question him. But he was pushy, and she could be, too. She loved him, and she wanted to know everything about him. "Does this have something to do with why you'll never shave off your beard?"

Sky chuckled at her perception. "Bull's-eye." At her inquisitive glance, he elaborated, "He died so suddenly, Brooke, so unexpectedly, that a lot of his friends didn't hear about it right away, or they didn't believe it. They'd run into me on the street and shout, 'True! Hey, True! I heard you were in an accident! Great to see you in one piece!'" His eyes clouded over, and he lowered them and drank some wine. "You probably can't begin to understand what it's like to be walking around with a dead man's face instead of your own. It was hell, Brooke, absolute hell. It was bad enough losing my brother, my closest friend my—" he sighed "—my twin. And then, for months afterward, having all his buddies accosting me and saying, 'Hey, True! You're alive!'" He groaned softly.

Brooke had never seen Sky look so desolate. "It must have been agony."

"It got so I didn't know who I was anymore. I felt as if my identity was slipping away, as if Sky Blue had somehow gotten nailed into the coffin with True." He sighed again, drank some more wine and forced a feeble smile. "When I was pretty sure I was over the edge, I went into analysis for a while."

"Analysis?" Brooke blurted out. She couldn't conceive of someone as confident and stable as Sky seeking an analyst's assistance. She could scarcely conceive of him enduring such anguish. Her entire picture of him was demolished, and she scrambled futilely to resurrect it.

"Analysis was a waste of time," he noted. "Growing a beard and leaving Oregon proved much more effective."

"I don't see how growing a beard and changing your address can enable you to overcome that kind of grief."

"It took more than the beard and the move. It took a lot of patience, a lot of effort. It took having to learn to accept things and keep going. It took a conscious decision on my part to be happy, to take what I had and run with it. Grief wasn't getting me anywhere. So I resolved to accept it and move on."

"To go with the flow," Brooke murmured.

He gazed steadily at her. "People who know my work often ask me how faces came to be my trademark, unusual faces, unique faces. It really makes a lot of sense, given my own experience. When I first arrived in New York, I spent hours staring at people, days, just watching the way their lips moved, the way their eyes focused. I was looking for life, for the joy of life in faces. And when I started making commercials, I put those faces on tape and celebrated them." He paused for a moment to think. "Yes, I go with the flow, Brooke, and it's made me happy again."

Her heart swelled in her chest, straining against her ribs. She felt overwhelmed by her love for Sky, by this new strength she'd discovered within him. He was happy because he'd *made* himself happy. It wasn't frivolity or carefreeness, but something quite the opposite, a solemn, thoughtful design to overcome the tragedy that life had handed him. He'd actively courted happiness until it became a part of him. Sky was the bravest, strongest man she'd ever known.

She bowed her head to his and kissed him. His hand reached for her hair, combed through it, then pushed her gently from him. "Don't do this," he mumbled hoarsely.

"Do what?" she asked, startled.

"Pity me."

"Pity you?" she echoed. "You think I'm kissing you because I pity you?"

"Yes," he said firmly. His gaze didn't waver as it traced the exquisite lines of the face above his. His eyes probed hers, infinite darkness to glittering hazel light, and he remembered how she had sounded that morning when she'd laughed. Maybe she did pity him, maybe she was kissing him because she felt sorry for him. Maybe the only way a woman like Brooke could love him was if she knew that he'd borne his own cross, that the world had been as capricious with him as it had been with her.

He despised the possibility that baring the misery of his past was the only way to reach Brooke's heart. If she loved him just because of his brother's death, he'd resent her forever.

But she bent to kiss him again, and his hunger for her swamped his ability to reason. He had accepted worse things in the past. And no matter how wrong it might be, he would accept Brooke tonight. He wanted her too much to refuse.

Chapter Eight

She wished there was some way she could explain her love to Sky. She had realized the truth of her feelings long before she knew anything about his brother, although her new knowledge of the sorrow Sky had endured made him seem even more special to her. She wished she could tell him that the plus list she'd composed for him was lengthening off the computer screen, expanding beyond her ability to enumerate.

But even if he hadn't been kissing her so forcefully, she couldn't speak such thoughts aloud. If she did, he'd accuse her of talk, talk, talk. So she let her body communicate for her, and her soul.

His tongue took full possession of her mouth, locating secret, sensitive places no man had ever discovered before. The fingers of one hand dug imploringly into her hair, holding her head immobile, and his other hand slid down to her waist and tugged the tail of her blouse from her slacks. He slipped his hand beneath the fabric to stroke the naked skin of her back.

Her flesh seemed to melt at his touch, softening, yielding to his urgent caresses. She broke the kiss, gasping for air, then applied her trembling fingers to the buttons of his shirt. Spreading apart the yellow cloth, she admired his hard chest, the upper portion of which was covered with soft black swirls of hair. She pressed her lips to the base of his throat and felt it vibrate as he groaned.

"I love you, Sky," she whispered, the words suddenly coming very easily to her.

"Ssh," he silenced her. His thumb meandered along the nape of her neck beneath her hair as she grazed downward, brushing her mouth over the silken tendrils adorning his skin. His rippling muscles and dark, tensing nipples spread a warm feeling of arousal through her body.

Sky rolled onto his side and drew her down next to him. He wrenched the buttons of her blouse open, then reached behind her to unfasten her bra. It was a plain white cotton garment, not a hint of alluring lace, not a bit of sheerness. He should have expected as much from Brooke.

He pulled off the blouse and bra, exposing her to the waist, and drew his hands forward to cover her firm breasts. They were small and beautifully shaped, and at his gentle massage Brooke gasped. His fingers worked toward their centers, teasing her nipples until they ached. He moved lower on the bed and covered one with his mouth. The unfamiliar sensation of his beard against her skin stimulated her beyond belief.

"Sky..." The word was moaned, not spoken.

"Don't talk," he cautioned her.

"Sky..."

"Just my name," he acquiesced, sliding his mouth to the other breast and running his tongue over the hard, pink tip. "Say my name."

"Yes, Sky." Her fingers raveled into his hair, holding him to her. "I love your name."

He made no indication that he heard her. His hands were already opening the zipper of her slacks, quickly stripping her naked. Without her assistance he removed the rest of his own clothes.

He was moving faster than she would have imagined, but she didn't mind. Clearly he was as eager for her as she was for him. She had only an instant to admire his tall, well-proportioned body before he lay down beside her again and wrapped his legs around hers. "Brooke," he said, his hands waltzing down to her waist and up to her breasts again, his lips wandering along her hairline, kissing her bangs. "You feel so good, so smooth."

She understood then that it wasn't talking he objected to. It was his fear that she would spoil the mood by becoming analytical that had caused him to stifle her before. She sighed, arching toward him, and set her hands loose across his warm, supple back. "You feel good, too," she murmured. "You feel wonderful."

His thighs released hers, and one leg slid between hers, flexing against her. She trembled as the heat of her desire spiraled through her. Again she felt as if she were melting, liquefying, transforming into the fluid of her name, washing over and around him. She shifted onto her back and he followed on top of her.

He bent to kiss her, and she nibbled his beard with her teeth. Brother or no brother, she loved his beard. She loved his face, his body. His hand gliding slowly down to her hip, playing across the softness of her bottom, slipping around her thigh to awaken her fully.

She closed her eyes and moved with him, emitting soft moans of delight. She wasn't terribly practiced when it came to lovemaking, and what experience she'd had didn't prepare her for the astounding spasms of blissful energy that spread up and into her from the gently insistent friction of his fingers over her damp flesh. She wanted the pleasure to last forever, the thrills coursing through her, forcing through her resistance, illuminating her in a way that had nothing to do with light and everything to do with love.

"Sky," she said breathlessly as her fingers floated hesitantly across the lean stretch of his abdomen, reaching for him. At her shy touch his entire body seemed to clench and then shudder. She touched him again, more boldly this time, and a strained groan passed his lips. He covered her mouth with his, then removed his hand and hers. He rose fully and surged deep into her.

She clasped his back, matching his rhythm, meeting his potent thrusts. Gradually their bodies seemed to burn away in the blaze of their want, leaving just their souls to touch, to merge. Water around rock, each shaping the other, surrendering to the seething current. Brooke felt it carrying her along, pulling her toward an edge and then over it in a cascade of sensation. The torrent raged through her, drumming against her, her clamorous pulse deafening her to her own choked cry of ecstasy.

Then Sky followed her over, hurling himself down, down into her, into the deepest, most intimate part of her. She felt the fierce release whip through him as he surrendered to a force far stronger than himself.

He continued to cling to her, kissing her, blanketing her until the fist of passion that had taken hold of him began to unfurl. His breath slowly grew more regular, his heart stopped pounding, his muscles slackened. He wearily lowered his head onto the pillow beside her and let out a ragged sigh.

Brooke turned her head to face him. She wove her fingers through his hair, brushing it back behind his ear. Her eyes glowed with contentment, with fulfillment. Incredible happiness, he defined the golden flush that illuminated her face.

He ought to have been relieved that he had pleased her so completely, but he wasn't. He had wanted Brooke, wanted her so much he'd been willing to have her any way he could. But he hadn't wanted her to love him out of pity.

He could scarcely bear to look at her, to see her wonderful face transformed by a love spawned in grief. Twisting abruptly, he sat up, then heaved himself off the bed. He prowled as far as the desk and leaned against it, trying to regain his equilibrium.

"What's wrong?" she asked, sitting up as well.

Good question, he muttered silently. What was wrong with him? Why couldn't he just accept this, this magnificent occurrence, this splendid sexual sharing? Brooke had given him more than she'd ever given a man before—he knew it instinctively—and still he wasn't satisfied. Why did he even care about satisfaction? It wasn't like him to be measuring, expecting, wanting so much.

And yet he wanted more.

"Sky...please say something."

He turned apologetically to her. Her face was shadowed with worry. The glow was gone from her eyes, and he hated himself for having extinguished it. "I'm sorry, Brooke,'' he murmured, unable to return to the bed quite yet.

"Are you really?'' she asked in a tremulous voice.

"Not the way you think,'' he hastened to reassure her.

As if his words offered any reassurance. "What way do I think?'' she challenged him. "You didn't want this to happen?''

"I...'' He swallowed, buying time to organize his thoughts. "I wanted it to happen with laughter,'' he explained haltingly. "I wanted it to happen when you were roaring with laughter. You're so stunning when you laugh, Brooke—''

"And I'm not stunning when I don't laugh?''

He wished to high heaven that he was better at expressing himself. Not certain how to continue, he crossed to his night table and lifted his glass of wine. He emptied it in several swallows.

It didn't help. Dropping onto the bed beside her, he exhaled and gathered one of her hands in his. It felt icy to him, and he lifted it to his lips and tried to warm it with a kiss. "Brooke,'' he attempted. "Brooke, I wanted you to want me when you were laughing, when you were happy and free. Not when you were thinking about how poor Sky lost his brother and needs some cheering up.''

"Is that what you think happened here?'' she asked incredulously. "Sky, I love you.''

"How can you say that now? You didn't love me when I was making the video or being pushy or calling you a stuffed shirt.''

"I am a stuffed shirt,'' she insisted almost boastfully. "And I did love you when you were making the video. And being pushy. And the whole thing. Sky, I ran you through my computer, and—"

"You what?" He couldn't stop himself from laughing.

Brooke grinned sheepishly, then bravely continued. "Yesterday, I did a calculation in the computer and it came up that I loved you. I don't necessarily reach conclusions in the same manner as you, Sky, I have my own style. I analyzed it." Sensing that he was about to object, she pressed her hand to his mouth to cut off his words of protest. "I analyzed it and this was the way it computed."

"You did this yesterday?" he asked doubtfully.

"Yesterday afternoon."

"Why didn't you say something last night?"

"I would have, but you went and conked out on me," she reminded him sternly.

He laughed again, his disappointment ebbing. "That'll teach you to drag me to some European stomp fest," he teased.

"Believe me, I learned my lesson," she muttered.

He sprawled out beside her, curling one arm about her shoulders and hugging her close. "You're so proper, Brooke, so...so contained. You seem like the sort of woman who'd feel sorry for someone like me. Rich Boston puritan and that whole trip. I bet you give to charity, too."

"I do," she agreed. "Sky, I'm sorry about your brother, but that's history, as you said. This is now. Admit it, Sky: You probably felt I was the charity case here, not the other way around."

"Maybe," he replied. He studied her face, despising himself for having spoiled the aftermath of their lovemaking. How could he have demanded more from her when she had given him everything? How could he have been so blunt, so cold, when she had been so warm and soft, so open to him?

He hadn't trusted her. For that one moment, when Brooke began to seduce him, the universe had suddenly seemed to reverse on him. Not because he was being seduced by her instead of initiating things himself, but because he'd been fraught with doubt. He hadn't been able to believe that Brooke could love him, just as she hadn't been able to believe a couple of weeks ago that he could love her.

He was shocked by his understanding. It was unlike him—everything that had happened when Brooke started kissing him was unlike him. She was altering him, eroding his strong surface, uncovering aspects of him that he'd long forgotten. Doubt, distrust, his fury with people who had expressed pity about his brother's death.

"Ah, Brooke," he said, sighing, wondering if there was any way to explain. "When I thought you were a—God, I don't like this phrase."

"What phrase?"

"Charity case."

Brooke smiled gently. "It's not very pretty, Sky, but admit it. You said right at the start that you thought I needed saving."

"Sinning, too," he refreshed her memory.

"Whatever." She shrugged.

He smiled, amazed by her willingness to talk this way, to accept this conversation. He knew she never discussed such things with other people, and her discussing it now without flinching fed his respect for her. "When I thought you needed saving, that wasn't what made me love you. What made me love you was seeing you at your strongest, not at your weakest.''

"My strongest?''

"Talking business. Organizing me. Arguing with Michael and Willow. You're so strong and sensible, Brooke. When I realized that, mere fascination turned into love.''

"And what's my weakest?'' she goaded him, only half smiling.

"Your weakest is when you run away.'' *Which was what I just did,* he muttered beneath his breath.

He lapsed into silence, relaxing on the bed, hugging her closer. His fingers described a consoling pattern through her hair, savoring its silkiness, exploring the evenness of its clipped ends. He had known, right from the start, that Brooke was different from him, that she was different from other women, that he was taking a big chance by chasing after her. But he'd always believed that she'd be the one to change, not he. He'd believed that she needed more changing than he did.

However, knowing her *had* changed him, in ways he would never have predicted. She was right about putting his business in order. He used to condemn compulsive orderliness, and his ignorance had cost him more than money. It had thwarted his plan for eventually starting up his own video business. He was always so busy being freewheeling and easygoing, the brilliant artist who couldn't be bothered with such mundane matters as saving receipts. He'd worn his impracticality like a badge of honor.

He'd been the same way with people, he admitted. He'd breezily fallen in and out of love, considering it all a part of life's flow. To take love too seriously, to take anything too seriously, didn't seem worth it. In retrospect, he realized, the only time he'd ever committed himself fully to love was with his brother. The love of two brothers, twins, two halves of the same entity, was a bond no outsider could ever understand. And he'd lost True. It had hurt so much he'd broken down completely, and like any normal person he loathed being hurt. So he'd vowed never to let himself be that serious about anyone or anything again.

But with Brooke, everything was different. The old Sky would have been quite content to have sex with her, to label his feelings love, to enjoy it while it lasted and move on when it ended. The new Sky, the Sky that Brooke had turned him into, was suddenly filled with dreams of perfection, ideals, hopes. His desire to love her only when she was strong, when she was laughing, was selfish and unfair. The love Brooke demanded of him had to accommodate her when she was solemn, when she was weak, when she needed him.

His epiphany frightened him. He felt raw and vulnerable. And in turn he had lashed out at Brooke, blaming her for his own shortcomings.

"I'm an ass," he announced glumly.

"What?"

"I'm an ass. I'm irresponsible, shallow, careless. You ought to run me through the computer again," he told her. "Even computers have been known to make mistakes."

She leaned back against his arm so she could see his face. "The computer didn't make a mistake with you," she declared in a firm, quiet voice. "You're not what I ever thought I wanted in a man, but I didn't make any errors with the data, and I trust my computer. If it tells me I love you, I'm not foolish enough to disagree."

"I like your computer," he murmured gratefully. "I'm not sure I trust it, but I like it."

"If you don't trust it, maybe you don't want me to continue doing your taxes for you."

"We'll chance it," he conceded. "We can always hope Uncle Sam won't catch on."

Gratified that his mood seemed to be improving, Brooke nestled her head against the cushion of his shoulder and sighed. "Tell me what it was like to be a twin," she begged him.

His fingers continued their soothing pattern through her hair as he spoke. "Sometimes..." He paused to reminisce. "Sometimes it was a royal pain," he confessed. "You'd run into someone and he wouldn't say, 'Hi.' He'd say, 'Which one are you?' People would frequently stare at True and me as if we were freaks. They'd point and gawk. Our teachers were always confusing us, messing up our school records. And it was difficult financially, too. My parents didn't have much money, and they always had to buy everything double: two cribs, two baseball gloves, two bicycles, two college tuitions at the same time. Money was always tight."

He paused again, then continued. "But the good things outweighed the bad. True and I were pretty mischievous—we loved playing tricks on people. Sometimes one of us would make a date with a girl and the other would go on it. Usually the girls didn't notice."

"Even your first true love in high school?"

"Even her." he remembered with a grin, then grew solemn. "True and I knew each other so well, Brooke, we hardly had to talk to each other most of the time. We always knew each other's thoughts. Sometimes we said things simultaneously. It's hard to explain." He struggled to find the words. "We just knew each other completely. When he died, I knew what it was like to die. Does that make sense?"

She nodded. "How did your parents feel when you took off the way you did? Didn't it upset them to lose you after losing their other son?"

"It upset them, but they understood it," Sky said. "They understood that what I went through was totally different from what they went through. I'm still close with them—we talk a lot on the phone, and I visit them often. They understand."

She digested his words, then sighed again. "I don't know how you could think I pitied you," she murmured. "If anything, I envy you."

"Envy me?"

"To be so close to your brother... My brothers and I are strangers who grew up in the same house and shared the same last name. We got so little attention from our parents, we were always competing, always viewing each other as rivals. And they were mean to me, Sky. They despised me for being a girl. They thought my parents loved me more than them because I brought in the money and they didn't. I would have given anything to have a brother I could love, someone I could share things with the way you shared things with your brother. Of course I envy you."

He eased onto his side and touched his lips to hers. "I'm glad things worked out for you the way they did. You've been storing up all that love inside you instead of using it up on your ingrate brothers, and I'm the lucky recipient.''

"I don't think it works that way," she argued, but he kissed her again and she no longer cared how it worked. She hadn't even been aware of how much love she had stored up inside her, but now it was pouring from her like an untamed river, washing its sweet tide over Sky. That, Brooke decided, was all that mattered.

SHE WOKE UP before him. The morning's sunshine filtered softly through the drapes covering the window, illuminating the room with a diffuse light. She propped herself up on her elbow and gazed down at Sky's face. He look even more serene now than he had Friday night when he'd fallen asleep in the theater. Obviously a bed was more comfortable than a theater seat, but Brooke allowed herself the flattering thought that his peaceful slumber was a reflection of his love for her and the night they'd spent in each other's arms.

She studied the thick, dark lashes fringing his eyelids, the warm nuances of his skin, the denseness of his beard. She wondered what he was dreaming about.

"See something you like?" he suddenly said.

His eyes were still shut, and she was startled by his having guessed what she was doing. But all she said was, "As a matter of fact, yes."

He opened his eyes and smiled at her. "For an overgrown virgin, you're a pretty sexy lady," he murmured appreciatively, his sparkling eyes conveying his contentment.

Brooke didn't argue. The night they'd just spent together made any argument on her part irrelevant. "Just trying to unload all that stuff I never used up in the past thirty years," she parried.

"Here's hoping you have an inexhaustible supply," Sky said, cupping his hands about her head and drawing her down for a kiss.

Brooke wished that they could lie there kissing forever, but reluctantly Sky pulled back, sinking into the pillow. His eyes seemed slightly glazed, and he issued an uneven groan. "The bad news," he whispered, "is that I've got to go to work today."

"But it's Sunday."

He nodded, then reached for his wristwatch on the table beside him and squinted at its dial. "I've got to go to the lab and have a look at yesterday's tapes. I can't very well put it off till tomorrow. Tomorrow is already reserved for Rickler's Candies."

"Sky, you're working too hard," Brooke admonished him.

"That doesn't seem like the sort of thing my business manager should say," he countered, pushing himself up. "If I get an early start, maybe I'll finish up by late afternoon and we can get together for dinner. How's that for an incentive?"

"If it's your best offer, I guess I'll have to accept," Brooke conceded, sitting up also.

Once they were both dressed, they ate a light breakfast of toast and coffee and then left Sky's apartment. The sun baked the street in springtime heat, and the window boxes decorating a neighboring building displayed the splashy yellow petals of daffodils in bloom.

Sky summoned a cab for Brooke, kissed her cheek and sent her on her way with another promise to phone her that evening when he was through at the lab. Brooke rode north to her apartment in a daze of love, her body still replete with the memory of Sky's profound tenderness and her mind still reeling with the new things she had learned about him. For someone who behaved so debonair and carefree he certainly was a complex person, and his complexity made her love him all the more.

The living room was empty when Brooke entered the apartment. But the Sunday *Times* was spread out across the dining room table, so she knew Nancy was home. Brooke crossed to the table and discovered the *Times* magazine open to the crossword puzzle, a pencil balanced along the crease of the spine. Nancy hadn't made any marks on the puzzle, which was surprising, since Brooke hadn't been around to quarrel with her over who would get to solve it.

"Hello?" she called.

"In here," Nancy's muffled voice emerged from her bedroom.

Brooke strode down the hall and pushed open her roommate's door. Nancy sat at the center of her bed, dressed in a garish fuchsia dressing gown, a box of tissues resting on the blanket beside her. She had obviously been crying.

"Nancy?" Brooke approached the bed. "Are you all right?"

"I'm fine" Nancy sniffed, then yanked a tissue from the box and blew her nose.

Brooke eased onto the bed beside her. "What happened?"

"Nothing happened," Nancy replied, lifting her baleful eyes to Brooke. "Bogdan's troupe left for Hungary."

"Of course they did," Brooke murmured. "Is that a surprise?"

"No, it's not a surprise," Nancy muttered, her voice wavering. "I'm just…just feeling a little low now that he's gone."

"But, Nancy, you knew he'd be leaving."

"Don't start in with I-told-you-so," Nancy warned her. "Just because I knew he was leaving doesn't mean I have to be happy now that he's gone."

Brooke examined her roommate and sighed compassionately. She was surprised that Nancy was taking Bogdan's departure so badly; she should have been prepared for it from the start. The man was loyal to Hungary, after all. He loved being surrounded by discos and Rubik's Cubes. Nancy certainly couldn't have expected him to stay in New York.

Besides, Nancy had had plenty of other brief love affairs and emerged from them jubilant and energized. What made Bogdan so different from the others?

This was no time for being analytical, Brooke reproached herself. Whatever the reason, Nancy was apparently dejected over having to say good-bye to Bogdan. She needed Brooke's friendship and support, not a lecture on her lack of foresight.

"I tell you what," Brooke said brightly. "Let's go to church."

Nancy gaped at her. "Church?"

Brooke hadn't planned to go to church, but she thought it would do Nancy some good to get out, and that was the first idea that came to mind. An excellent idea, too, she decided. "Come on," she said, rising from the bed and urging Nancy to her feet. "Put some clothes on."

"Brooke, I'm not a Methodist," Nancy protested.

"I doubt that God will notice," Brooke pointed out.

Nancy scowled, then moved reluctantly to her closet. She surveyed its contents and her scowl deepened. "I'm borrowing something of yours," she announced, brushing past Brooke as she left her bedroom.

"Be my guest," Brooke said as she returned to the living room. She crossed to the table, picked up the pencil and then lowered it. If anyone needed the diversion of solving a crossword puzzle today, it was Nancy. Brooke wouldn't fight her about it.

She settled on the couch with the newspaper's business section and waited for Nancy to dress. Eventually Nancy joined her, clad in Brooke's seersucker A-line skirt and a demure white blouse, her frizzy mop of hair fastened into a somewhat tame ponytail with a tortoise-shell clasp. "Do I look churchy?" she asked.

"Practically ready for sainthood," Brooke assured her. "We'd better get going if we don't want to miss the first act."

As it turned out, they arrived at the church after the service had already begun. They inconspicuously took seats in a rear pew.

Nancy immediately pulled a hymnal from the rack before them and leafed through it, feigning boredom. Brooke settled on the oak bench and listened to the tonic harmonies of the hymn the choir was singing.

As a child she had attended church regularly with her family, but she'd come to resent the weekly ritual. She was irked by the hypocrisy of her family, which connived and bickered and played power games for six days of the week and then expected, miraculously, to discover grace on Sunday. As Brooke matured, she came to realize that church was little more than a social obligation to her parents, an opportunity to show off their latest elegant clothing purchases and to remind Brooke's aunts and uncles that Brooke was the first girl born into the family, the one blessed with her grandmother's name. By the time Brooke started college and moved into her dorm, she was convinced she'd never set foot inside a church again.

But in time she found her way back into a chapel. She didn't consider herself devoutly religious, but she liked the tranquillity she found in a church, the feeling of communal solitude that enabled her to meditate and reflect, to work out her thoughts in peace. Sometimes the sermons moved her and sometimes they didn't, but she appreciated the quiet time church offered her.

The minister began his homily on the subject of brotherhood and Brooke's thoughts turned to Sky. She thought about the brother he had lost, and about how it was better to have loved and lost than never to have loved at all. She thought about how Sky's loss had strengthened him, how it had helped to make him the man he was today. She wondered if she would have loved him if she'd met him eight years ago, before he'd been forced to make his own sense of life's cruel blows.

She thought about her own brothers, the isolation she had known as a child, the frustration of realizing that no matter what she did, her brothers would never accept her and befriend her. It was probably sacrilegious to think about reincarnation in a Christian church, but Brooke couldn't help praying that if her soul ever returned to earth in another body, she'd want it to be the body of a twin.

As soon as the final hymn was sung, Nancy headed for the door, Brooke scrambling to keep pace. "That is definitely not my style," Nancy declared as they started down the street.

Still, Brooke thought Nancy looked less mournful than she had when Brooke had arrived home from Sky's place, and she decided to press her luck. "Why don't we buy some Italian ices and take a stroll through the park?" she suggested. "It's such a glorious day."

Nancy glared at her. "This isn't like you, Brooke," she mumbled. "Since when are you interested in junk food?"

Brooke ignored her, her attention drawn to the window of a candy shop on the block. "Wait here," she ordered Nancy before vanishing into the store.

She emerged after several minutes carrying a brown paper bag. "What did you buy?" Nancy asked suspiciously.

"You'll see," Brooke replied mysteriously, leading Nancy across the street toward the park.

They found a vacant park bench beneath a leafy arbor not far from the Sheep Meadow. Brooke sat and pulled Nancy down beside her, then removed a box of chocolates from the bag. "Chocolates?" Nancy hooted. "Brooke, this isn't like you at all."

"They're Rickler's chocolates," Brooke explained. "Sky makes their television commercials."

"They must be persuasive commercials if you'd go out and blow real money on a box of empty calories," Nancy muttered, studying the arrangement of light and dark chocolates in their festive paper nests. After careful deliberation, she selected a candy and bit into it.

Brooke took one for herself. "I honestly don't remember if I've ever seen any of his Rickler's ads," she confessed. She bit into the chocolate-covered nougat and her taste buds rejoiced at its sweet flavor. It reminded her of kissing Sky. "What do you think, Nancy?" she asked. "Should we order cable television?"

Nancy's eyes grew round. "Cable? Since when did you get addicted to the boob tube?"

"I was only thinking, if we subscribed to cable we could get the station that shows rock videos."

Nancy helped herself to another candy and scrutinized her friend. "To what do we attribute this gross transformation in your character?"

"I'm in love."

Nancy groaned. "Great. What timing," she said sarcastically. "Here I am in the pits, and now, out of the blue, you decide you're in love."

"Nancy, the timing's perfect. This way I'm high enough to yank you up from the pits." She eyed her roommate, dressed in such proper attire and acting so dour, and suppressed a laugh. She wasn't used to reversing roles with Nancy, but Nancy had exerted great effort to buoy Brooke over the years they'd known each other, and now it was Brooke's turn to buoy Nancy.

She thought about Nancy's usual behavior, her fickleness with men, her cheerful relationships with them that swung from friendship to passion and back again. Brooke used to be awed by Nancy's insouciance, but now she recognized that sometimes one's heart could play tricks. Sometimes genuine feelings slipped in when one wasn't expecting it, and the result could be terrible sorrow. She wondered whether any of Sky's love affairs had ended the way Nancy's fling with Bogdan had ended, surprising him with the sting of regret.

For the first time in her life, Brooke was glad that she'd never been casual about love. Having never allowed herself to fall in love had meant many long years of an even, dull existence, but now that she was in love, the sheer novelty of it gave it its special meaning, its unique luster.

"So you're in love," Nancy mused, examining the chocolates thoughtfully. "What led to this great revelation? Is the guy great in bed?"

"You have a crass mind," Brooke scolded indignantly.

"Okay, he's great in bed," Nancy surmised. "What else? I'll grant you he's an eyeful, but honestly, Brooke, he looks like a geriatric hippie. You said yourself he wasn't your type."

"I was wrong."

"Well, I suppose congratulations are in order." Nancy and Brooke simultaneously reached for the same truffle, but Brooke quickly deferred to Nancy, selecting instead a chocolate-covered almond. "I thought being in love is supposed to make you lose your appetite," Nancy asserted.

"Sometimes," Brooke allowed, recalling her computer list.

"On the other hand, being depressed is supposed to make you go on binges," Nancy declared, plucking yet another candy from the box. "But who cares? It's your skirt. If I pop the button it's your fault."

Brooke firmly set the lid back on the box. "In the interest of preserving the button on my skirt, you've had enough. Let's take a walk."

"What a regimen," Nancy complained as Brooke hustled her along the path at a brisk pace. "First salvation, then sin, and now salvation again. Wake me up when we get to the next sin."

The next sin turned out to be a huge lunch at a sidewalk café, complete with rich pastries for dessert. But salvation soon followed in a double-time march back through the park and west to their building. An afternoon spent reading the newspaper with the television set turned on constituted the next sin. Brooke watched every single commercial, but none were for any of the products Sky had mentioned as his clients.

When the telephone rang at five, Brooke raced to answer it. She was absolutely stuffed, and she hoped that Sky wouldn't mind if she didn't want to go out to a restaurant for dinner. "Hello?" she answered breathlessly.

"Brooke? It's your mother."

Brooke sagged against the kitchen counter. Her mother always identified herself this way, not "Mom," not even "Mother," but "your mother," just in case there was any question in Brooke's mind as to whose mother the woman was. "Hello, Mother," she said emotionlessly, wondering what might have precipitated the call. Her mother never called unless she had something concrete to report.

"I'm calling," her mother obliged, "because Grandmother Brooke thinks she's had another stroke."

"*Thinks?* How can you *think* you've had a stroke?"

"Her doctor said it wasn't a stroke, but she doesn't believe him. He claims it was just a spell of dizziness. She's nearly eighty-eight years old, for goodness' sake."

And chronically dizzy, Brooke muttered soundlessly. "Is she all right?" she asked, forcing her tone to reflect patience and respect.

"Yes," her mother replied in a disappointed voice. Brooke's mother and her siblings knew there was an enormous inheritance awaiting them if Grandmother Brooke ever succumbed to her final dizzy spell. "Brooke, as you know, her birthday is coming up. In light of this latest incident, she's decided to move her annual birthday dinner forward to this coming Saturday evening."

"Is this an invitation?" Brooke asked testily.

"She does expect you to come," her mother noted. "She's getting on, Brooke. It would be a smart idea for you to come."

To get myself written into the will, Brooke grumbled to herself bitterly. She had dutifully attended her grandmother's annual birthday dinners even after moving from Boston, but they were a trial that she was growing less and less able to tolerate. Like her grandmother, she, too, was getting on in years, and the older she got, the less able she was to stomach her family's Byzantine politics. She would just as soon not be included in her grandmother's will.

But all she said was, "I'll think about it. This isn't much notice."

"Of course, you'd be welcome to spend the night at our house if you so desire."

If I so desire, Brooke thought. Had ever a more gracious invitation been extended by a mother to her daughter? "I'll see what I can arrange" was as far as she would commit herself.

"Very well, Brooke. As you know, a family gathering isn't complete without you present."

Brooke grimaced but managed a pleasant farewell before hanging up the telephone. Almost at once it rang again, and she lifted the receiver. "Hello?"

"Hi, Brooke." Sky's warm, husky voice spun through the wire, erasing all her vexation. "I just got in. Correction: I got in five minutes ago and your line was busy. Tell Nancy to stop tying up the phone."

"I was the one tying up the phone," Brooke informed him. "Mea culpa and all that. My charming mother called to invite me to my charming Grandmother Brooke's eighty-eighth birthday party." A sudden whimsical thought occurred to her. "It's next Saturday night, up in Boston. Will you come with me?"

"Oh, Brooke..." He sighed. "I'd love to."

"No, you wouldn't," she teased him. "It's going to be stultifying, and I'm sure you know it."

"I'd love to spend the weekend with you," he clarified, "but I can't. I've got to do more taping next weekend, some close-up work with Willow. She came out awful on the tapes. She wasn't even close to synchronized. There's no way I can match up what I've got of her with the record."

Brooke remembered the foul mood Willow had been in on Saturday. "That's too bad," she said. "You could have used a weekend off."

"I could always use a weekend with you," Sky murmured. "But work is work. If anyone knows that, my business manager ought to."

What his "business manager" knew was that holding down a full-time job in advertising and moonlighting as an independent rock video maker was going to lead to a physical collapse if Sky wasn't careful. She didn't like to think of him spending the prime of his life dozing at concerts because he was too exhausted to stay awake past suppertime.

On the other hand, she also knew that he was wise not to quit his full-time job at this point, when he was just starting out and getting himself established in a new field. Perhaps after this summer, when he'd completed the other two videos he'd been contracted for, his reputation would be a bit more solid. But when she considered the shape he'd be in by September, working on those two videos in addition to his nine-to-five job, she shuddered. Her free-as-the-breeze lover would turn into a workaholic drudge if he didn't take care—if his "business manager" didn't watch out for him.

"Well," she said with a sigh. "If you can't join me next weekend, you can't. Your work is important. I don't want to lead you into temptation."

"Please do," he replied. "Tempt me till I beg for mercy. You can start this evening at dinner."

"Okay," she accepted. "But, Sky, I've got to warn you, I've been gorging myself on candy all day. I'm not going to be able to eat much."

"Candy?" he asked, surprised.

"Rickler's Candies. Would you like me to write to the company and tell them how your brilliant ads led to my downfall?"

"I'd like you to tell me that I led to your downfall," he teased. "I'll pick you up in half an hour."

"I'll be waiting," Brooke promised.

SKY SET THE TELEPHONE back in its cradle and grinned. Brooke gorging on candy was an image he found incredibly appealing. He stared at the telephone for a long minute, assessing its placement on his desk and wondering what the tax law was regarding the use of one's office phone for private calls. Was he supposed to drag the telephone across the room to his night table when he was making a personal call? He'd have to ask Brooke about that.

But now that she was succumbing to the delight-fully wasteful activity of gorging on candy, he doubted whether she'd be able to give him a straght IRS by-the-book answer.

In fact, he doubted she'd even care.

Chapter Nine

Sky picked Brooke up at her office after work Friday.
It had been another week of having to visit each other
over the telephone instead of in person. Sky had spent
every evening negotiating with Willow and Michael,
rounding up technicians and obtaining the necessary
permits for a second Saturday of filming at Bethpage
State Park. His exhausting efforts showed clearly in his
face. He looked harried and haggard to Brooke, his
lips resisting their usual easy smile, his eyelids heavy,
his brow creased.

At her insistence, they didn't dine out, but instead
stopped at a grocery store on the way to his apartment and bought two steaks to broil for dinner. As
soon as they were done eating, they cleaned up and
then relaxed on Sky's bed, his stereo radio turned on
to a classical music station. After the week he'd had,
Sky claimed, he couldn't abide the thought of listening to rock music.

Brooke curled up next to him on the bed and pondered the draining week he'd endured. Apparently,
he'd spent every single night of the week engaged in
heated combat with Willow and Michael. Willow had

argued that Sky was being too fussy and demanding, that any shot displaying her gorgeous face had to be, by definition, fabulous. Michael had harangued Sky about the cost overruns the extra taping would entail and about the difficult time Willow's record company was giving him in releasing additional funds for the video. Sky had in turn protested that he was unwilling to produce a shabby tape, that his own reputation as well as Willow's was on the line, and that if she wanted a good rock video for her new record she had to give it her all.

One evening things had grown so acrimonious that Michael had telephoned Brooke from Willow's apartment while Sky was there. "Honest to God, Brooke, I need another business brain here," Michael had complained. "I'm stuck here with two raging *artistes*, and I'm doing my damnedest to stay mellow, but it ain't easy."

Brooke had suspected that Michael's attempt to stay mellow was being made with the assistance of some of his funny pink cigarettes, but she had refrained from issuing a pious lecture on sobriety.

"Any chance I can entice you over here to inject some sense into the proceedings?" Michael had cajoled her.

Much as Brooke wanted to see Sky, she certainly hadn't wanted to impose herself on the fracas unfolding at Willow's jungle abode. "Michael," she'd said rationally, "there's absolutely nothing I can do about Willow's ego. As far as the money goes, I don't see why the budget should be a problem. Haven't you got a contract with the record company?"

"Well, yes."

"Then why don't you read it and see if it contains any clauses about cost overruns?"

"What an excellent idea. I'll do that. Take it easy, Brooke."

They all needed business managers, she'd snorted after hanging up. Even Willow's business manager needed a business manager.

Now, lying in the comforting enclosure of Sky's arms, Brooke realized how much he needed a manager. He was truly running himself ragged, and it was all Willow's fault for having been so stubborn and sulky last weekend. "I'm worried about you," Brooke gently told him.

"Me? Why?"

"You look so tired, Sky, so fatigued. That's not to say that exposing yourself to my grandmother's hideous party tomorrow night would do you much good, but it would be better than having to knock yourself out retaping everything for Willow."

"Tomorrow won't be so bad," he assured her. "It's just going to be close-up work with Willow. I'm going with only one camera and a few technicians. We won't have to leave the city before sunrise. It shouldn't be too bad."

"Even so..." She studied his face, then ran her fingernails tenderly over his beard. "I hate to see you working yourself to the bone."

"Afraid I don't have enough energy left for you?" he asked, his eyes twinkling mischievously.

"Afraid you don't have enough energy left for yourself. Are they paying you something extra for having to make additional tapes?"

"I wish." He sighed. "My deal with them was a flat fee plus residuals."

"From here on in," she instructed him, "I want you to make sure that the contracts you sign for independent work contain a stipulation guaranteeing you extra payment if you have to do extra taping."

"Yes, ma'am," he promised. "You see how I need you to keep me from blowing things? Oh, by the way, I've got something to show you."

He lifted himself slightly from the bed and reached into the hip pocket of his corduroy trousers for his wallet. He pulled out a small, stiff rectangle of paper, bright blue, and handed it to her. She read: "Sky Blue, Video Artist." The bottom left-hand corner contained his home address, the bottom right-hand corner his telephone number.

She grinned broadly. "I like it," she declared enthusiastically. "Especially the color." She reread it, then set it on the night table. "Why 'Video Artist'? How come you didn't mention rock videos?"

"I don't know if rock videos are all I want to work on," he explained. "There are other free-lance things a video maker can produce. Who knows? The next Hungarian folk dance troupe to visit the United States might want to make a tape for broadcast on public television."

"Keeping your options open," Brooke murmured. "Very smart. You're beginning to think like a businessman."

"Heaven forbid!" he objected, cuddling her close to him again.

Her fingers drifted across his chest to his loosened necktie. "How tired are you?" she asked.

He brought her hand to his mouth and kissed it. "Close to unconscious," he announced. "You'll have to do all the work."

"Work?" she protested. "Who said anything about work?"

"You'll have to do all the play, then," he amended as he set her hand back on his chest. "Undress me, wench."

"That," she said indignantly, "is a very sexist remark." Yet she eagerly freed the tie from its knot and began to unbutton his shirt.

"What's sexist about it?"

"The word 'wench'."

"I'll never let it slip past my lips again. Far be it from me to want to insult my best chick."

"Chick!" Brooke cried, jabbing her fingers along his ribs until he squirmed and laughed. Clutching her hands, he pulled them off his body and pinned them behind her. Then he dropped back onto the pillow, Brooke tumbling down with him, and they kissed.

"Brooke," he whispered, rejuvenated by the languorous kiss, "I'll miss you tomorrow night. I don't suppose we would have been able to make love this weekend anyway, not at your parents' house."

"We could have if we took a hotel room," she pointed out.

His eyes widened at her unexpectedly seductive comment and he smiled. "You're full of surprises, aren't you? I know I told you to tempt me until I begged for mercy. I may have to start begging soon."

"Later," she suggested. "Not now."

"Not now," he agreed, covering her mouth with his again.

She did surprise him, and he had no complaints. Never had he expected when he first met Brooke that when he unstuffed her shirt he'd discover such a passionate woman inside. He forgot about how tired he was as he slaked his thirst for her with an all-consuming kiss. As soon as he freed his arms from the sleeves of his shirt he tossed it onto the floor and pulled her fully on top of himself, sliding his hands down her spine, over the flowing skirt of her dress to the backs of her knees. The warmth of his palms penetrated the sheer nylon of her stockings, and he drew his hands up her legs toward her hips, anxious to remove the stockings and feel her skin.

Unexpectedly he *did* feel her skin. The tops of her thighs were exposed to his touch, and he broke the kiss in astonishment. "What the hell are you wearing?"

She pulled back from him, startled. "What?"

He slid up the hem of her dress to her waist and discovered that she had on real stockings, fastened to a garter belt. Brooke Waters wearing a garter belt? He couldn't believe it. But he loved it.

She studied his face, then his hands trailing along the tan band trimming her stockings. It wasn't as if her garter belt were black lace with red ribbons dangling from it. It was a plain item of beige cotton, with elastic at the waist to hold it snugly in place. Yet the way Sky inspected it was inexplicably embarrassing to her. "Panty hose are too warm in the summer," she explained bashfully. "And I've got to wear stockings for work. This is just a little bit more comfortable on a hot day. That's the only reason I wear it."

"Don't shatter my illusions," he muttered, slipping his fingers beneath the stockings' edges and tantalizing her inner thighs with delicate caresses. "Do you have any idea how sexy you are?"

"Sky." She laughed nervously. "I thought you promised no mortification."

"Don't be mortified," Sky said, his voice a low rumble. He hastily pulled her dress and half-slip over her head, then removed her bra and panties. "Oh, God," he breathed, examining her in her unintentionally enticing stockings and garter belt. "Oh, Brooke...the last thing in the world you should be is mortified."

"What should I be?" she whispered as he urged her onto her back and ran his hands the length of her legs.

"Be a woman." He bowed to kiss the exposed flesh of her upper thighs.

Her body stiffened as a bolt of fire swept through her. "I thought I was supposed to do all the work," she whispered shakily, buffeted by another bolt of fire as his tongue ventured over her skin. "I thought you were tired."

"Comatose," he murmured before letting his mouth reach its ultimate goal. His intimate kiss shocked her, stunned her, left her reeling in a whirlwind of emotion and longing. No, not a whirlwind, a storm, an ocean storm. This was no friendly forest brook running its delightful course. Her body seemed gripped by a great, surging tide, a curl of surf rapidly gathering momentum, sweeping her ahead of itself as it careened wildly toward the shore.

At first she tried to swim through it, but then she gave up, surrendering to its superior power. Sky's lips and tongue conquered her with their exquisite movements. The wave picked up speed, swelling larger, and

Brooke moaned as her body was propelled toward the breaking point.

The tide crashed over her, shattering, dragging her down in its rapturous undertow. She felt herself drowning in the sublime sensations that washed through her flesh, wave after wave, pulsing, presenting her soul to Sky.

He lifted himself up to view her tear-stained face, her lower lip caught in her teeth as she tried unsuccessfully to contain the sobs that filled her throat. The first time they'd made love, he had been sure she had given him everything, but now he knew that she was giving him even more of herself, more than he could have dreamed possible. And he knew that he, too, had given her more than she'd ever had before.

He bowed to kiss her brow, her cheeks, the salty teardrops captured in the webs of her long eyelashes. Her hands circled his back and he held him, held him as if he were a raft in the turbulent sea she was floating on. She held him as if her life depended on it. For a crazed moment, she was sure it did.

"Are you all right?" he asked when at last she stopped trembling in his arms.

"I love you, Sky."

He knew it was the truth. He wondered how he could ever have doubted her love when she responded to him so completely, so generously, when she let him bring her such incredible happiness. He kissed away the last of her tears, knowing as he did so that crying was something Brooke rarely did. Witnessing her tears was as exciting in its own way as witnessing her laughter. He removed her stockings and the rest of his clothing, and as he bound himself fully to her his heart followed his mind in understanding the depth of her love for him. His weariness burned away in the blaze of her love, a love strong and vast enough to consume them both.

He loved her, too. His sweet, shy Brooke. Not a wench, not a chick, not an overgrown virgin, but a woman, an enchanting, beautiful woman. He loved her.

SKY DIDN'T HAVE TO LEAVE for Long Island precisely at dawn, but he did have to get an early start, and after a quick breakfast, Brooke wished him luck and left his apartment for her own. The train she had decided to take to Boston was scheduled to depart from Penn Station at twelve-thirty and reach Boston at five. She didn't want to arrive at her grandmother's house a minute before she had to.

Entering her apartment, she found Nancy in the living room, serving coffee to a wiry young man dressed in a color-coordinated jogging suit. "Brooke, I'd like you to meet my friend Darryl Ephraim," Nancy introduced the stranger. "We met at the Korean fruit stand on Broadway. Darryl knows everything you'd ever want to know about ginger root."

Which isn't much, Brooke mused, though she was delighted by Nancy's improved spirits. "Pleased to meet you," she said, offering the young man a cheerful handshake. "If you'll excuse me, I've got some things to do." She winked at Nancy and departed for her bedroom.

She rummaged through her closet in search of something to wear to her grandmother's party. Everything she owned looked too...appropriate.

Brooke wasn't the same person she'd been at her grandmother's soiree last year. Why should she dress like a pompous prig when she was now liberated and proud of it?

She tiptoed from her room to Nancy's and pawed through her things. She didn't want to go overboard. But maybe an outfit just a little flashy, a little shocking...

She pulled a shapeless dress of unbleached muslin from its hanger and slipped it over her head. Though it fell past her knees, the hem curved upward toward the side seams like a nightshirt. The fabric was wrinkled, the sleeves trimmed with oversized cuffs. A polished teak button fastened the neckline above a deep slit.

Twirling in front of the mirror, Brooke scrutinized her reflection and guffawed. It was a wretched dress, she decided, which made it ideal for tonight's family gathering. Especially if she wore it with the snake bracelet and the eyeball ring. And the purple feather boa.

The clothing she packed in her overnight bag to wear back to the city Sunday was suitably conservative. But for tonight she was determined to shake up the Jennings clan. It had done Brooke good to be shaken up over the past several weeks; perhaps her family would have a similar reaction. It couldn't hurt.

"Nancy," she said as she emerged from her bedroom, carrying her overnight bag and a purse. "Do you mind if I borrow this outfit?"

Nancy's guest was clearly jolted by Brooke's appearance, which offered a stark contrast to Nancy's atypically normal outfit of neat blue jeans and a T-shirt. Nancy only laughed. "Are you sure the boa's right with that dress?" she inquired.

"I'm sure it's utterly wrong," Brooke replied. "That's why I'm borrowing it."

"Be my guest," Nancy said with a shrug. "But listen, Splash—if they boot you out, spend the night at a motel. Don't take a late train back to New York or you'll be pulling into Penn Station at an unsafe hour."

"I'm not a fool," Brooke brushed off the unneeded advice. She cast Darryl a playful glance. "Appearances to the contrary," she added. "So long. I'll see you tomorrow."

"Have a good trip," Nancy called after her as she swung out of the apartment. "Don't let them get to you."

"Dressed like this, they won't get within ten feet of me," Brooke said with a laugh.

Clothing does not the woman make, she contemplated an hour later as her train rolled out of the station. While Brooke didn't regret having chosen to wear such preposterous apparel, she felt undeniably disconcerted as the passengers sharing the car with her gave her stares of undisguised horror. She buried herself in the issue of *Forbes* she'd bought to read during the ride, and found herself convulsed with laughter when she considered the picture she must present: a woman wearing a ratty feather boa and a potato sack of a dress, carrying a suitcase and resembling something akin to a bag lady, reading a conservative business magazine, of all things. A month ago, if she had encountered a woman in such an outfit on a train, she'd have surely gawked. Now she was not the gawker but the gawkee. She wondered if the astonished stares she was receiving were anything like those Sky had gotten when he appeared in public as one half of a set of twins.

At the station in Boston, she stopped at a kiosk to buy her grandmother some flowers. Brooke's grand-mother adored cut flowers, and Brooke wondered momentarily whether that was the reason for her own aversion to them. She purchased a showy bouquet of red tulips and then headed outside to summon a cab.

The driver whose eye she caught seemed dubious, but a fare was a fare. When he pulled up to her grandmother's genteel town house on Beacon Hill, she gave him a lavish tip for having not commented on her appearance.

She tripped up the front stairs and rang the door-bell. It was answered by Grandmother Brooke's housekeeper. Because of her age and frailty, Brooke's grandmother kept on hand a small retinue of house-hold staff: the housekeeper, a cook, a full-time nurse. Of course, with her extensive family fawning and doting on her, she was well taken care of.

A large number of Brooke's relatives were already in the parlor when she entered, many of them hover-ing over the family's matriarch. Tiny and white-haired, Grandmother Brooke sat in her tufted satin easy chair like a queen on her throne. At Brooke's en-trance, the room grew still, the buzz of conversation instantly ceasing as all her tweedy, stuffy relations turned to stare at the flabbergasting vision of purple feathers that had intruded into their proper midst.

"Oh, my God, it's the Drip" came a low, coarse grumble. Brooke instantly identified the voice as that of her brother Larry.

She swept grandly into the room to present the flowers to her grandmother. "Hello, Grandmother Brooke. Happy birthday."

Her grandmother squinted up at her. "Brooke," she cackled, "you certainly are a sight."

"For sore eyes, Grandmother?" she asked airily.

"Just a sight." Her grandmother clucked in bemusement. "We'll leave it at that. Someone get me a drink." Three of Brooke's cousins collided in the doorway as they scampered to satisfy Grandmother Brooke's request, each hoping to score points with the woman.

"How are you feeling, Grandmother?" Brooke asked politely. The room's glacial silence made her uncomfortable.

"Dizzy," her grandmother replied. "Looking at you makes me dizzier."

"Oh, come now, Grandmother," Brooke chided her, "I look awesome and you know it."

"I will not quibble," Grandmother Brooke conceded, then turned to the cousin who had succeeded in delivering her a stiff martini and offered him an artificial smile. "You look awesome," she said as she twisted back to Brooke. "Feathers give me headaches. I do wish you'd remove that vile thing."

"When I'm ready," Brooke said nonchalantly. Anyone else in her family would have stripped off the boa and tossed it out the window just to please Grandmother Brooke.

Slowly the gathering came back to life, Brooke's relatives falling into small clusters and chattering softly. Brooke's mother approached and grabbed Brooke's arm, tugging her out of the parlor to the stairs. "Brooke," she said in a low taut voice, "whatever are you up to?"

How predictable of her mother to assume that Brooke had some devious plot up her sleeve. "I'm not up to anything," she answered honestly. "I thought it would be fun to dress like this."

"You are going to give your grandmother apoplexy," her mother scolded.

"Mother, Grandmother Brooke has survived countless strokes by her own diagnosis, and she's fomented more intrigue in this family than Rasputin instigated in pre-Revolutionary Russia. My clothing isn't going to kill her. If anything, she ought to be amused by it. I've recently taken a fancy to purple feathers, and—"

"Brooke! This could be your grandmother's final birthday. Why are you bent on destroying it?"

"Destroying it? I thought I was livening it up. Think of it, Mother: I'm providing the family with a new topic of conversation for the next decade. Now you won't have to keep reverting to discussions of money all the time. You can talk about little Brooke and her outlandish boa."

"You are your grandmother's namesake," Brooke's mother reminded her, as if Brooke could ever forget. "You owe her some respect."

"And you, Mother, owe *me* some respect," Brooke asserted. What in the world had gotten into her? She had never talked to her mother that way before. Brooke had always retreated and receded at family gatherings, gritting her teeth and counting the minutes until she could tactfully leave.

But that was before she had fallen in love. That was before she had learned that she could hold her own in the company of a green-haired rock singer, that she could rescue her chronically cheerful roommate from an unexpected case of the doldrums with her common sense and a box of chocolates, that she could lose control of herself to an amazing man with a bushy beard and an enchanting spirit. That was before she had learned how to experience incredible happiness.

She was incredibly happy now, even at this dismal gathering, surrounded by well-dusted antiques, Ming vases on trestle tables, musty portraits of previous generations of Humprhieses and Jenningses glowering from the walls, and thick Oriental rugs vacuumed into faded submission. Brooke was happy because, like Sky, she had learned to let herself be happy. She was happy because she had learned not to resist the universe's hidden currents but to go with them.

"I've come to the party because you want me here," she now explained, meeting her mother's steely gaze. "But I'm determined to enjoy it. I'm here, and that's all you have a right to expect." She pivoted on her heel and returned to the parlor, leaving her mother scowling and shaking her head and clutching the newel post at the foot of the stairs. Probably calculating what Brooke's sudden rebelliousness was going to cost in Grandmother Brooke's will, Brooke thought with a sniff.

Her relatives valiantly managed to converse with her, and a few of them seemed visibly relieved to hear her chat about her work at Benson & Broderick, the "Women and Numbers" panel she'd served on at Hunter College, the Hungarian folk dance troupe she'd recently seen performing at Town Hall, and the tickets to Mozart concerts she had reserved for the summer. Apparently cousin Brooke hadn't gone off the deep end, they presumed. Dressing weirdly and behaving a bit more robust and forceful than usual, but not yet a candidate for some discreet and exclusive sanitarium in the mountains.

To her utter pleasure, Brooke actually found that she was enjoying herself. She enjoyed the pots of cut flowers set about the house. She enjoyed kneeling on the floor to experiment with her nephew Andy's new top, which he privately complained was a dinky toy but Great-Grandmother Brooke had given it to him and his daddy told him he had to play with it. She enjoyed advising her cousin Jane that she was wasting her youth on bridge games when she could be contributing her time and energy to some worthwhile cause. She enjoyed describing to her neighbors at the elongated dining-room table the gummy green paste she'd eaten not long ago at a vegetarian restaurant a rock star she knew had insisted on visiting.

"A rock star?" Brooke's aunt Delphine nearly choked on the forkful of pressed duckling in her mouth. "You know a rock star?"

"Yes, and she's dreadful," Brooke bragged. "The first time I heard her sing I thought I was listening to a sickly cat. She has green hair, too. Her name is Willow."

"Willow?" Brooke's nephew Larry, who was ten years old, clearly knew more about rock music than his parents might have approved of. "You know Willow? Wow, Auntie Brooke. That's ba-a-ad!"

"Don't talk that way," Brooke's sister-in-law silenced her son with a frantic glance at Grandmother Brooke, who was seated at the far end of the table, waiting impatiently for her nurses to finish mincing her meat for her. Evidently Brooke's sister-in-law feared that a bit of pre-adolescent slang would jar the elderly woman into another undiagnosed stroke.

Brooke enjoyed herself. The only thing that would have made the party more enjoyable, she realized, was Sky's presence. She was sorry he had to spend the day out on Long Island working with Willow when he might have been here. Together, they would have spent most of the evening dissolved in laughter. Brooke would have been stunning with laughter if only Sky were here to share the occasion with her.

After dinner, Brooke's grandmother declared that she wanted to relax in her private sitting room at the end of the hall. The rest of the family congregated in the parlor, the men to sip cognac and the women demitasse. The housekeeper entered and announced that Grandmother Brooke would meet with her relatives one at a time. Brooke's uncle Philip was summoned, and the rest of the family pretended to be totally unconcerned about the private conference taking place at the other end of the house.

Brooke sensed a palpable tension in the room, even as the family gabbed idly about meaningless things. She mused that the atmosphere in the parlor must be comparable to that of a waiting room for witnesses subpoenaed to testify at a murder trial.

Her uncle Philip returned to the parlor, located his snifter, and emptied it in a long, unsteady swig. "Her will," he announced in answer to the unvoiced question in everyone's eyes. No one dared to ask him for details about what Grandmother Brooke had said to him. When Brooke's mother was summoned next, her patrician cheeks went slightly pale as she threw back her shoulders and followed the housekeeper from the parlor.

Not potential witnesses at a trial, Brooke corrected herself. Condemned prisoners awaiting sentencing. "Come on, Andy," she beckoned him, dropping onto the floor. "Let's play with that top of yours. Everyone's acting like such stuffed shirts around here."

Eventually her turn came, and she let the housekeeper escort her down the hall. She wasn't at all anxious: nothing her grandmother could say to her would upset her. She had no interest in her grandmother's will. She didn't even feel any rancor toward her grandmother. Sky had taught Brooke to accept that she was her name and her name was her. He had very nearly convinced her that she had a beautiful name.

The sitting room was a small, square room furnished in cloying pastels. The tulips Brooke had brought her grandmother stood in a crystal vase on a table, surrounded by several other, gaudier bouquets. Grandmother Brooke sat on a tufted satin chair, her legs propped on a matching ottoman with a plaid wool blanket spread across her lap.

"Come close," she commanded Brooke. "I think my hearing's failing."

Brooke didn't believe that for an instant. She suspected that her grandmother was able to hear anything and everything she wanted to hear. But she obediently approached the horsehair chair beside her grandmother's and dropped onto it.

She studied her grandmother's face. Graceful lines laced the older woman's cheeks and chin. Once she had had skin as smooth and clear as Brooke's. Physically Brooke strongly resembled her grandmother. Both had long, straight noses, pointed chins, proud cheeks, and pale eyes. Gazing into her grandmother's face, Brook felt as if she were gazing into her own future. The notion unnerved her.

"Tell me, child, why the change?" her grandmother asked, sounding more interested in Brooke than she'd ever sounded before.

"I'm in love," Brooke replied candidly.

"I see. Well, I suppose it's about time. You're no spring chicken," her grandmother bluntly observed. "Does the gentleman like purple feathers?"

"The gentleman likes me," Brooke stated. "I don't think what I'm wearing matters that terribly much to him."

Her grandmother nodded, then wove her withered hands together in her lap. "Is he well fixed?"

Brooke could have told her grandmother that Sky was an exceptionally talented man with a very comfortable income, but she didn't. Beyond finding the question insufferably nosy, Brooke reacted to it as a professional, which entailed never divulging a client's private financial information. "That's really none of your business," she said in as calm as a voice as she could muster.

Her grandmother appeared unruffled. "I ask only because, as you know, I am getting on in years and planning for the inevitable. If you are in love with some poor boy, I would want to be able to help you if I could."

"I don't want your money," Brooke said firmly.

Her grandmother leaned forward slightly, her narrow shoulders hunching beneath her silk blouse. "You never have wanted my money, have you, Brooke?" she retorted.

"No, Grandmother," Brooke confirmed. "I never have."

Her grandmother peered at her for a long time, her eyes as clear and keen as Brooke's. "I'm sorry you've always hated me," she said without a hint of sadness.

Brooke took a moment to recover her wits. "I don't hate you, Grandmother Brooke," she maintained.

"What is it, then? Supply a better word. I'm so dizzy these days I've been having difficulty with my crossword puzzles."

Brooke wondered if, when she herself reached her eighty-eighth birthday, she, too, would have trouble with her crossword puzzles, and the thought evoked a strange empathy from her. "I don't hate you," she repeated. "But..." She hesitated and tried to collect her thoughts. Maybe the family—and the woman who headed it—were correct. Maybe Grandmother Brooke would never see another birthday. This could be Brooke's last opportunity to express the pain and disgust that clouded her relationship with her family. "I've always hated being named Brooke Waters. It's a ridiculous name. And it's your fault that I'm stuck with it."

"My fault?" Grandmother Brooke seemed astonished by the possibility.

Could it be that Grandmother Brooke's mind was fading? How could she have forgotten the hand she had played in naming Brooke? "Of course," Brooke reminded her. "You announced a big fat money reward for whoever named a daughter after you. Don't you remember? My parents won the reward by naming me Brooke."

"That's right," Brooke's grandmother swiftly agreed. "*They* named you. I couldn't believe how grasping all my children were, creating their own little baby boom all because they wanted my money. I suppose it's my fault in that I raised them, and I guess I rather botched up the job of teaching them values. But when I made that offer to them, oh, some thirty-six years ago, I did it hoping to prove that they weren't as grasping as I feared they were. I prayed in my heart that they'd ignore me, that they wouldn't prove as greedy as they seemed."

Her eyes glazed with memory, then sharpened on Brooke once more. "I was wrong, of course," Grandmother Brooke admitted with a sigh. "I usually am. You probably don't remember your grandfather; he died when you were just a wee thing. But he always told me I was wrong, and not a very good mother. I imagine he was correct. I raised a pack of money-grubbing louts, didn't I?"

Brooke's grandmother looked so pathetic that Brooke's heart brimmed with sadness for her. A year ago, a month ago, she would have dismissed her grandmother's claim as just so much self-pity and self-justifying. But now that Brooke had come to terms with her name—and her heart—she found that it had room in it even for this embittered elderly woman who had, indeed, raised a pack of money-grubbing louts.

"It was your parents who ought to have realized that Brooke Waters is a silly name," her grandmother continued. "But they were too avaricious to think things through to that degree. If I'd asked them to name you Ethelred Petunia, they would have done it. Now I'm an old lady, with too much money and no way to spend it all, and my children are still at it, all still trying to wrangle more than their fair share. I'm sorry your parents named you Brooke Waters, dear, but it was their decision. Not mine."

Brooke nodded. Impulsively she reached for her grandmother's gnarled hand and squeezed it. She addressed the hand more than her grandmother's face, studying the slender fingers and wondering whether her hands would age similarly. "It was difficult growing up with the name," she confessed. "I couldn't help but blame you for it."

"What was difficult," her grandmother gently suggested, "was growing up the daughter of your parents. Your brothers aren't bargains, either, I dare say. If I'd done a better job raising your mother, you could have been named Ethelred Petunia and never minded it all."

Brooke nodded again. "The man I'm in love with— his name is Sky Blue."

"Sky Blue? Good Lord! It sounds like the name of an actor, or a gigolo. Is he a decent man, this Sky Blue?"

"Very decent," Brooke said with a small laugh. "He loves his name, Grandmother, because it was given to him by parents who loved him."

"Then you understand," her grandmother said hopefully. "I must accept my share of the blame, Brooke, but I don't want to go to my grave thinking you hate me."

"Don't even think about going to your grave," Brooke scolded lightly. "You're a tough old lady, Grandmother, and always have been. If you don't think so, go spy on the vultures in the parlor, complaining because you're still kicking and they can't get their grubby hands on all your loot."

Grandmother Brooke snorted. "Vultures. You're the one wearing feathers, but they're the vultures. I'm glad we've had this talk, Brooke. Promise me we'll talk again soon."

"Of course," Brooke vowed, standing as she discerned that the interview was at an end. "No discussion of your will, though. I'm really not interested."

Her grandmother gazed up at her. "I'm proud to think that you carry my name," she said softly. "Go back to New York and have a fine time with the man you love."

"I will," said Brooke. She bent and kissed her grandmother's cheek, then waltzed from the room.

Being in love, she realized, was a truly remarkable thing. It gave one the strength to forgive. It gave one the strength to overcome past sadness and resentment and move on. She couldn't change her heritage any more than she could change her name. Her grandmother, her parents, her brothers were all a part of Brooke, and she had to accept them.

Now that she had learned, with Sky's miraculous help, how to be happy, she could do so. His love gave her the strength and freedom she needed. She couldn't wait to return to New York to tell him what he'd done for her.

She left Boston after breakfast Sunday morning, choosing not to attend church with her parents and instead catching an early train back to New York City. Nancy wasn't home when Brooke got to the apartment, and she moved directly to her bedroom to unpack Nancy's dress from her suitcase—as if she ought to be worrying about wrinkling the dress.

Before she had a chance to finish unpacking, the telephone rang. Brooke raced to answer it, hoping it was Sky.

It wasn't. "Brooke?" Michael's voice shot across the wire. "Do you know where Sky is?"

"No," she told him. "I've been out of town. I just got back. Why do you ask?"

"I think he and Willow have run off together."

Chapter Ten

"Don't be silly," said Brooke.

"I'm not being silly," Michael insisted. "They left yesterday around eight o'clock to shoot on Long Island, and I haven't heard from either of them since. I think they've run off together. You know Willow's got the hots for Sky. I think she must have gotten through to him. Pretty weird, huh?"

More than pretty weird, Brooke thought. Totally unbelievable. "Why didn't you go out to the taping with them?" she asked.

"Willow asked me not to," Michael replied. "I figured, what the hell. Whatever she wanted, just so long as she didn't get into a snit and ruin another day of shooting. So I stayed home."

Brooke shifted from foot to foot, determined not to let Michael's news disturb her. "There must have been technicians present," she pointed out. "Haven't you spoken with them?"

"Yeah. They said Sky was being really attentive to Willow all day, playing up to her and the whole thing. After the shoot he told the techies to head back to the city, that he and Willow were going to have dinner by themselves. The techies were kind of surprised, because after a shoot Sky usually likes to go out to dinner with the gang, you know, to celebrate the day's work and all. But Sky said, 'Not today, boys and girls, just me and Willow.' And then they cut out and nobody knows where they went—or where they are.''

Brooke's head began to pound. She really didn't want to believe Michael's story, yet she knew he wasn't lying. Certainly Sky must have had a good reason to go off with Willow. There had to be a plausible explanation for their disappearance.

There was, of course, and she didn't like it. Michael could very well be outlining the most plausible explanation. "Michael," she said slowly, endeavoring to remain calm, "why are you alarmed? I thought you and Willow had an understanding about such things."

"Sure. I don't care if she wants to get in a few innings with Sky. I'm only worried because she's got an interview with some guy from *Rolling Stone* magazine tomorrow morning, and if she doesn't show up soon, I'll throttle her. It's an important promo piece, what with the new record and the video coming out. I've got to track her down. I had hoped to prep her tonight for the interview. And now she's done a disappearing act with Sky."

"Sky wouldn't do anything to jeopardize Willow's career," Brooke maintained, struggling to keep her tone steady.

"If she thinks she's got an outside shot at him, she's not going to tell him she has an interview lined up. Come on, Brooke, Willow's a gorgeous, sexy lady.

Stronger men have succumbed to her. Why shouldn't Sky?''

Because he's the strongest man in the world, Brooke wanted to say. Because he thinks green hair is stinko. But maybe Michael was right. Maybe with Brooke out of town for the weekend Sky couldn't resist Willow's strange allure. In certain lights Willow's hair didn't look quite so green, and she did have a pretty face. Teenage boys by the thousands had bought posters of her to hang on their bedroom walls, Willow had once boasted to Brooke. Evidently some people found her gorgeous and sexy.

But Sky loved Brooke. He had told her he loved her, and she believed him. "Michael," she said, "be logical. Sky isn't the sort to do something so completely out of character."

"Out of character?" Michael laughed. "Come on, Brooke. You've known Sky long enough by now to know how he is with women. Madly in love with Lady A on Monday, and by Wednesday it's on to Lady B. You know how he is. No strings, no ties, love's a lark and the whole trip. He's in it for the fun, and I can tell you from experience that when she wants to be, Willow is a lot of fun. Well, listen," he said with a resigned sigh, "if you happen to learn of their whereabouts, give me a call, okay? I've got to do some more searching."

"I'll keep my eyes peeled," Brooke promised before taking down Michael's telephone number and saying good-bye. Hanging up the phone, she felt her knees weaken beneath her, and she wilted against the counter. She anxiously tried to clear her mind.

The idea was ludicrous. No way would Sky run off with Willow. Brooke couldn't conceive of such a possibility.

She lifted the receiver and dialed Sky's number, certain that he'd answer and provide some perfectly sound explanation for Willow's disappearance. But the phone rang and rang, its continuous purring rasping against Brooke's nerves, causing her head to throb. Exhaling, she slammed down the phone.

She wandered as far as the living-room sofa and sank onto it. What had Michael said? "You know how he is with women.... No strings, no ties, he's in it for the fun."

"No," she said aloud. But uttering the word didn't automatically make it true. Sky had told Brooke that he loved her, but he'd also told her he'd been in love before, in and out of it. He'd told her without a flicker of shame or sorrow that he considered such casual relationships legitimate love. Perhaps that was what he felt for Brooke: a legitimate but transient love. Perhaps he assumed that once she loosened up a little she wouldn't be so hung up on love, so serious and analytical about it.

A low sob tore from Brooke's throat. She'd gone as far as she could with the flow, but love wasn't just a river to her. It was the rocks in the river, the unmoving bits of earth that remained in place, permanent and committed as life's currents swirled around them. She loved Sky the only way she could—completely and faithfully. Maybe Sky loved her the only way he could, too, but it wasn't her way. He wanted to have a ball on his journey to the grave. He was free and easy, flexible, in it for the fun. Brooke couldn't have expected more from him. She shouldn't have made assumptions that Sky's love resembled hers. They were too different to have stumbled onto an identical definition of love.

This was what happened when one lost control, she thought morosely. She had left herself vulnerable to pain, to betrayal. To relinquish control meant to set herself up for heartbreak. She had known the risk, and gone ahead and fallen in love with Sky anyway. And now she was paying for her stupidity.

She should never have let herself forget that Sky was completely unlike her. She should never have let herself succumb to his persuasive arguments in favor of loosening up and letting go. She should have remained herself, in control of her emotions, self-protective.

But chastising herself for what she should or shouldn't have done didn't erase the pain she felt now. She knew even as she returned to the kitchen to try Sky's telephone number again that he wouldn't answer. Wherever he was, he was undoubtedly with Willow—or someone else—happily falling in love again.

Dropping the receiver into place, she tried to fight down her rising despair by being analytical. Loving Sky hadn't been a total mistake, she consoled herself. Loving him had given her the strength and spirit to face her family undaunted, to reconcile with her grandmother, to accept her name. Loving him had allowed her to come to terms with who she was. Sky had never offered her a guarantee that if she flowed like a brook she wouldn't encounter thorny twigs and contorted roots in her path. All he had taught her was that she had to learn to move in the best route she could over or around the obstacles lying in her path.

Understanding that didn't lessen her pain, however. In a way, she was an overgrown virgin, a thirty-year-old woman having to recover from her first bout with love. If she'd been like Sky, learning about love as a high school adolescent, she'd have been adept at dealing with it by now. But she wasn't. She was inexperienced, unknowledgeable, ignorant enough to approach love by running it through her computer. Maybe computers were fallible, after all.

When Nancy arrived home that evening from an afternoon date with Darryl Ephraim, she found Brooke agonizing over her idiocy at having fallen in love with a man who had never made promises, never vowed monogamy, never declared his unshakable commitment to Brooke. Nancy suggested that they go out to buy a box of Rickler's chocolates, but Brooke didn't want candy. She didn't want to describe her weekend in Boston. She didn't want to do the *Times* crossword puzzle or watch television. All she wanted to do was crawl into bed to lick her wounds. Nancy considerately left Brooke alone as she dialed Sky's home one last, futile time and then shut herself in her room for the night.

She didn't expect to fall asleep, and her expectations bore out. She lay beneath the lightweight blanket, remembering the physical ecstasy Sky had introduced her to in his bed. How in the world had she let herself believe that a man who viewed a very practical garter belt as something sexually suggestive could ever be serious about love, she wondered mournfully. How could she have let herself believe that the misery

Sky had experienced in his brother's death signified that he was a deep, feeling person? Loving one's brother didn't necessarily equate to loving a woman.

At eleven o'clock the telephone rang. Brooke assumed that Nancy was already asleep, and since she herself wasn't, she sprang from her bed and darted to the kitchen to silence the ringing. "Hello?" she mumbled groggily.

"Brooke. I'm so glad you answered," said Sky. "I was hoping I wouldn't disturb Nancy."

"Instead you're disturbing me," Brooke snapped, then bit her lip. It wouldn't do to let Sky hear how hurt and angry she was. He'd accuse her of having regressed, reverting to her old prim and proper personality. That was exactly what she was planning to do, once she had her wits about her, but she didn't want to hear Sky berate her for it.

"I'm sorry I'm calling so late," he said, sounding genuinely contrite. "I just got in."

"Quite a long taping session, wasn't it?" Brooke muttered. "Did you decide to do some filming in the moonlight, too?"

He cursed, not at Brooke but at some inner irritation. "Brooke, I'm absolutely wiped out. I can hardly keep my eyes open. I'm sorry, but I had to hear your voice before I dropped off." He illustrated his point by issuing a deep groaning yawn. "How was Boston?"

"Boston?" Good Lord, he was behaving as if there were nothing at all unusual about his having disappeared for a weekend with Willow. Brooke felt her tenuous composure crumbling, and she raged, "Why the hell do you want to hear about Boston? What business is it of yours?"

When he next spoke he sounded completely awake. "What do you mean, what business is it of mine? I've just barely survived a pretty lousy couple of days, and now you're jumping down my throat. What's wrong with you?"

"What's wrong with me?" she nearly shrieked. "You're the one who went running off with Willow. If it turned out lousy, that's your tough luck. Don't expect me to be overflowing with sympathy because Willow didn't turn out to be a legitimate love for you."

He hesitated before responding. "I think I'd better come over," he said softly. "I'll be at your place in fifteen minutes." The line went dead.

Brooke slammed down the phone and stormed from the kitchen. She had absolutely no desire to see Sky. She didn't want to hear him fabricate some ridiculous story about what had happened between him and Willow. Or worse, to hear him tell her the truth. She wasn't flaky and flighty; she didn't want to be a part of some open-ended free-as-the-breeze relationship with Sky. She didn't want to see him.

But there wasn't a thing she could do to keep him from coming to her building. She supposed she could refuse to let him into the apartment, but the night doorman was a bit of a gossip, and if Brooke adamantly refused to allow a handsome male visitor into her home, it would be the major topic of conversation among the building's tenants for days to come.

That was just a cheap excuse, she chided herself as she stalked to her bedroom to fetch her bathrobe. Doorman or no doorman, she knew she'd have to see Sky.

After tying on her robe, she trudged back to the living room and clicked on a lamp. Then she dropped onto the sofa to wait for him.

HE REALLY WAS BUSHED, but he had to see Brooke, he had to find out what in the world was bothering her. Sane, logical Brooke Waters was acting like a woman scorned, for crying out loud! After the weekend he'd endured, he didn't need Brooke turning into a crazy lady on him. He'd had enough of crazy ladies to last him a lifetime.

Besides, he fumed as he slumped in the cab's backseat, what had happened was all Brooke's fault. She'd been the one to lecture him about Willow's importance to his career. She'd been the one to point out that he was a novice in the field, and that Willow was an essential client, and that he had to grasp the import of the situation. Brooke was knowledgeable about such business matters, and Sky had presumed she was right regarding Willow. Under the circumstances, he thought he deserved her congratulations, not her wrath.

He was surprised that Michael wasn't with Willow when she emerged from her building Saturday morning and climbed into the rental car beside Sky. "Michael can't join us," she explained blithely. "He's got other plans."

Sky didn't bother to question Willow further. She was looking radiant—as radiant as a woman with green hair could look. Her mood was bright and chipper, so Sky thought it best to keep his mouth shut and count his blessings.

"Where's Brooke?" she in turn asked him. "How come she isn't tagging along?"

"She's in Boston for the weekend," Sky replied casually.

Willow shrugged and smiled. "Looks like both the cats are away, so we mice had better play," she said with a giggle.

Not only was Willow bright and chipper, but she was surprisingly co-operative as the taping proceeded. She didn't squawk about having to dangle from the tree's limb, and she concentrated on synchronizing her lips to the words of the song as his sound man played the audio tape. She was behaving like a real trouper, and Sky encouraged her with praise and affection as the day wore on.

He took some shots of her in the tree, some on the ground, some beneath a shrub. Willow didn't complain once. Sky was elated. If Michael and Brooke were right in their assessment of Willow's feelings for Sky, he was glad Michael and Brooke weren't present. Quite possibly it was their absence that made Willow so easy to work with. It made her seem awfully petty and immature to him, but again, he kept his mouth shut and counted his blessings.

He finished taping a little before five o'clock. The shoot had gone splendidly and he was convinced that he'd be able to create a superb video from the material he had. He called it a wrap, and as his technicians packed up, he decided he'd treat them to dinner. He could write the dinner bill off as a business expense, he mused. Brooke would be proud of him for thinking along those lines.

But Willow stymied his intention by slinking up to him and purring, "Sky, honey, I've been such a good girl today. Why don't you and I have dinner, just the two of us, so you can thank me for being so good?"

Again he recalled Brooke's cautionary words about not offending his most vital client. Of course Brooke was right. It was more important to coddle Willow's ego for an evening than to slap his assistants on the back. So he agreed to Willow's request and sent his technicians back to New York without him.

He and Willow drove to a restaurant not far from the park. Sky was distracted by thoughts about the splicing work that awaited him in the city, but he resolutely forced his attention to Willow, who clung to his arm as they entered the restaurant and gushed about how talented he was and how glad she was that he'd directed her video.

Before they could be seated, they were besieged by a swarm of ga-ga fans who recognized their musical idol and clustered around her. They touched her hair, her dress, her arms; they shoved cocktail napkins at her face and begged for autographs. By the time Willow was done satisfying their demands—and relishing every minute of it, Sky suspected—she no longer wanted to eat in the public restaurant. "We won't have a moment's peace," she predicted, her smile curiously pleased. "I've got a better idea. Let's buy some take-out and go back to the park for a picnic."

It seemed liked a patently stupid idea to Sky, who wanted only to return to his apartment and rest up for the following day's labor at the lab. But once more he reminded himself of Brooke's warning: He had to bear in mind the import of the situation. It wouldn't do to insult Willow. Reluctantly he agreed to her plan.

They bought some Whoppers and milk shakes and drove back to the park. Although the park closed at sundown, the lots were unguarded, and he and Willow carried their meal to the picnic table near the grove where they'd spent the day filming. Willow's spirits remained cheerful throughout their meal; she cooed about Sky's boundless talent, about the joy of working with him, about the many videos she hoped they'd make together in the future, and Sky decided that Brooke had been right in urging him to accommodate Willow's moods. Naturally, he wanted to continue working with her. She wasn't a chart-busting star yet, but she was on her way, and the success of his work for her would lead to more commissions for him, more videos, the opportunity to quit his advertising job and make a full-time career out of independent projects.

"How about it?" he said as he gathered up their litter and dumped it into a wastebasket near the table. "We've still got a long drive ahead of us. Shall we head for home?"

"Oh, Sky, don't be such a drag." Willow pouted coquettishly. "I'm just beginning to have fun."

He sighed wearily. "I'm just beginning to nod off," he complained, his patience wearing thin. "It's been a long day for me."

"Let's make it a long night," Willow suggested, twining her arms around him.

There were limits to coddling important clients, and Sky had reached his limit with Willow. "No, thanks," he said curtly, peeling her hands from his neck.

"What do you mean, no, thanks? Come on, Sky. Just one night. Why not?"

"Because I said so," he replied, realizing at once that that was a dumb answer.

"Yeeeech!" Willow wailed. "Sky Blue, what's wrong with you? I'm *Willow*! You saw the way my fans reacted to me. I'm offering you something any red-blooded American male would give anything for."

"Maybe my blood's on the purple side," Sky suggested. When she refused to smile, he said, "Willow, I know you're a lovely woman and very popular with your fans. No hard feelings, but I think of you as a friend. That's all."

"So? Friends can't mess around a little? Since when did you join the International Society of Prudes?"

Since I met Brooke, Sky contemplated. In the old days he wouldn't have turned down an offer like Willow's. Well, maybe an offer from Willow—her hair really was repulsive. But that was academic now. He wasn't interested in a fling with another woman, no matter how casual and uncomplicated, no matter what color her hair. He had pampered Willow enough for one night. If his continued working relationship with her depended on his willingness to bed her, he'd stick to advertising and forget about establishing an independent enterprise.

"Willow," he said gently. His eyes coursed over the thickening shadows of the park as the sun slipped below the horizon. "Willow, I'm saying no. Okay? Don't take it personally. I appreciate the offer, but no."

At that she flew into a rage. She was *Willow*, damn it, and he had some nerve insulting her this way. She pounded the table, zigzagged furiously through the grove, kicked pebbles, then plopped herself in Sky's lap and nuzzled his beard, her anger spent. "Please, baby, please don't be so mean," she whimpered. "I thought you liked me."

"I do like you," he insisted.

"Then will you take me to Montauk Point to watch the sun rise?"

That was definitely preferable to taking her to bed, he decided. If it preserved their ability to work together, he figured it wasn't that onerous a request.

He was wrong. They drove for hours to the eastern tip of Long Island. They ought to rename the damned island Extra-Long Island, he muttered to himself. Tortuously Long Island. By the time they reached the easternmost point, his back and shoulders ached with fatigue, and his eyelids felt as if there were hundred-pound weights attached to them.

But he had to humor Willow; he had to keep his mind on the import of the situation. So he collapsed beside her and stared at the black water and counted approximately three thousand seconds until the sluggish sun finally poked its orange head out of the water to mark the start of Sunday.

Willow announced that she wanted breakfast. It struck Sky as the first normal idea she'd had since they'd finished shooting the video, and he readily agreed. They located a restaurant, part of an elegant hotel resort, and as soon as they entered, several patrons leaped from their chairs to accost Willow.

Last night she'd found such attention flattering, but this morning it irked her. She issued a strident complaint. The maître d' wrung his hands in apology.

When she demanded that she be given a private room for breakfast, the hotel manager hastily complied to avoid a scene. Sky cringed.

He didn't want to be in a hotel room with Willow, but suddenly there they were. He sensibly recommended that she telephone Michael to inform him of her whereabouts, but she flew into another rage. Michael didn't own her, she fumed. She was an independent woman. "I am strong!" she whined. "I am invicible!"

"That song was recorded years ago," Sky reminded her. "And it's not your style. It's too melodic."

Willow took his comment as a grave insult. She burst into tears.

"I'm sorry," he consoled her, though he honestly wasn't.

"Show me how sorry you are," she demanded feistily. "You've been insulting me all night. Make it up to me now." With that, she began to strip.

Sky ducked out of the room to catch his breath. The entire episode struck him as a farce, and not a very funny one. He was angry with Willow, angry with Michael for not having accompanied them to the park on Saturday, angry with himself. Especially angry with Brooke for having persuaded him to think like a businessman around Willow.

Willow locked the door on him. Then she began to throw the breakfast dishes around; he heard the shatter of china against the walls. He summoned the hotel manager. Willow refused to let anyone inside. When the manager tried to open the lock with a master key,

Willow screamed "Rape!" and barricaded the door with furniture.

Eventually the police were called. A local newspaper reporter showed up at the hotel to write a scoop on the obstreperous rock star who was trashing a chic seaside resort's room. Sky found himself wishing he were in a nice, dull profession such as corporate tax accounting.

After several hours Willow emerged, dressed and subdued. The manager insisted on filing a damage report at the police station, and Willow threw a tantrum. She was *Willow* she told anyone who'd stand still long enough to listen to her. She was famous. She didn't liked being treated like a vandal.

"You *are* a vandal," the hotel manager insisted, and declared that if she didn't agree to pay for the broken dishes he would press charges.

Sky tried to telephone Michael several times, but the line was constantly busy. Finally he wrote a check to cover the damages Willow had incurred, and the police released her.

She was too embarrassed to go home right away, she sobbed as they left the police station for the car. "Please," she begged Sky. "Give me a chance to pull myself together. Michael'll kill me when he finds out what I did."

If Michael decided to kill her, Sky mused, he'd volunteer his assistance. But he courteously drove her all over Long Island while she shopped for some sort of gift she could bring Michael as a peace offering. Michael was hung up on Willow's public image, she explained tearfully. When he found out she'd had a run-in with the law, she wanted to be able to present him with a token of penance. A conch shell, she resolved. One of those big shells he could hold up to his ear and hear the ocean inside. Also a plant. She would bring him a plant.

"Just what he needs," Sky muttered as he drove from one nursery to another in search of one that was open for business that early on Sunday. All he could think about was, plant or no plant, shell or no shell, Michael had better reimburse him for the broken dishes. Sky didn't care that the cost was probably tax-deductible. He wanted his money back.

Overtired and edgy, he finally delivered Willow to her front door on Central Park West at eight. She implored him to come up to the apartment and help her explain to Michael what had happened, and he agreed only because he wanted to get money from Michael. Not only for the broken dishes, he resolved, but for the extra day's rental on the car. He was able to think like a businessman enough to know that his working for Willow was supposed to result in a profit, not a deficit.

Michael understandably became rabid when Willow told him about her adventure. Sky had to witness their argument for a full hour before Michael got around to paying Sky for his unexpected outlays of money. Hardly able to focus his eyes on the city traffic, Sky somehow managed to get the car back to the auto rental place and himself to his apartment. He desperately wanted to go to sleep. But even more than that, he wanted to touch base with Brooke.

And what did that get him, he grumbled bitterly to himself as he paid the cabdriver and disembarked at

Brooke's building. His beautiful, sane woman, his stable Brooke, had practically bitten his head off.

He waited impatiently for the doorman to announce his arrival to her, and wondered whether she would permit him upstairs. She did, and he stumbled wearily to the elevator and rode it up.

She said nothing as she admitted him into the apartment and locked the door behind him. He dropped onto the sofa and groaned. "Independence isn't worth it," he complained disconsolately. "I'll stick to advertising."

"What are you talking about?"

His eyes slowly sharpened on her. Clad in a set of unflattering pajamas and an equally unflattering bathrobe, she looked like a mother whose child had just gotten home an hour after curfew. Yet he relished her appearance. How like Brooke to look so...so delightfully ordinary. His lips, stiff from the grimace they'd been frozen into most of the day, magically softened into a smile as he gazed upon her. "I love you," he whispered.

The words seemed to mollify her, though she left several feet of space between them on the sofa when she took a seat beside him.

Without much coaxing, he described his wretched weekend to her. "Oh, Brooke," he concluded, his voice hoarse with exhaustion, "if there was ever any doubt, there isn't now. Prim and proper ladies are definitely my type."

Brooke slid toward him and let him arch his arm around her. "You have only yourself to blame for doing business with a weirdo," she chided him.

"I have you to blame for making me think of business matters. You were the one who said Willow was important for my budding enterprise."

"You did think like an entrepreneur under the circumstances," she complimented him. "However..."

"However?"

"This is one time you should have booted the spoiled brat out of the car and left her to fend for herself."

"Would you have done that to one of your clients?"

"My clients don't have green hair," Brooke reminded him, then laughed. "But yes, if one of them behaved that way, I would have told him where to get off. Speaking of which," she added, cuddling closer to Sky, "I wore Nancy's purple feather boa to my grandmother's party."

"You did?" Sky asked in amazement.

"I did. It was my own way of telling my family where to get off. They were aghast. My mother implied I'd get cut out of my grandmother's will for dressing so brazenly. On the other hand, I scored points with my nephew because I told him I knew Willow. He's heard of her."

"Most people have," Sky noted. "If her little bout of vandalism makes the papers tomorrow, she'll be a household word all over the country."

"Her dream come true," Brooke said with a laugh.

"What did your grandmother say about the boa?" Sky brought Brooke back to the subject she'd introduced.

"She said it made her dizzy. We had a delightful chat, actually." Brooke gathered Sky's hand in hers. "I told her I was in love."

"Oh? What did she say?"

"She said it was about time, since I was no spring chicken."

"You're more of a chick," Sky mocked her. "A wenchy sort of chick."

"And you're a macho pig," she countered. "I'm not wearing stockings, pal, so clean up your act."

"And here I was hoping you'd invite me to spend the night," he complained. "I'm in dire need of tender loving care, Brooke, and all you can say is that I should clean up my act."

"You know I like clean, neat men," she said playfully before growing somber. "Tomorrow's Monday, Sky. I've got to get to work in the morning."

"So do I. After this weekend, I'm almost tempted to tear up my little blue business cards."

"Don't talk that way," Brooke reproached him. "Life can be unpredictable, and sometimes things get out of control, but you've just got to go with the flow." It was a lesson Sky had taught her, and she knew in her heart how true it was.

He did, too. "Okay," he agreed. "I won't tear up my little blue business cards. I wouldn't have the strength right now, anyway."

"Meaning I'm going to have to do all the work?" Brooke protested as she stood up and hauled Sky to his feet.

"Who said anything about work?" he teased as she led him to her bedroom.

THE TAPE LEFT HER SPEECHLESS. Never in her wildest imagination had she thought Sky would put together such a seamless montage of shots. The actor-animals were definitely surreal, and Willow blended right into the pastoral setting, her green hair flowing over the tree limb, her lips perfectly co-ordinated with the song, her reedy body merging with the graceful branches surrounding her.

But it was the final shot that stunned Brooke the most. As the song dissolved into a coda of syncopated drums and nasal guitar twangs, the video cut to a clearly human figure clad in street clothes twisted up on a picnic table bench, convulsed with laughter. "Sky!" Brooke blurted out. "How could you? How could you put me in the video?"

"How could I resist?" he defended himself. "It's the perfect ending, Brooke. I know these things. I'm an artist, don't forget."

"But—but—" she sputtered, then surrendered to a laugh. "You might at least have asked me first."

"You want to be paid union scale?" he asked. "All right. It's deductible."

"I don't care about being paid, Sky, but really!" She continued laughing, her shaking shoulders lifting off the pillow on Sky's bed, where they were sitting. He had recently purchased a videotape player for his apartment—a business expense, Brooke assured him, and he dutifully saved the receipt in the cubbyhole of his desk designated for such receipts—and before he showed the tape of Willow's video to anyone else, he wanted Brooke's opinion of it.

"So? You hate it?"

"I like it," she confessed, dabbing the tears from her eyes as her laughter waned. "It's odd, but I guess that's the right style for this sort of thing. It's effective, anyway."

"And viewers won't pay too much attention to Willow's voice," Sky added. "I think the actors did a fantastic job."

"They did."

"Including you."

"I'm not an actor," she objected.

He shrugged dismissively. "I often use inexperienced actors in my commercials. If they've got the right face, I approach them wherever I find them, and when they hear how much they can earn they usually agree to work for me. One of my favorite techniques."

In the past several weeks, Brooke had finally viewed some of Sky's television commercials. While she hadn't been aware that the advertisement's performers weren't seasoned professionals, she'd been acutely conscious of their unusual faces. Sky was justified in considering faces his trademark. "So I had the right face for this rock video?" Brooke asked.

"The right face, the right laughter. I think that final shot is what makes the whole thing work."

"If you say so," she conceded. "As you said, you're the artist."

He stood up to shut off the tape player and the television set. Then he returned to the bed and gathered Brooke into his arms again. "I'm glad you like it," he murmured with satisfaction. "I think it's pretty good myself. The guy I've been negotiating with about doing a video this fall says that if his tape is as good as he expects it to be we've got a deal."

"I don't think you've got any worry there," Brooke assured him. "He's sure to love it."

Sky nodded and leaned back into the pillow. His fingers twirled absently through Brooke's hair as he ruminated. "It's going to be a hectic stretch for me. Two more tapes this summer, one already lined up for the fall...I should be a basket case by Thanksgiving."

"Unless you quit your advertising job," she pointed out.

His fingers paused for a moment, then continued their gentle meandering through the tawny silk of her hair. "You're my business manager," he posed. "Do you think I should?"

"You can afford to," Brooke observed. Having completed his amended tax return and organized him for the current tax year, she knew whereof she spoke.

"Even if I give up all the perks?"

"Insurance is expensive, but it won't bankrupt you," she said. "What will bankrupt you is working till you drop. Imagine what your health costs would be then." She mused, then commented, "Maybe you could work out something part-time at the agency."

"Maybe I could," he allowed. "I'll talk to my bosses there and see what we can figure out." He bent to kiss the crown of her head. "You are the most intelligent woman I've ever met," he said. "What would I do without you?"

"Is that a rhetorical question?" she countered.

He chuckled, then drew her even closer. His shoulder felt firm against her cheek, his chest broad and inviting as it stretched below her arm. She played her hand across the fabric of his shirt, delighting in the subtle movements of his muscles beneath her palm. "Here's a better question," he murmured. "One that only someone with a sound business head on his shoulders would ask: Does Benson and Broderick offer insurance coverage for spouses of employees?"

Brooke broke away to stare at him. "What did you have in mind?" she asked.

"Marriage," he replied simply.

"You want to marry me for insurance coverage?"

"It's a sensible idea, don't you think?" he remarked. At her frown, his beard spread in a delicious smile. "Probably the least important reason in the world to marry you, Brooke, but you see how you've got me thinking? I'm very analytical now," he declared proudly. "I haven't got a computer to run you through, but I think if I did, it would compute that I ought to marry you."

"Oh?" She permitted herself a small grin. "What other data have you got to run through this imaginary computer?"

"Besides insurance benefits? Well," he reflected, "you wear garter belts."

"Only in the summer."

"We can negotiate on that," he said, his dark eyes glinting wickedly. "Then there's the matter of your wonderful face."

"You were supposed to say my pretty face." She pretended to sulk.

"It isn't a pretty face, Brooke, but it's wonderful. Beautiful. Breathtaking. I could look at it forever. Important bit of data, that." He urged her back against him. "You've made me view the world more seriously," he continued.

"Is that a plus or a minus?"

"A plus. A definite plus. I used to associate seriousness with sadness, but I was wrong. I'm serious about you, and that doesn't make me sad at all."

Brooke's smile expanded as she nestled against him. "What else?" she asked.

"Fishing for compliments?"

"You started this list with Benson and Broderick's benefits for employees," she reminded him. "I could use some reassurance."

"I need you," he said unflinchingly. "That's a damned big plus."

"It certainly is," she whispered.

"I need you and I love you. And given that you were as much a charity case as I was—" he stifled the protest taking shape on her lips with a resounding kiss "—you need me, too. And you've said you love me. You're honest. I believe you."

"That's very wise of you."

"And here's the biggest kicker of all," he announced triumphantly. "The way I figure it, if we get married, we can hyphenate our names. We can both be 'Blue-Waters'."

"Ugh!" she shrieked, bolting upright. "Are you crazy? *Blue-Waters*?"

His smile was firm but mirthful. "Sure, why not? Sky Blue-Waters and Brooke Blue-Waters. Don't you think that sounds great?"

"I think it sounds like a misplaced tribe of Chippewas," she argued.

"Nobody would take you for a Native American, not with your coloring," he assured her. "Unless you make a habit of wearing purple feathers."

"Blue-Waters," she mumbled glumly. Then something softened inside her and she murmured the hyphenated name again. "Blue-Waters. I don't know. It does have a certain zing to it."

"It seems like the perfect name for a stuffed shirt from Boston, don't you agree?"

She chuckled. "I think it would make Grandmother Brooke dizzy." She stopped smiling as she remembered her recent encounter with her grandmother. "Sky, I'm no spring chicken, you know. I'm thirty years old."

"And?"

"And...in a few years, I may be too old to have children."

"Then we'll start right away," he resolved.

The idea surprised her with its appeal. She had always wanted to have children; it was only recently, when the likelihood of her ever meeting a man she could truly love seemed to be growing ever more remote, that she had put thoughts of becoming a mother out of her mind. "I'm afraid to ask what you'll want to name them," she muttered.

"Hmm." He considered. "If we have a girl, Crystal. If we have a boy, Clear."

"Crystal Blue-Waters and Clear Blue-Waters," she said aloud. "I've recently become partial to Ethelred Petunia, myself."

"What?"

"It's a long story," she said with a laugh. "For another time." She lapsed into a brief silence. "We might just get lucky and have twins."

"Not probable," Sky told her. "It usually skips a generation. We'll have twin grandchildren."

"Planning for the future, aren't you?"

"Funny thing about that," Sky returned. "Until I met you, I never thought about the future. And that's a plus," he concluded, anticipating her question. He

used his thumb to tilt her face to his and kissed he
again. "Here we are talking about grandchildren and
you haven't even accepted my proposal."

Her eyes brightened with mischief. "I've got to run
it through the computer, too, Sky. We would get less
of an exemption as a married couple than we do fil
ing singly. But with the Schedule W adjustment for
working couples, it might just balance out."

"You want to figure out the tax benefits of mar
riage before you say yes?" he accused her with a
frown. "Now I'm the one who could use some
reassurance."

Brooke kissed his soft beard before sliding her
mouth to his. She ran her tongue over his lips until
they parted with a husky groan. "You were the one
who said I loved you," she whispered when the kiss
ended. "I can't imagine you need any more reassur
ance than that."

"Just in case, you'd better kiss me again."

She did, and his arms closed around her. Their love
flowed around them, a sweet, powerful current that
neither of them was foolish enough to resist. So they
went with it, willingly, unquestioningly, accepting that
wherever the blue waters carried them was exactly
where they wanted to be.

Harlequin Intrigue

Because romance can be quite an adventure.

She fought for a bold future
until she could no longer
ignore the...

ECHO OF THUNDER

MAURA SEGER

Author of **Eye of the Storm**

CHO OF THUNDER is the love story of James
allahan and Alexis Brockton, who forge a union that
ust withstand the pressures of their own desires and the
allenge of building a new television empire.

uthor Maura Seger's writing has been described by
omantic Times as having a "superb blend of historical
rspective, exciting romance and a deep and abiding
ssion for the human soul."

EYE OF THE STORM

MAURA SEGER

A powerful
portrayal of
the events of
World War II in the
Pacific, *Eye of the Storm* is a riveting story of how love
triumphs over hatred. In this, the first of a three-book
chronicle, Army nurse Maggie Lawrence meets Marine
Sgt. Anthony Gargano. Despite military regulations
against fraternization, they resolve to face together
whatever lies ahead.... Author Maura Seger, also know
to her fans as Laurel Winslow, Sara Jennings, Anne
MacNeil and Jenny Bates, was named 1984's
Most Versatile Romance Author by *The Romantic Time*

Take 4 books
& a surprise gift
FREE

SPECIAL LIMITED-TIME OFFER

Mail to   **Harlequin Reader Service**®

In the U.S.   In Canada
2504 West Southern Ave.   P.O. Box 2800, Station "A"
Tempe, AZ 85282   5170 Yonge Street
                           Willowdale, Ontario M2N 6J3

YES! Please send me 4 free Harlequin American Romance® novels and my free surprise gift. Then send me 4 brand-new novels as they come off the presses. Bill me at the low price of $2.25 each —a 11% saving off the retail price. There are no shipping, handling or other hidden costs. There is no minimum number of books I must purchase. I can always return a shipment and cancel at any time. Even if I never buy another book from Harlequin, the 4 free novels and the surprise gift are mine to keep forever.

Name _____ (PLEASE PRINT)

Address _____ Apt. No. _____

City _____ State/Prov. _____ Zip/Postal Code _____

This offer is limited to one order per household and not valid to present subscribers. Price is subject to change.   DOAR–SUB–1